PRAISE

"Part *Twilight*, part *Beauty and the Beast*, readers will eat up the lush settings, mystery, and romance of *Never Call Me Vampire*. Tamara Grantham has created a high-stakes story rich with history, myth, and legend."

— ANGELA LARKIN, CO-AUTHOR OF THE
BEYOND SERIES

"[T]he plot is suspense-laden, delivering the perfect adrenaline-filled cocktail for an entertaining and exciting read. The characters display a near-perfect balance between normal and paranormal traits....Readers will love the delightful ending..."

— JM LAREEN, *IND'TALE MAGAZINE* (FOR
NEVER CALL ME VAMPIRE)

"I found *Never Call Me Vampire* mesmerizing and worth reading in one sitting. Tamara Grantham takes the enchanting theme of vampires and builds on their reputation and thrilling mystique to create a novel that will haunt you until it is finished...I could not put this book down and look forward to seeing what could happen next at Crimson Hollow."

— PEGGY JO WIPF, *READERS FAVORITE*

"*Never Call Me Vampire*...is the amazing start of a promising paranormal series. If you've been longing for a good vampire novel with a new spin, your search ends here....Grantham throws off the shackles of traditional vampire stories and gives us one that we can sink our teeth into....This author is exceptionally skilled at building a world we can believe in..."

"[T]his story works well because of the value that Tamara Grantham adds to the theme, which makes it hard to put down once you start reading."

"A sparkling fantasy."

"Grantham is prepared to make her mark in the urban fantasy scene with this one."

"Springs to life from the very first sentence."

THE 7TH LIE

THE 7TH LIE

TAMARA GRANTHAM

BABYLON BOOKS

For Bridger
Thank you for always being there when I need you most.

Shoot for the moon. Even if you miss, you'll land among the stars.

— NORMAN VINCENT PEALE

Synthetic sunlight warmed my skin. I stood in the field running my hand over the ripened wheat stalk, spikes tickling my fingers, until I plucked off the plant's top and ground it between my hands. When the kernels detached, five grains sat on my palm.

My eidetic memory took over, opening like the pages of a book.

Scientific name: Triticum. Family Poaceae. Order: Poales. Kingdom…

Shaking my head, I clamped my hand around the kernels. On the horizon, miles of golden wheat fluttered like waves on an ocean.

If I'd really been here, I would've smelled the sweet scent of fresh growth. Still, I breathed deeply, imagining the air to be something other than the recycled, metallic oxygen they pumped through the facility's vents.

Tossing the seeds aside, I noticed how uniform they looked as they tumbled to the ground, each one the same shape and size. No variations in color or diameter. Most people wouldn't have noticed such minute details, but I wasn't most people.

Doctors had a name for my extra perceptiveness. They

called it ECP. I tried my best not to read too much into the label. Being different meant social isolation in high school. It wasn't a trait I hoped to carry with me.

"Agent Sabine Harper," Fifteen's voice came through my earpiece. "Is the simulation working?"

I pressed my finger to the earbud. "Yes. I'm in the field by my old house." My gaze wandered to the two-story homestead. Paint peeled from hundred-year-old boards. "What's my target?"

"A needle," he answered, his voice hinting at a British accent.

"A needle?" I asked. "Like a sewing needle?"

"Yes," he answered stiffly, his voice emotionless.

I almost laughed. "A needle in a wheat field. Got it."

A butterfly fluttered past in a dazzling array of turquoise and copper, its wings more vibrant than any common land insect.

A distraction.

Focus. The target.

They would have used the wheat to their advantage and camouflaged the needle. I ran my hands over the stalks once again, training my eye on any inconsistencies. Rows of gold passed me by as I walked. It wouldn't be among the spikes, which would have been the best place to hide it, where a silver needle would have been almost indiscernible from the gold.

But I would have looked there first.

And they knew it.

No. It wouldn't be with the spikes.

They would have put it somewhere they didn't expect me to look.

I paced from one row to the next. A tractor's engine rumbled in the distance. My heart ached at the thought of Dad out there somewhere.

Was he okay?

Even in a simulation, the reminder of him distracted me,

and I found myself looking out across the field, hoping to spot him somewhere. I shook my head and kept going, cataloging each plant, mentally checking them off, until a glint near my feet stopped me.

I paused, then crouched by the plant. A snail's shell reflected the sunlight.

Standing, I continued, using all my senses to train on a single silver needle. I spent another fifteen minutes wandering from one row to the next, looking for anything out of place, until I spotted the roots of a plant peeking from the soil.

Strange. Winter wheat roots grew deep. Seeing them near the surface wasn't a good sign. Dad would have never allowed a plant to grow like that. Then again, this wasn't Dad's field.

I knelt. Cold dirt dampened the knees of my cargo pants. When I spread the roots apart, something sharp pricked me.

"Ouch," I mumbled, still pulling the shoots apart, until a thin piece of metal stood out against the brown soil. I picked the needle out of the tangle of roots, then I stood, holding it up to the light. The sliver of stainless steel glinted. A tiny speck of my blood tipped it.

"Got it," I said to Agent Fifteen. "What was my time?"

"Seventeen minutes, six seconds."

"Hmm." I pursed my lips.

"Did the distractions slow you?" he asked.

"The butterfly? No. But the tractor..." I trailed off, looking once again at the house, then tucked the needle in my pocket. Wind gusted. Long strands of my dark hair brushed my cheeks. When I reached to brush it back, the sun drenched my skin, chasing away my chills.

This place seems so real sometimes.

I shook my head. It wasn't real. Virtual reality and computer code couldn't replace home. Still, with the cameras functioning inside the house, maybe I would get to see Dad and Mima June—the real them, and not holograms—that was, if I could convince Agent Fifteen to let me.

"Can we switch the VR to the indoor cameras? I'd like to see inside my house if that's okay."

The line went silent.

"Agent Fifteen?" I asked.

Only a phantom wind answered. Had a solar flare cut him off?

The line crackled. "I'm here," he finally said.

"Good. What happened? Another flare?"

"Not a flare, Agent Harper, but we do have a problem. Seeing familial relations puts you in danger as well as them."

"Why?"

"If they made you lose focus now, they'll do it again."

"No. That won't happen. I promise," I said, determination in my voice. "They'll be in no danger. You saw how the tractor slowed me down. Let me see them, and maybe the interruption will be minimized if I can see them before I go through the dome."

The line went silent again. "If that's your wish, Agent Harper."

"It is."

"Very well," he replied.

The field broke apart in pixelated cubes. Sleek mirrored walls of the VR sphere appeared around me until another scene formed.

I stood in my living room.

The box fan hummed in the corner. Pictures of generations of Harpers hung on the wall. Great Grandpa standing by the fence. Great-Grandma Blue sitting in her chair, wearing her thick-framed glasses, her crochet in her lap as a smile made her eyes squint. When I'd been younger, there were times I'd thought I'd heard the laughter of the children who'd lived here. Heard the pattering of tiny footsteps on the stairs.

I looked to the recliner where Mima June usually sat, but I saw only an empty seat. Still, my memory served to show her there, sitting where yellow foam peeked from the cushion, beside the table with the box of UNO cards, magnifying glass, and folded newspaper. The last time I'd sat with her, she'd held my hand and asked if I had a boyfriend.

I laughed at her comment. Told her I'd never met anyone worth dating. A few casual relationships, sure. But most men were little more than children more interested in partying and acting like idiots. I wasn't sure there was a single mature male left in the world. No. If I ever met someone intelligent, someone who cared more about helping others than his own personal pleasure, then maybe I'd consider dating again.

She'd told me to give it time. I just needed to find the right person.

I didn't share her confidence.

Before I left, she told me to give her one last kiss goodbye.

That was six months ago.

I took a step toward the chair, staring around the empty room. The quiet noise of the TV blended with the whir of the fan. Mima June's picture sat on the coffee table. She was seventeen, maybe, standing by a fence post with her knife tucked in her belt. She had a willowy frame. Her long lashes shuttered almond-shaped eyes, and her wisps of raven-black hair framed her angular face.

I stiffened as I stood staring at the empty recliner. Where was she?

A chair in the dining room creaked, and I turned my attention to Dad.

He sat at the table with his head in his hands, a stack of papers strewn around him.

"Transfer to the dining room camera," I said to Agent Fifteen.

"Are you sure?"

"Yes. Go there now."

"Of course," he said with a sigh.

The scene shifted. I stood over Dad. He filled out a form, and I peeked over his shoulder to get a better look.

Application for Certificate of Death
Name: June Amelia Harper

Panic gripped me.

I reread the paper. Something was wrong. This couldn't be right.

"Fifteen," I said, my voice calm, though my heart had stopped. "What's happening? Is something wrong with the VR?"

"The VR is functioning properly, although I can run a diagnostic—"

"No." I stopped him. "Did something happen to Mima June?"

"I can check." He paused. "Checking... I'm sorry. There's no information available in Vortech's database."

"None? Check again." Did he hear the desperation in my voice? "Search outside Vortech's database if you have to."

Another pause. My mind raced, and my stomach felt queasy.

"I found something in the Independence Daily Reporter," he said. "It's in the obituary section."

Oh no. "Read it to me." I spoke calmly, though my heart raced so fast, I thought it might beat a hole through my chest.

"It says June Amelia Harper recently passed away from complications of cancer. She is survived by a son, Thomas James Harper, a granddaughter, Sabine Amelia—"

"Stop," I said. "That's enough."

My gaze stayed on Daddy.

Why didn't you tell me? I wanted to ask.

I exhaled a long, shaky breath. Closing my eyes, I tried to process my new reality, but how could this be? She'd been fine when I left.

"Fifteen, do I have any recent emails from Dad?"

"Let me check." Static crackled as I waited. "No new emails, Agent Harper."

"None?" I questioned. "Did you check all the folders?"

"Yes," he answered. "All but one."

"One?" I asked. "Which one?"

"The restricted file."

"There's a restricted file?" I fisted my hands. Anger and grief warred within me. "Why wasn't I told about it?"

"Vortech's privacy policy," he stated matter-of-factly.

"Override it. I'm going on my last mission, and if my father had a message for me, I need to know what it says," I said. "Please," I added.

"I'll have to get this approve—"

"No. Keeping my own messages from me is unethical and questionably legal. If Vortech wants me on the next mission, you'll read that email to me, or I'll walk. I'll leave the mission right now, Fifteen," I challenged. "Let me have access to that email."

"Understood," he said after a pause. "I'm opening the email now. Would you like me to read it to you?"

What do you think? "Yes. Please."

"The email says: 'Beanie Girl, I hope you're doing well. I hate to bring sad news, but your grandmother passed away this morning in her sleep at home. Her health started going downhill after the flare. Losing access to her treatments took its toll. When she finally got access to chemo again, the doctor said her cancer had spread too far to control it. But she's no longer in pain. Thank the Lord for that. And my own cancer is in remission. We're holding a small service next week. I don't expect you to attend as I know how busy you are. I can't believe you're at the top of the world. Who would've thought a Harper would've traveled so far from home on such an important mission? Mima was so proud of you.

Keep fighting the good fight.

-Dad'"

A stone dropped to the pit of my stomach.

I stood over Dad, unable to speak to him.

Taking a step back, I tried to swallow the knot in my throat. I prayed something was glitching with the VR. This was all some stupid joke. Mima was fine and sitting in her chair as usual watching *Price is Right.*

"Fifteen, take me out. I've got to talk to Logan. I have to go home. I can't stay here anymore."

"Harper, I would advise against such an action."

"I don't care," I bit out. "I'm going home. Dad needs me."

"Are you sure?"

I stood looking at the image of Dad through the cameras. If I could've hugged him, he would've smelled of Zest soap and engine grease. Laugh lines creased his careworn skin, and if I could've sat at the table with him, he would've grabbed my hand and told me how proud he was of me. How I'd joined Vortech and was the youngest to be picked for the elite program. How he knew I would change the world someday.

Harpers never quit, he'd tell me. *They finish with honor.*

He folded the paper and placed it in an envelope. A hole opened at the bottom of my heart.

We'd never have the money to pay for his chemo if his cancer came back. He'd end up just like Mima.

He looked up and, though I knew he couldn't see me, why did it seem recognition lit his eyes?

He didn't want me to abandon my mission, and he didn't want Mima June's death to be a distraction. I had nothing in Kansas. No future. No prospects.

Wind whispered through the open window, ruffling the curtains.

I swallowed a lump in my throat and squared my shoulders.

I would finish my assignment with Vortech, and I would come home.

"Fifteen, take me out," I said.

I cast one last glance at Dad, then at the wall filled with photos of my ancestors, and the empty Lazy Boy with the worn cushion, yellow foam peeking through the torn fabric.

In a blink, it seemed as if Mima June sat there once again, smiling as she always did, and though I was on a tiny island north of the Russia mainland, so very far away, I swore I heard her words whispering on the wind.

Give me one last kiss goodbye...

2

Freezing wind gusted as I stepped outside the facility. I pulled my hood over my head and followed Agent Logan through the snow.

"You ready?" he called, his frame hidden under bulky layers of clothing and a gray overcoat, a red-letter *V* stitched over the breast pocket.

I hesitated before answering. I'd spent half my night wondering if I'd made the right decision by staying. Finally, I'd sent off a quick message to Dad, telling him I loved him, I would come back. I was sorry about Mima June. My emotions were too raw to know what else to say.

"I'm ready," I called back.

"You got everything?"

I straightened my backpack's straps. If he was asking if I had all my material things, then the answer was probably not, as I was famously lousy at remembering everyday things like a toothbrush and underwear. If he was asking if I had everything in my head—all the knowledge of Champ Island, the Bering Sea, the weather patterns, the gateway cave, the dome and the little information we knew of what was under it—

then the answer was yes. I hadn't spent the last six months of my life in training for nothing.

"I'm good," I yelled back.

He nodded, then sat on his snowmobile, pulled his goggles over his eyes, and cranked the engine. The roar mingled with the howling wind. I cast one last glance at the facility.

The stark metal building loomed against a churning white sky. A single red light flashed from the antennae reaching up into the storm, as if it were a beacon screaming for help. I wasn't sure it had stopped storming since I'd arrived half-a-year ago. I'd had no idea what I was getting into.

My nerves on that first day had been unbearable. After joining Vortech and making the cut to elite status, they'd sent me here to the top of the world, to a tiny, unknown island north of the Russian mainland. A place filled with mysterious sphere-shaped boulders that pocked the unforgiving landscape.

That's when I'd learned about the dome, and my Kansas way of thinking—of Earth and everything in it—had been shattered forever.

After cranking my snowmobile's engine, I pushed the throttle. Snow spewed behind me as I sped forward and followed Logan. I allowed myself to revel in the rush of wind, the crispness of the air, and the taste of ice on my tongue, something unfamiliar after being trapped inside the facility, with only a few trips to the outside world on my survival expeditions.

We sped past the wreck of the old immigrant's ship. Weathered wooden planks comprised its hull. In some places, the boards stuck up like the bones of a whale's skeleton. Whatever storm had pushed it to the top of the world must've been massive in scope.

The ship conjured images of the pages of a book I'd read as a child. *The Lost Shipwreck of Champ Island.* The book opened as if I were reading it again. Black-and-white photos and their captions popping out at me. *How the ship got here is still a mystery. The immigrants' disappearance is a mystery, too. After fifty years of study, scientists are beginning to fit the puzzle pieces together. No bodies were recovered, and in extreme temperatures such as those found on Champ Island, their remains would've been easily preserved. Some scientists believe they may have found a cave to take shelter in, yet no evidence of such an event has been recorded.*

Beyond the ship lay an expanse of snowy wasteland. I dodged sphere-shaped boulders, some as small as ping-pong balls, others larger than my snowmobile. A blanket of white covered their tops, as if to hide their secrets. Lines of text from the *Atlas of Champ Island* jumped out in my mind.

Perfect spheres don't exist in nature. Scientists have discovered the boulders were formed by water. However, because of the extreme temperatures, there are no recorded civilizations living on Champ Island, and no conclusive evidence that the spheres were formed by human hands.

Ice crystals crunched under our snowmobile's skis, bringing me from my thoughts. I shook my head. Sometimes this photographic memory thing was a pain. I couldn't stay focused on anything long enough before a book page hit me out of nowhere, and my concentration got jerked from one idea to another.

A howling wind echoed through the expanse. This far away from civilization, I imagined what it would feel like to be a shipwreck victim out here alone, with the screaming wind and the numbing cold. Where would I have gone from here?

The void of white faded with the setting sun, leaving the world drenched in gray. As we approached the substation, only the blinking red lights gave any indication we were near the bunker. The roaring engines grew quieter until we shut them off, leaving me with ringing ears in the sudden silence.

Logan removed his goggles. "You good?"

"Fine," I called back.

We got off our snowmobiles and headed for the entrance. I flexed my stiff fingers. Despite my gloves, the cold managed to seep through, straight to my bones, until numbness settled inside.

The black metal hatch loomed, a block letter 'V' etched into the plate. We trudged through the snow until we reached the keypad. Logan removed his gloves just long enough to press his thumb to the fingerprint pad. A red laser scanned his finger, then the pad turned green, and the hatchway opened.

Snow particles blustered around us. I stepped onto the metal grating and inside the bunker, then I walked with Logan down a metal staircase, our footsteps echoing with hollow clangs. The door sealed shut above us. Panic of being caged in weighed heavy in my chest, but I gripped the railing.

Get it under control, Harper.

We descended into an abyss of computer screens and mirrored walls. The room held the sterile scent of a hospital. The sharp odor of rubbing alcohol conjured visions of endless injections during Vortech's tests. My stomach churned at the unbidden memories, so I focused elsewhere. Scientists wearing lab coats sat at computer stations. They stood as we entered, and Agent Steele paced toward me.

He walked with an exaggerated swagger. His plastered-on smile and muscled torso reminded me of a model on a body-builder equipment infomercial. He looked the part, too, with his gelled sandy brown hair. A fake tan stained his face, and his teeth had been bleached whiter than the snow outside.

"Agent Sabine Harper," he said in a voice too quiet to match his beefed-up frame. He extended his hand. I took it, though I didn't bother with removing my gloves. "I can't believe today is finally here. I hope the trip over to the bunker wasn't too bad. I know what that weather's like out there."

"It wasn't too bad today." I glanced at Logan. He stood in a military posture with hands behind his back. "Logan and I have been through worse."

"I'm sure you have. Champ Island is a hostile place. Easy to lose your way out there. Well, let's not waste any time. It's been ten years since the last flare, ten years since we've sent anyone through the portal. As you can guess, we're more than a little excited you passed the tests. We've got high hopes for you, Agent Harper."

The room quieted as eyes focused on me. I swallowed the nervous lump in my throat. "Yeah," I said with a shrug. "I hope I don't disappoint you."

"You'd better not," he said with a laugh. "Anyone who's been through as much of a vetting process as you had better come back alive." He spoke with an easygoing tone, though I detected a hint of seriousness lingering in the dark glint of his eyes. "If you'll follow me, we've got station two ready to go."

I followed him past rows of computers and mirrors. When we rounded a bend, the gateway portal came into view. Seven lights blinked around its outer shell. A network of thick cables ran to each of the lights.

I felt like I'd entered a sci-fi movie. This was so far from the familiar, I almost wondered if I were dreaming.

Beside the gateway, a chair was arranged by a medical desk, where rows of needles lined a tray. My stomach soured.

"I'm hoping these are my last shots."

Logan chuckled behind me. "Once you're through, I doubt you'll have to worry about it."

A middle-aged woman wearing white scrubs neared us. "Remove your coat, please," she said in a robotic tone. "Then have a seat."

I did as she said. The plastic squeaked as I got settled on the chair. Scientists and medical techs hovered around me, taking my temperature, pulse, blood pressure, looking at my pupils with a pen light. I'd gotten used to it by now.

"We're giving you a final series of inoculations," Agent Steele explained. "While we don't know the diseases the locals carry, we can take educated guesses. We're also going to draw your blood to compare your cellular structure to its behavior after passing through the gate."

"I understand," I said as the nurse tied a rubber cord around my arm. The needle pricked as it slid under my skin. A thin line of red filled the tube.

Agent Steele rolled a chair to me and sat as the nurse worked. Logan remained standing at my side, like a soldier on watch. "You don't have to hover," I whispered to him.

"Says who?" he answered with a wink.

"We need to discuss a few things." Steele clasped his hands on his lap, his skin stained the same fake tan color as his face, as if he were trying to recreate sunlight in a place where there was none. "You've read all the atlases and history. You know the science behind the gateway discovery. I'm assuming you know what you're up against?"

"Partially," I said. "I know what you've told me. There's more I haven't been told."

He raised an eyebrow in an accusatory gesture. "What makes you say that?"

"You're Vortech." I laughed. "You rely on secrecy. Most of the world doesn't know you exist. The people who do fear you. For good reason."

A cold wipe chilled my arm as the nurse cleaned my shoulder. "This is the first one," she said. "It'll bite a bit."

"Got it."

"Do tell, Agent Harper." Steele waved a hand at me. "What is it you think we haven't told you?"

The needle pricked my arm. I did my best to ignore the sting. "The reason I'm going in. This isn't some scientific research mission. If it were, I'd be cataloging, bagging and tagging, exploring, that sort of thing. Instead, all you care about is cerecite. You only care if I come out with it. Nothing else. You've made the seven pieces of cerecite my primary mission. Why?"

"Your question is noted." His eyes narrowed, but he smiled. "Any other questions?"

"Yes," I continued, though I noted his lack of an answer to

my question. "The survivors of the shipwreck. It doesn't take a genius to figure out they made it under the dome two centuries ago. They've been living in an alternate reality ever since." Talking about an alternate reality out loud sounded absurd even to me, but after spending six months isolated on the island, I'd had time to give it some thought. Too much thought.

He pinched his lips. "You may be too clever for your own good, Sabine."

Sabine. He'd used my first name. I must've been getting under his skin. It was just as well. I was done with the song-and-dance. If Vortech wanted me under the dome, they'd do it by being honest with me.

"You're wrong on one thing, however." Steele crossed his arms. "This alternate reality, as you call it, is something more. Something we haven't determined. The shipwreck survivors were the first to discover this cave and what was in it. A bridge to an extra dimension." He nodded toward the glaring gateway, then he leaned forward. "The dimension they entered varied from our own by one major component. The rocks you see lying around this island were on theirs as well, except those stones were made up of cerecite, an extremely rare mineral that possesses incredible qualities.

"With it, they were able to create a dome that sheltered them from Champ Island's harsh weather."

The nurse injected me with the second shot. I winced, but I didn't flinch. "You should've told me this sooner," I said. "Why did you keep it a secret?"

"Because, as you said yourself, Vortech relies on secrecy. Secrets are power." He tapped his fingers on the tabletop in a nervous gesture, as if pondering how much to tell me. "Harper," he said softly, though his eyes bored into mine with enough intensity to make me flinch. "How much do you know about the flare?"

I shrugged. "As much as anyone else. It hit us ten years

ago. Knocked out our electronics and GPS for months. Millions of people died because we lost access to breathing machines. Medicines spoiled. Smaller flares are still affecting us now. Cancer has tripled in our population because of the radiation." That was a fact I knew too personally.

I chewed on my bottom lip as I pondered his question. He must've been getting at something else. "That's why I'm here, isn't it?"

His eyes narrowed, but he didn't reply.

"This was never a scientific mission. You need the cerecite for a power source."

"Yes," he said with a single nod. "The seven pieces of white cerecite can power our entire planet without the need for electricity."

Logan cursed. "You would own the planet," he said quietly. "You'd bankrupt every power company in the world. Is that what this is about? Money?"

Steele's eyes hardened. His shoulders stiffened. "No," he snapped. "Not money. It's about saving our world."

"Saving the world?" I asked. "What do you mean?"

He glanced away and pursed his lips. "There's a reason we haven't told you everything until now. There are some things not meant for the public, and this is a secret you can tell no one. Understood?"

I glanced at Logan. Did he know about this? If so, he'd done a good job hiding it. I turned back to Steele. "I understand."

"Good." He clasped his hands. "A month before the first flare, a coronal mass wave was recorded at four-hundred times the normal limit. We didn't think much of it. Most waves are barely detectable. But a month later, you know what happened. The sun erupted. It took out everything." He shook his head. "The government is lying to us. Has been since the flare. They say they're handling it. That another flare—statistically speaking—will never happen again in our lifetime, and if it does, they'll be prepared." Steele leaned forward. "But what if I told you that we recently detected another coronal mass wave. This one is three times larger than the last one. Harper, it will be strong enough to wipe every grid off the planet. Fossil fuels. Wind energy. Nuclear power. They'll be useless after this one."

Fear chilled me straight to my core. I sat speechless. What could we do? What could anyone do?

"Surely it's not that bad," Logan cut in. "We survived the first one. We'll do the same for this one."

"No," Steele said with certainty. "The only way to survive the next flare is to find an alternate power source. We need cerecite."

I imagined Mima's body lying in a casket, eaten by cancer that could have been treated if not for the flare. The same would happen to Dad if his cancer came back.

"It's a terrifying situation," Steele continued. "One that has one answer. We're not trying to control our planet, Agent Logan. We're trying to save it."

My gut twisted with unease. "So…" I said, my voice haunted. "If I don't recover the cerecite…"

"Then we lose our planet," Steele answered.

Panic shot like lightning down my spine. But beyond my fear, confusion plagued me. There was so much that didn't make sense. "Steele, you must realize how absurd this all sounds. You're literally telling me we're going to lose our planet, and I'm the only one going through the dome to save it. There are too many risks." I pointed to the gateway. "What if I die in there? Which is a very likely situation given we lost all the agents before me."

Steele steepled his fingers. "You're right, Harper. And believe me when I say we understand your concern. Trust me, we'd love to send a squadron through the dome and take every last piece of cerecite in there, but we've only got the tech to send one person through. Anyone else who enters gets crushed in the transition." He shook his head and sighed. "We've gone over every possible scenario. We ran millions of simulations. Our greatest chance for success was to send a single person into the dome—and that person couldn't be just anyone. They needed specific qualifications."

"You're referring to my EPC."

"Yes. Among other things." He rubbed his neck. "Eidetic Perceptive Cognition only exists in about one-one-thousandth of the population. Among those, only one-one-hundredth can function in society. We're lucky to have you, to be honest. If it weren't for the rigorous recruiting process our agents enacted, we never would have found you.

"With your enhanced abilities, you can focus on details with the laser focus of a supercomputer. You may be the only person on the planet who can find the cerecite in enough time to save us from another flare."

Another flare. I rubbed my forehead as a headache pounded. It was too much to take in.

Logan leaned forward. "Agent Steele, why weren't we told this sooner?"

"What good would it have done?" He spread his hands. "Telling you would have changed nothing."

"I don't buy it." Logan crossed his arms. "Surely the government has other options."

"Yes." Steele mimicked Logan and crossed his arms. "They do. They're working on alternate solutions to the problem. But we're not with the government. When Harper returns with the cerecite, we deliver it to the government. No questions asked. It's in our contract."

"How much have they agreed to pay you?" I asked.

Logan's jaw ticked, as if he were annoyed by my question. "As I said before, this isn't about money."

I studied him. Was there a possibility that there was no second flare coming? That they were using scare tactics to get me to do their work for them?

But what if they were telling the truth? Dad's life was on the line, and that was a risk I couldn't ignore. I'd already lost my mother and Mima to the last flare. I couldn't afford to lose anyone else. The thought of losing Dad shattered me.

"This is your final injection," the nurse said, punching the needle into my arm, then pulling it out with a quick jerk of her hand.

"You'll have some bruises to show off," Logan said, attempting a cheerful tone.

"Yeah." I laughed nervously, Steele's words haunting me, though I did my best to shrug away the fear. "I'm sure everyone under the dome will care." I glanced up at Steele, who stood and started pacing nervously.

Flare or not, lingering fear chased me. One thing I knew —I needed all the information I could get, and with Steele available to answer my questions, I would take my opportunity.

"What else can you tell me?" I asked. "Why haven't you told me about the immigrants? Don't you know anything about them?"

"No." He stopped pacing to stare at me. "Trust me when I say we don't have that information. Getting a clear idea of what's going on under the dome isn't easy. Our communications are slim to none, which is why we've equipped you with your Agent Fifteen unit. The AI is programmed to respond with all the Vortech protocols. Plus, it can communicate with you better than any of us. As far as their civilization goes, we placed an informant inside. His name is Ivan Nordgren. He's expecting you."

I scrutinized him. "What if I refuse to go?" Maybe it was a stupid question, but one that needed to be asked.

"That would be unwise." His voice took on a hardened edge. "Keep in mind, you weren't some random person we picked from the streets. We'll never find someone to replace you. Your EPC is necessary to find the seven pieces of cerecite. Use it to your advantage. Come back to us with the seven stones. That's all we're asking."

I closed my eyes to calm the nerves fluttering in my stomach. "All right," I answered. "Send me through the gateway. I'm as ready as I'll ever be."

Standing, I grabbed my backpack off the floor and faced the looming arch of glowing lights. Whatever was there, I was about to find out.

3

I squinted my eyes against the blinding fluorescent lights lining the gateway's outer edge. My image reflected in the mirrorlike façade. My tall frame reminded me of the photo of Mima June standing by a fence post with her knife strapped to her belt. The reflection wavered, as if it were made of quicksilver. I reached for it, but I hesitated before touching it.

"I wouldn't touch it if I were you," Logan said behind me.

"Why not? I'm going to walk through it, aren't I?"

"Sure, but it could cut your fingers off or something."

I forced a nervous laugh. "I doubt it."

Logan stood between me and the gateway, blocking the glare so I could see again. Scruff grew on his wind-chapped face. Wrinkles lined the corners of his eyes and around his mouth. I'd never thought of him as handsome, but at forty-something, he did remind me of my dad, and I had this insane urge not to disappoint him.

"Hey, kid, be careful out there, wherever you're going."

"I will."

"You got your weapon?"

"Always." I bent and pulled the knife out of my boot. The pearl-inlaid handle had worn in the places where Grandma's hands had held it. I wasn't sure my fingers fit as well as hers. "I'd bring the Sig-Sauer, but you know, it wouldn't be civilization appropriate and all that."

"Yeah. I know."

"Maybe they've got lightsabers on the other side," I suggested. "Or phasers. That would be cool."

"Nerd," he joked.

"Army brat," I countered.

He nodded at my knife. "The locals are most likely using pitchforks for all we know."

"I doubt it."

"Why?" he asked.

"They've got cerecite. They built a dome. There's technology out there."

"Probably true." He sighed. "Hey, Harper, be careful, all right? I'd hate to have trained you just for you to turn up dead. Wouldn't look good on my resume."

"Ha ha," I said sarcastically.

"I'm serious. We don't know why the last fourteen agents never came back. There's something dangerous on the other side. Just watch your back."

"I will," I answered. "I have no intentions of dying."

"Good. I have no intentions of waiting around forever for you to come back. I'm giving you a month, tops, then I'm headed to Hawaii for a much-needed vacation. If there's another flare on the way, I'm going out in style."

"Wonderful. I'll think of you when I'm huddled up in some igloo freezing my ass off."

He smiled. "And I'll think of you when I'm sitting on the beach drinking a piña colada watching the sun explode."

With a heavy sigh, I turned to the gateway. "It's a scary thought, isn't it? Another flare."

"Yeah," he answered with seriousness.

Silence pressed between us. The gateway shimmered like a

wall of liquid mercury. What would it be like to walk through it?

"You'll be fine," Logan said, as if he sensed my unease. "The other agents reported making it through, though I hear it's a rough transition. Just don't pop a lung and you'll be fine."

"Pop a lung? That's a new one."

He waved his hand. "Or get a concussion or break an arm or whatever it is the others reported."

Agent Steele approached us, looking businesslike as he carried a chrome-plated tube resembling a flashlight and handed it to me.

"What's this?" I asked. The metal weighed heavy and chilled my fingers. "My lightsaber?"

"No," he said without humor. "A scanner. You'll be able to detect elemental substances, including cerecite. Your AI unit can tell you how it works. Just be careful with it. Those instruments inside are fragile, which is why your bag is lined with Kevlar. The scanner will be protected if it's in your backpack."

"Got it." I unzipped my pack and stuffed it inside.

"Also." He held up a leather band decorated with a tarnished silver disc. "You've got some new jewelry. Once you get on the other side…" he lifted the band to reveal a letter "V" etched into the sliver disc… "press this button to communicate with Agent Fifteen. Wearing an earbud will be a dead giveaway you're from another dimension."

"And this?" I unzipped my mom's old bomber jacket and pointed to my sweater printed with the words *Red Shirt. I May Not Make It.* "Not sure if they've heard of *Star Trek* over there."

"Right. Wait till you get to the other side. The informant will have a change of clothes for you."

"Understood," I said as I strapped on the leather band, then took out my earbud and handed it to Steele.

"Ready?" he asked.

"Yeah. How about you stop asking me that and let me get on with this."

His hesitant smile told me he was either amused or put out at my snark, but I had to have a sense of humor through all this. Otherwise, I was certain I'd lose my mind, especially with the revelation of another flare. A gaggle of scientists gathered around us as I faced the gateway.

One of the scientists stepped to me and placed a pulse lead sticker on my neck. "We'll measure your vitals until you get to the other side. After that, you're on your own."

"I understand," I said, then gave a pointed look at Logan. "You'll tell my dad... if I don't make it back..." This was harder to say than I imagined.

Logan gave a single nod. "He'll know."

"Thank you," I managed.

As I crossed toward the portal, a clammy sweat broke out on my skin. "I'm doing this to save our world," I whispered to myself. *No. Not good enough.*

Another step.

"I'm doing this to find out what's out there." *I can do better.*

One more step.

I'm doing this because I love Dad. Because he deserves to be happy, to have a daughter who finishes what she starts. Because I need him to survive, or else I'll die with him.

The gateway's quicksilver surface reflected my image. It showed the determination in my eyes—and the fear.

I stepped through the gateway.

4

S ilver encased me.

The air escaped my lungs, and a boom blasted.

I fell. My stomach dropped, and I landed hard on a stone floor. Stars replaced my vision. My wrist screamed with pain. The fall would have knocked the wind out of me if I'd had oxygen in my lungs.

Gasping, I used my good arm to push to a sitting position. I blinked until I could see.

Glass lay in shards around me. Thousands of tiny slivers were all that remained of the computer screens and mirrors. The quiet came as a shock. Rubbing my forehead, I tried to think through the blinding pain in my head and my wrist.

Nausea welled in my stomach. Spots danced in my vision.

A door banged loudly, pulling my gaze up the staircase and to the open doorway on the landing above me.

The room looked exactly the same as the one I'd come from, down to the computer monitors and steel-plated walls, except everything here was smashed. Glass lay in glittering shards over the floor. The portal gateway was twisted, and the metal blackened. A mangled mess of wires and metal casing replaced what had once been the outer shell. What had happened to it?

I climbed to my feet and pulled my backpack up with me.

My rational brain noted the blood pooling on the floor and dripping behind me. With a quick glance at my hands, I saw cuts slicing across my skin, although adrenaline masked the pain.

I fumbled my bag open and pulled out some gauze with my good hand, then did a sloppy job of wrapping it around my cuts. Logan would be appalled, but it was better than leaving the wounds open to the air.

After closing my bag, I studied the remains of the gateway door, touching a piece of cold metal. "No wonder it almost killed me to come through it."

Glancing around the room, I forced my mind to slow down and think through my situation. I most likely had a concussion. A sprained or broken wrist. Judging by how swollen it had gotten, my bet was on the latter.

I needed to find the informant, and I needed help.

With a wince, I managed to press the button on my leather band, thankfully wrapped around the uninjured arm.

"...Harper..." a staticky voice chirped. "You...made..."

"Hey, Fifteen. I'm alive. I'm here, wherever that is." I turned in a circle around the room, my boots crunching over glass. "This place is pretty destroyed. I don't think I'll be going home this way. Can you tell me where I should find this informant?"

"Not far. Half-a-mile to the east... last known location. Latitude. Fifteen degrees... Longitude. Thirty degrees...West. Coordinates. Fifteen. Ten. Twenty... Four-fifty-six."

"You're cutting out. Can you repeat?"

His voice came through, but the static made it impossible to hear.

"Fifteen. Repeat."

The static stopped. The silence came back, more deafening than before. Glancing around the room, I swallowed the bile rising in my throat.

Alone. In a foreign reality. Communications were shot. Multiple injuries. Well, at least it couldn't get much worse.

"Says the girl about to be attacked by aliens…" I muttered as I crossed to the stairs. Every step sent pain shooting down my spine, and the tiniest movements made my wrist scream. When I reached the top landing, I slung my backpack over my shoulder. The open door slammed backward in the wind, hanging awkwardly off its hinges. I stared past the door leading to my new reality. The snowy landscape stretched. Snow crunched underfoot as I stood on the bunker's threshold. Wind howled, and ice crystals blustered past. In the light of the storm, blue globes radiated light over the barren waste.

Steele's words came back to me.

The difference in this reality is the round stones. They're made of cerecite on this side. I went to the closest one and ran my gloved hand over it, dusting the snow off the top, then knelt to be eye-level. The turquoise glow danced like firelight inside the stone.

"Beautiful," I said to myself, looking from one stone to the next. They lit my path through the storm. As I walked from one glowing rock to the next, I unhooked my compass from my backpack and got my bearings.

The compass needle danced in slow circles. I bumped it several times until it turned a lazy circle to true north. When the needle lined up, I turned to face west.

The sun hung low on the horizon, a gray, shadowy ball behind thick clouds. Icy wind burned my cheeks as I trekked over the snow-packed ground. I licked my cracked, dry lips. Oxygen froze in my chest.

Whoever had destroyed the gateway bunker had done one hell of a job. I was lucky to be alive. The only reason I'd survived was because my side of the gate still functioned.

It bothered me that the gateway had been destroyed. Not

only did it mean I didn't have a ride home, it also meant someone had made some enemies here.

"I can't wait to meet them," I mumbled, my exhale coming out in a puff of wispy white air.

My boots sank into the powdery snow. I kept my hood down as I trudged, using the boulder's light to guide me.

On the horizon, evergreen trees appeared. I stopped, narrowing my eyes, making sure I wasn't seeing things.

Trees.

There hadn't been any trees on the Champ Island I knew. But this was a different reality.

Hiking to the forest, I spotted a thin line of smoke churning from a chimney and a log cabin tucked inside the woods.

Excitement spurred my movements. The informant. Had to be.

Still, if I were wrong. If the person were hostile…

My hands shook with cold as I grabbed my knife out of my boot. Wind blustered, and I wiped the flakes of snow off my face before approaching.

"Stop," a gruff voice barked behind me. "Drop the weapon."

I stiffened. Should've known he would've been outside. Then again, if this were the informant, maybe I could negotiate.

"Who are you?" he demanded.

"My name's Harper," I answered. "Sabine Harper."

A moment of silence ticked past. "You're with Vortech?"

Anxiety trickled through my blood. If he were hostile and I admitted to being Vortech, what then? But I had to take that chance. I would be dead out here if I didn't find help soon. "Yes," I answered.

"Turn around," he commanded.

I did as he said and spun to face him. Fear darted down my spine. A mammoth of a man loomed over me. His grizzled, graying beard and his weathered skin, sunburnt in patches on his cheeks and nose, hinted at a life spent outdoors. Malice exuded from the hunch of his shoulders to his narrowed eyes. Snow particles blew around him, blustering his coat of animal furs. He drew a bone hilted machete from a sheath at his waist. Blood splotches marred its tarnished surface.

"I'm Ivan Nordgren. Your informant." He pulled the furs away from his hand, showing me a leather band around his wrist. The round, metal disc gleamed. It looked identical to mine. He nodded at my blade. "You can put that away."

"You first."

He shrugged, then stuck the machete in its sheath.

I held my knife for a second longer, then placed it back in my boot. As I straightened, he narrowed his gaze at me.

"You're the next lab rat, huh?" He spat a glob of brown spit on the ground. "You from the states?"

"Yes. Kansas. You?"

"Alaska. Wilderness guide before I came here. That was thirty years ago. Looks like you made it, though. Wasn't sure you'd get through the gateway in one piece."

"I made it. Not sure about the one-piece part." I nodded to my sling.

"Injured, huh?"

"Yeah. Broke my wrist. Hit my head, too. That was one hell of a welcome."

He reached inside his fur-lined vest and pulled out a metal flask. "This should help. There's green cerecite mixed in it. Should fix that injury."

"Green cerecite?"

"Yes. Helps with healing."

I cocked my head. "I'm supposed to find cerecite. What's it doing in your drink?"

"You're looking for white cerecite. The pure stuff," he clarified. "There's all sorts of cerecite on this island. Blue, yellow. Green. We use green for healing, so you'd better drink up."

I took the flask from him, unscrewed the lid, and sniffed the contents. The pungent scent burned my nose. "It smells delicious."

"Don't knock it." He laughed. "You won't find anything better at healing than green cerecite."

"I'll take your word for it." I looked inside the flask where a dark greenish liquid swirled, then I pressed the opening to my lips. The drink slid down my throat, tasting of wheat grass juice. I swallowed, then shoved the flask back to him.

"I've tasted worse."

He smiled as he stuffed the metal container back into his vest.

"Let's get you inside. There's a lot you need to know before you start hunting white cerecite."

He stepped to the cabin when a glowing wolf bounded to us and jumped on Ivan's legs.

"Whoa there, Brutus. We've got a friend here." He patted the beast's head before turning to me. "Say hello to Agent Harper."

I approached the wolf, curiosity tugging at me as I inspected the blue strands of its fur. "Your wolf is glowing."

"Mystik wolf," he explained. "All the animals on this island look the same."

I knelt by the creature and patted its head. My photographic memory jumped out. Wolf. Canis Lupus. The individual strands of fur were soft to the touch, though they resembled crystals, and I assumed they must've been feather-like to be so smooth.

I glanced up at Ivan. "What causes the glow?"

"It's the green cerecite that does it. Someone who takes in this stuff all their lives—well, it changes their cells. After they die, a portion of their DNA stays around, gets turned into something else. Mother Nature's way of recycling. You'll see these creatures roaming all over the place."

"This is incredible."

The wolf barked, and I gave it a playful pat before standing up.

"Let's head in," Ivan called, waving, as he trudged to the cabin. I followed him through the snow, the wolf trotting in front of me.

A million questions swam through my mind. I'd expected this reality to have its differences, but this? Glowing wolves and miraculous healing potions? Where did it all come from?

When I stepped through the door, warmth exuded from a fireplace at the far wall. A table and a few chairs decorated the room. Shelves with books and knickknacks lined the wall to my right, and a cot strewn with worn blankets took up the floor space nearby.

"Sit." He pointed to a roughly hewn chair by a makeshift table.

I placed my bag on the ground and rested on the seat, the wood creaking.

Exhaustion crashed with me. I could sleep right here in the chair and be refreshed come morning.

Ivan busied himself around the room, placing a kettle on the fire and taking a loaf of bread from a cupboard.

"Vortech sent me word last week you were coming." He placed a loaf of bread and some butter in front of me. I tore off a piece and popped it in my mouth, only now realizing how hungry I was.

"Tell me about the other agents," I said. "Vortech says they don't know what happened to them."

His eyes narrowed. "Vortech said that, huh?"

I paused before taking another bite. "Do you know what happened to them?"

He heaved a long sigh before answering. "Most of the agents found a few pieces of cerecite, then turned up missing.

I've searched but never found them. This last agent to come through, her name was Rodriguez. Rosa Rodriguez. She got closer than all the others. Found six of the stones. I really thought she had a chance."

He placed two mugs of tea on the table, then sat across from me. Brutus lay at his feet, propping his head on his paws, his wide eyes peering up at us.

"Don't you have any idea what happened to her?" I asked before sipping the tea.

"I followed her trail out near the caves past Edenbrooke. Found a few of her things. And this." He stood, removed a book from a shelf, and placed it on the table in front of me. "Her journal."

I opened it, finding the pages filled with sentences written in Spanish and a few crude drawings.

"She'd had the six pieces of white cerecite with her when she went missing. When I found her, the cerecite was gone."

I narrowed my gaze at him. "Any idea where it ended up?"

He nodded. "The palace," he answered gravely. "Happened every time. An agent recovers the cerecite, they go missing, and the cerecite returns to the palace." He leaned forward. "Someone in the palace is causing the agents to disappear. Vortech will tell you not to get involved with the royals. It's not your business. Stick to finding the cerecite. But you'd be a fool to ignore what's going on in that place. When Rodriguez disappeared, she was onto something. Vortech says her ECP made her go crazy. She got paranoid. But the truth is, she knew too much. Something with the royals put her on edge, some big secret only they knew."

"You think Vortech knew?"

"No idea. But there's no doubt the royals are guarding the cerecite. Have been for centuries." Ivan tapped his fingers on the table in a nervous gesture. "They've got a problem with it, though. A big one."

Pondering his words, I took a bite of bread. "What kind of problem?"

"It's the nature of the stuff. You've probably realized by now that this side functions differently than yours and ours. Scientific principles aren't the same. The white cerecite, for example. In its true form, it looks like a ball of white glass. But it doesn't stay that way. It mimics objects around it. Put it in a room full of pots and pans, and it changes to look like one of them."

Processing his words, I sipped my tea. If my muddled head were from a concussion or trying to make sense of this place, I couldn't be sure. "Let me get this straight—the past agents found the cerecite, then they went missing. The cerecite ends up back in the palace, but it mimics objects around it, making it hard to find again."

"Right."

"If that's the case, then how am I supposed to find it?"

Brutus paced. Ivan gave him a scratch on his head before he sat in front of the fireplace.

"Vortech gave you a scanner?" he asked.

"Yeah. In my bag."

"Good. Keep it. That'll tell you if you've got white cerecite. Finding it in the first place is trickier. That's why they sent you. My guess is you're good at picking up on details."

"I'm okay, I guess."

He chuckled and crossed his arms. "Don't be modest. There's a reason Vortech sends your type. Once you're in the palace, you'll need to pay attention. After ten years, I imagine the objects will be spread around a bit. The royals have tried to keep the objects locked up, but the nature of white cerecite makes it impossible to keep them in one place for long." He reached across the table and patted Agent Rodriguez's journal. "She put clues in here as to what form they may've taken. For example—" He placed his mug at the table's center. "We see an ordinary mug." He spun it around. "Nothing out of the ordinary. But when cerecite takes the form of something, it's always changing. It's the chemical nature of the thing. There's too much radiation for it to contain, so it shifts slightly to keep from going nuclear. You'll see a cup with a chip one minute. The next minute. No chip." He took a sip from it, then placed it on the wood with a thud. "That's why Vortech sent you. You're good at spotting the little differences no one else notices. ECP, right? Just like Rodriguez." He nodded at the journal.

"Yeah, about that. My high school Spanish is rusty."

"Then you'll have to ask for help from your AI unit once it calibrates with this reality. That could take some time, so while you're waiting, you may as well get familiar with the palace and the people in it."

He stood and crossed the room to a bookshelf. Some of the books caught my eye. *Ithical-A History. The Tale of the Green Dragon. Mystik Creatures of the Island.*

Books.

Like the trees, they came unexpectedly, and this new reality was something I'd need time to process.

The fact that there were books on the island meant the shipwreck victims must've done more than just survived here. They'd built a civilization.

Ivan slid a leather-bound folder from between two books. When he returned to the table, he placed the folder on top of the journal.

"What's this?" I opened it to reveal a map on the top of the stack.

"This is your new reality. Welcome to Ithical Island."

"Ithical Island?" I questioned.

"That's right. You can't think of this as Champ Island anymore. Some of the landmarks are the same, the location of the gateways are in the same place, and the positioning of some of the boulders match the other island. But the similarities stop there. This island is immensely bigger than Champ. I don't know how many square miles, but as far as I've traveled, I can tell you it's large enough to be a continent."

I tilted my head. "How is that possible?"

He shook his head. "I'm no scientist. I can't even start to guess. Also, another difference, the cerecite shaped this reality into a place you won't recognize." He tapped the map. "Might wanna glance at this while you've got the opportunity."

"Got it."

I smoothed a hand over the parchment. Inked lines connected the villages, a broad lake in the southern portion and mountains in the northeastern half. One city, labeled *Ithical City*, dominated the center of the circular island. Several small villages, *Harpsinger, Grimwillow Grove, Edenbrooke, Fablemarch Vale*, surrounded the capital. A palace rose at the center of the main city.

On the next page, I found photos and a list of the royals.

The dark eyes of one the pictures caught my attention. A man in his early twenties stood apart from the rest, though I wasn't sure what made me focus on him. Maybe it was his lips pressed to form a thin line, as if he were trying to keep a secret. Or maybe it was his pale skin indicating a chronic illness. Or the angular, masculine shape of his jaw. Whatever it was, I had trouble pulling my gaze from the picture.

MORVEN ALEXANDER TREMAYNE the photo was labeled.

"Who's this?" I asked.

"The crown prince," Ivan answered. "Soon to take the throne on his next birthday. We don't see him often. Word is he's sick. He only makes appearances every now and then. Doesn't speak much. Keeps to himself." He leaned forward, and his gaze fixed on me. "This kid's parents died just before Rodriguez went missing. Then, no one saw the prince much after that."

"You think whoever made Rodriguez disappear had something to do with the death of the royals?"

Ivan shrugged. "Just keep your eyes open in that palace. That's all I'm saying."

I scanned the other photos. Ivan pointed to a picture of a middle-aged woman with arched eyebrows and a smug smile. "This is the queen regent. She's not well-liked, though to be fair, none of the Tremayne family has made a good impression on their people. There's been trouble with the cerecite miners lately. Wage disputes and working conditions, that sort of thing. The palace has doubled their guards. Damn near impossible to get into that place."

"Interesting." I gave him a guarded smile. "You do realize I had no idea any of this was here. You'll have to forgive me if this comes as a shock."

He chuckled. "You wouldn't be the first agent to admit it."

I tapped my fingers on the paper. Unanswered questions filled my mind. "If the cerecite is in the palace, and it's impossible to get inside, how am I supposed to get access to it?"

His smile showed a hint of his teeth, though the gleam in his eye spoke of danger. "Easy. The prince is always in need of a caretaker. They just fired the last one. I happened to find a young woman from a local fishing village called Fablemarch Vale who'll fit the bill. She'll start work in the morning."

I raised an eyebrow. "As the prince's caretaker?"

He grinned and gave a single nod.

Sitting back in my chair, I rubbed my forehead. "Wasn't expecting that one."

He shrugged. "You'll only have to keep up the charade until you find the cerecite."

I tapped my fingers on the table, then pushed the envelope aside and opened Rosa's journal.

El sonido es una mentira.

El tiempo es una mentira

La ubicación es una mentira.

La materia es una mentira

La luz es una mentira.

El mundo es una mentira

¿Veneno?

"This word." I pointed to *mentira*. "Any idea what it means? It's repeated in every phrase except the last."

"I'm not sure, but there are seven words on the list."

"Seven, as in the seven pieces of cerecite. You said she found six, and six are crossed out. Do you think mentira means cerecite?"

He scratched his beard. "It's possible."

Sighing, I scanned the other words. Some I understood.

Tiempo. Time.

Luz. Light.

Mundo. World.

I flipped to the next pages, but the writing grew illegible, all except for the word mentiras written over and over.

"What happened here?" I pointed to the writing.

He gave a sigh and shook his head. "Rodriguez, well, she got a little cracked at the end. Started thinking Vortech was after her. It's a shame really, what happened." He sipped from his mug and looked toward the room's only window, though it was too dark to see anything.

I studied him a moment, picking apart the pieces of his unspoken words. "Ivan, may I borrow your books about Ithical Island? Anything that will help me understand this place better? Vortech wasn't much help."

"Sure. In the bookshelf. I've got a few histories and an atlas. Feel free to look through them." He pointed to the shelves lined in leather bound tomes. Ivan stood and grabbed my empty mug. "You can take the cot. I'll sleep out in the woodshed. Got a nice bunk out there, a little yellow cerecite lantern for heat."

"You're sure?"

"Sure as anything. Haven't had any guests out here in ages. You'll need the rest more than me, after all. It's you looking for the cerecite." He took the dishes to a washbasin, humming as he worked.

I got to my feet and shuffled to the bookshelf, grabbed a few tomes, and sat on my cot. My stiff muscles burned, and a dull headache pounded behind my eyes. The fire crackled as I got settled on the canvas frame.

After I unlaced my boots, I settled down with the books. I read for a while until I couldn't keep my eyes open any longer. As sleep took me, all I could see was the face of the prince, and the haunted look I'd seen on his face.

Ivan sang a tune as I drifted off.

When you look in the mirror,
The only map you'll see,
Is of the tear trails,
Running down your cheeks.

5

I stood by Ivan overlooking Ithical City. I'd removed my sling, and nothing but a little soreness remained in my broken wrist. Wiggling my fingers, I rotated my hand.

"Does the green cerecite always work so quickly?" I asked, gingerly pressing the tendons, feeling nothing but a bit of pressure.

He smiled. "Usually does, yes."

"Nice. I could get used to a reality like this."

Brutus barked playfully, and Ivan patted the Mystik wolf's head.

"Stay here, Brutus," Ivan said. "I won't be taking you into the city today. We've got to get inside that bloody capital." His gaze wandered out to the skyline. Glittering towers and elegant copper domes reflected the sun. Marble statues stood as tall as wind turbines, and waterfalls tumbled from hanging gardens. Glittering golden rails ran above the city atop Grecian-style pillars.

"They have trains here?" I asked.

"Yes. Think of this place like a time capsule. When the survivors built this world, they did it with nineteenth-century technology in mind, building trains and buggies. But with the aid of cerecite, their tech advanced quickly. That's why you'll see everything powered by it."

"What makes the rails shimmer like that?" I asked, pointing, as a train whistled in the distance.

"Yellow cerecite. Works great as a power source. Don't touch it, though. It's poisonous if you ingest too much." He chuckled.

"What's so funny?"

He shook his head, and a smile creased his mouth. "Not long after I first arrived, I was waiting at a rail station. Saw a little girl, maybe four, trying to lick the rails. She said they looked like honey sweets. Her parents had to pull her away." He hooked his thumbs in his belt loops. "You see a lot of things when you're here as long as me."

"It's an incredible world," I marveled. "I don't understand how this exists and our reality knows nothing about it."

"Vortech," he answered. "They're good at one thing, I'll give them that. Keeping secrets is what they're best it."

"But it's also the trouble with communications, isn't it?" I asked.

He nodded. "We can't send messages of more than a few sentences every now and then, and that's a problem. The only way out of this place is to open a gateway, but you've seen what our side of the gate looks like."

"Yeah. It's unrecognizable. How are we supposed to get out of here without a functioning gate?"

"Never fear." He patted Brutus' head. "There's more than one way to skin a cat. There's a larger gateway on the north side of the island. Once you find the seven cerecite stones, it'll be easy enough to power the gateway and get back to our reality."

A breeze rushed past as we stood under the cover of trees. The air didn't hold the aroma of spruce as I would've imagined. Instead, a metallic scent got caught on the wind, tasting sharp on my tongue.

"That's odd," I said.

"Odd?" he asked.

"The air," I clarified. "It doesn't smell right."

"Yes. You'll have to get used to that. Being under a dome means the air gets filtered." His gaze wandered to the sky, and I noticed a purplish tint to the blue, as if I looked at a screen rather than something organic.

"Have the people ever tried to escape the dome?" I asked.

"I'm sure some have. Never been successful. The thing is, the people live in Utopia, so there's no motivation to leave." He sighed, looking out toward the city. "We should go. The queen holds an audience at ten AM sharp, and she's expecting me to introduce you. Follow me." He waved over his shoulder, and I descended the hill beside him.

I adjusted my new bag's straps, one Ivan had loaned me, with drawstrings instead of a zipper. The buckles on my new boots jangled as I walked. The supple leather rose to my knees, and I kept my knife tucked inside. Ivan had supplied me with new clothes, too. The pants fit comfortably, and the white shirt's sleeves billowed, made from a light, airy fabric. I picked at the buckles on my vest where pockets covered the front and lined the inside.

I may've looked the part of a commoner, but I'd have to brush up on my acting skills if I wanted to pass as one. Ivan had instructed me on how to pronounce my r's and draw out my o's, use the name *da* for dad or father, slight nuances that would aid in blending in. Thankfully, the Scottish brogue of yesteryear had been replaced with less of a distinct accent, and Ivan assured me not to worry about sounding out of place. Diverse dialects from each village were common enough, and I could always blame a slip of accent from being from a distant settlement.

We made it out of the forest and took a road leading to the city. Vehicles sped past us, and I did my best not to stare at the chrome-plated machines with whirring engines, crawling along like caterpillars with rows of twenty glowing yellow wheels. Some were bulkier and moved slower, resembling beetles lumbering down the copper-paved street.

When we entered the city, people bustled past us. Some cast wary glances at Ivan, who was less than inconspicuous with his furs and bone-handled machete. I walked casually, hoping to blend in, trying not to gawk as I passed through the lanes with Grecian-style and modern structures lining either side. Gold and glass gleamed. Art mixed with functionality.

We approached a town square where vendors and food carts packed the space. The scent of cooked meat and pastries wafted, and my stomach growled. Ivan bought us a few platters of thinly sliced steak and grilled onions. He ate with his fingers, and I was too hungry to make a fuss, so I scooped the food and shoveled it in my mouth as I trailed behind him. The seasoned meat fell apart in my mouth, and tender onions added a savory flavor, nothing like MREs and protein bars.

I raced to keep pace with Ivan. We marched down a broad road that led us to a bridge crossing a deep gorge. Glacier blue water rushed beneath us. Ahead of us rose the palace.

"That's the capital building and the home of the royals. That big tower on the bottom is where they hold government matters. The two higher levels are where the nobility lives. That's where you'll be spending most of your time."

I followed his line of sight to the two top towers, and a sudden onslaught of nerves twisted in my stomach.

As we stepped off the bridge, we came to a row of guards stationed outside the wall encircling the castle. They wore black leather pants and breastplates. Links of silver chainmail glinted through joints in their plated armor. Plaid robes were arranged over their left shoulders, held together with a dragon-shaped brooch, a glittering green jewel for the eye. Copper masks covered their faces. Each guard held a long pike. A dark green banner, tied below the blades, flapped in the chilly breeze.

"Halt," two of the guards barked in unison as we approached the main gates. They crossed their pikes with the clanking of metal.

"State your name and business."

Ivan pulled a scroll from his vest pocket and handed it to one of the guards. "Here to meet with Her Majesty the Queen Regent, if you please. This young lady is to be the new caretaker for His Highness, the prince."

Through the narrow slit in his mask, the guard's eyes shifted to me. A chill ran down my spine. The other guard took the scroll and studied it.

"Is this faked?" he asked.

"No, sir. I've got the queen regent's own signature there. You can check it if you like."

He placed his hands on his hips. "Are you in the habit of telling the queen regent's guards what to do?"

"I... ah..." Ivan shifted, casting a worried glance at me before turning back to the guard. "No, sir."

The guard loomed closer. "Keep your mouth to yourself, brute, or your neck might end up on the wrong end of a noose." He pulled a metal, square object from his pocket. With a click, a blue light glowed, and he held it over the scroll. After replacing the light in his pocket, he gave the scroll back to the first guard. "It checks out," he said quietly.

"Very well. We'll let you inside, *brute*," he said the name mockingly. "But just so you know, the queen regent has doubled the guard due to the troubles with the miners. Don't give anyone a reason to notice you." His eyes shifted to me. "Same goes to you."

The guards stepped aside, and the man on the right pulled a lever on the wall. With the sound of rotating gears, the massive bronze gates swung inward. When we stepped through, I exhaled my pent-up breath.

"That was tense," I said. "Did they have to be so rude?"

Ivan shrugged. "It's their job."

I eyed him. "You aren't upset?"

"They're only protecting the castle. Everyone's on edge. Soldiers with jobs like theirs can't afford to be nice."

We walked down a footpath to a garden area. The intersecting copper-tiled walkways created a network of square patterns. Patches of neatly trimmed grass grew between the squares. The vivid color and perfect texture bugged me.

"Ivan, wait." I knelt beside a grassy patch and ran my fingers over the blades.

"What're you doing?" Ivan asked.

"This grass looks unusual." I plucked a piece, studying the perfect tip of the sword-like blade, the flair of the stem, and its perfect green hue. Still, I couldn't tell what seemed so out of place, so I picked another blade, then held it beside the first. Their shapes matched up perfectly, the tip and the curve, even the stems running through the center were the same width.

"They're exactly the same." I glanced up at Ivan.

"Cerecite." He shrugged. "Haven't I told you? That's the answer to everything."

"Cerecite makes them the same?" I plucked another blade, comparing it to the first two—the three matched, down to the tiny veins running throughout.

"Yes. Engineers on this side use green cerecite to create plants. How else do you think anything could grow in the frozen waste of the Bering Sea?"

"I don't know. But it does remind me of something."

"Remind you of what?"

"Nothing." I shook my head, not wanting to explain the uniformity of the wheat kernels in Vortech's VR sphere, not sure he'd understand my suspicion—as I didn't understand it myself.

Glancing up at Ivan, I wondered how much he knew, and how much he was keeping secret.

"Ivan," I asked casually. "Is there anything else I should know about this reality? Anything you haven't told me?"

He shifted and glanced away. His eyes darted, and a dark look haunted him for a half second. It was such a brief expression, I almost missed it. But I'd seen that look before. Logan's training on truth detecting and social cues came back to me with full clarity.

Ivan knew something. A dangerous secret? Perhaps.

"I believe I've told you all the important things," Ivan said. "Just remember." His eyes darkened. "Keep your eyes open in there." He nodded to the looming palace behind him. "Whoever put the cerecite in there also had something to do with the disappearances of the other agents. You seem capable and smart. I'm rooting for you, Harper. Don't disappear like they did."

"I'll keep that in mind." After standing, I tossed the grass aside and stood to face him "Ivan, that's really all you can tell me? This world." I motioned around me. "Something seems off. You don't know anything else?"

"No," he said, a hardened edge to his voice that I hadn't heard before. "Now, let's go. No time to waste, Harper. You know the stakes as well as I do. We can't afford to wait for the second flare to hit."

He turned and marched away, and I followed.

Doubts crowded my mind. Ivan's reminder of the flare put me on edge. It seemed any time I questioned something, Vortech's answer was to remind me of the flare. But I had to admit, I'd seen no evidence of a second flare. No news reports. No scientific articles. Not even the conspiracy theorists were talking about it. Were scientists around the globe and world governments really able to keep such a giant secret? Or was something more sinister going on? Something Vortech wanted to be kept a secret?

I shook my head. Whatever was going on, I would find out, but first, I had a job to do. I caught up to Ivan who was hurrying down the path, though I couldn't shake the image of the grass and the metallic scent in the air, and I had to refocus my attention on my current surroundings to keep the suspicious feelings away.

A few soldiers milled around. Some cast lingering stares, but none stopped us, though I did notice Ivan carried his scroll in plain view.

We traversed to a courtyard leading to the palace's main entrance. The wind carried the sound of bagpipes. The music grew louder as we approached the sprawling staircase leading up to an entrance hall overshadowed by a Grecian-style gable. Carvings of people riding horses decorated its façade. At the center of the carving stood a dragon, its wings outstretched.

Two men played bagpipes in the atrium. The acoustics beneath the domed entry amplified the harmonized resonance of the instruments. Ascending the steps in such a foreign place while listening to the familiar sound of the bagpipes made the hairs on my arms stand on end. The melody created a magical aura that floated around the pillars and carvings, unseen, yet felt.

We crossed through the main vestibule, past a statue of a dragon created from oxidized bronze, and we entered the palace through a pair of carved marble doors.

The ceiling soared ninety feet overhead. Its square copper tiles glimmered in the light streaming through the walls of windows.

"Amazing." My voice echoed, then faded in the room's expanse. Only a few servants wearing uniforms of black and dark green plaid milled about as we strode into a hallway.

Paintings of knights wearing armor and the image of an imposing green dragon filled the pictures adorning the walls.

We exited the hallway and entered a room larger than the foyer. Gold leaf covered the pillars, walls, and ceiling. Our footsteps rang out over the marble floor of midnight blue streaked with veins of swirling gold.

No wonder Ivan had called this place a utopia.

At the back of the room, in front of a curtain with golden sashes, a dais rose. Two thrones sat atop it. A woman occupied one of the chairs. Several people stood on the steps leading to her. Guards stood at the alert behind her, and several more paced the outer perimeter of the room.

We stopped behind the group of people who spoke in hushed tones, though I caught bits of conversations.

"…petitioning for the sale of wheat and barley in the eastern…"

I peeked around them to get a better look at the woman on the throne. I recognized the Queen Regent from Ivan's picture. Pale skin stretched across her skeletal cheeks and collarbones. She wore a black dress decorated with a dark green tartan. A dragon-shaped brooch held the sash in place. She sat with stiff hands folded in her lap. Her lips were pressed together as she scowled.

"The queen looks better in her picture," I whispered to Ivan.

He chuckled quietly. "She's severe, to be sure. You'll need to address her as Queen Regent Tremayne, or Your Highness is also acceptable. Be careful of what you say. She's been known to throw out servants for serving her butter too warm or not styling her hair to her liking."

"Wonderful," I muttered.

The line dwindled until only we remained. A servant stood beside her, holding a platter with a goblet. He offered her a drink, and she took a small sip before motioning us forward.

I followed Ivan up the stairs. The queen's unforgiving eyes followed my movements.

Ivan knelt at her feet, and I did the same, though I lowered too quickly and rammed my knees into the floor.

Ouch. I hoped the queen didn't notice.

"Rise." She drew out the word, her tone bored and uninterested.

We stood, and Ivan took a step forward, then held out the scroll he'd been carrying so prominently with him. "Mr. Ivan Nordgren, Your Majesty. I've come with the girl I wrote to you about."

"Ah." She took the scroll from him, opened it, and read it quietly. "Yes, I remember. The caretaker. We're anxious to find a replacement." Her words carried a slight Scottish accent. She stood and glided forward, her gown softly rustling as she moved to stand in front of me. I clasped my hands behind my back to hide my nervousness.

She eyed me, then fingered the ties on my collar before circling me. "What positions have you held before?"

I swallowed a hard knot in my throat, my nervousness threatening to overwhelm me, but my training kicked in, and I stood with a straight back, my head up, the way I would do if Logan was drilling me.

"I've had several months of training, Your Majesty."

"Months?" She tsked her tongue. "That's it?" Her eyes grew shrewd. "You are awfully young. How old are you?"

"Twenty-one, Your Majesty."

She frowned. "Nearly the same age as my nephew. That's hardly appropriate." She waved her hand. "I'm sorry, Mr. Ivan. She's much too young. I wish you would've written to me of her age sooner, but she won't do. It's a shame." She turned to sit on her throne, and Ivan shot me a panicked glance.

"What now?" I mouthed.

He only shook his head. My mind went into overdrive. I had to get this job. Finding the cerecite would be impossible without it.

"Your Majesty," I called.

She glanced over her shoulder. Her eyebrows rose in a perturbed gesture.

"With all due respect, I believe I'm more than qualified for this position."

"Is that so, Miss—"

"Harper," I answered. "Sabine Harper."

"Well then, do tell, Miss Harper." She waved her hand dramatically. "What makes you think I should let you stay here?"

"Because I'm observant," I spoke boldly. "I can tell when anything is amiss. I'm also well-educated. I've spent years studying not only Ithical Island, but the world outside our dome. Your nephew will be the most qualified king in all Ithical. I'll do as you say, and I won't cause problems. If you want your nephew to be a wise ruler, then you'll hire me."

The queen laughed, then looked at Ivan. "Bold claims. Mr. Ivan, is that all true?"

"It is."

"Well." She placed her hands on her hips. "In that case, you should know I will expect you to be more than his caretaker. He's a headstrong young man, and despite his age, he hasn't spent nearly enough time learning to be ruler. If I hire you, I expect you to be his tutor. You answer to me. If I feel he isn't progressing in the areas I deem important, then you lose your job. Is that understood?"

"Completely, Your Majesty," I answered without breaking eye contact.

"Very well then." She finally looked away. "You may stay."

"Thank you." I spoke too loudly, the relief evident in my voice, and she cast me a sharp glance. I cleared my throat and stood straight, doing my best to hide my smile.

She returned to her throne. "You'll start work right away. The prince is in desperate need of some education, and I'll not allow him to while away his time. We're severely understaffed. We've recently lost our housekeeper, but you can speak with Mrs. O'Connor in the kitchens to loan you a uniform and show you to a room."

She sat on her throne. Behind us, a line of petitioners gathered.

"Dismissed," she said with a wave of her hand.

"Sorry, where are the kitchens?" I asked.

"Dismissed," she repeated with steel in her voice, and I had no choice but to turn around and follow Ivan out of the throne room.

"Ivan," I whispered. "Where are the kitchens?"

He shook his head. "I don't know. Maps of the palace are hard to come by. Royals like to stay secluded. This place is built like a labyrinth, too. But the kitchens…" He rubbed his chin. "Could be on the second tier."

We reached the massive foyer and back to the doors leading out. He stopped walking to face me. The warning in his eyes caught me by surprise. "You remember what I told you about the royals?"

"Yes."

"Good." His gaze darted, and his voice lowered to a whisper. "Don't trust everything Vortech tells you. Whatever happened to Rodriguez, it has something to do with the royal family. Remember that, and you might survive."

I felt Mima's knife tucked safely in my boot, warm against my ankle. "I'll remember," I answered sincerely. "Will I see you again?"

He shook his head. "Most likely not. But you know where I live. If ever you need help, I'm not far."

I nodded, and he held out his hand. I hesitated but placed my fingers in his. As expected, I flinched, and the urge to recoil nearly overwhelmed me, which always happened with extra perception. Sure, I could find things no one else could, but touching people was another story, and it took all my willpower not to snatch my hand away.

He didn't seem to notice, or perhaps he'd had experience with people like me and knew what to expect. When the handshake ended, he walked away, and I couldn't help but feel

I was losing the last piece of my world. While I was here, I walked in a foreign place among strangers—and possibly those who would make sure I went missing if they found out my identity.

Clasping one hand around my leather bracelet, I turned to search for the kitchens.

6

A maze of hallways and staircases blurred in my vision, though wandering the castle did give me an advantage. Memorizing the castle's patterned layout would help in my search for cerecite.

As I paced down a hallway, I paid attention to every detail. The table with the vase of flowers—red and white frilly petals, though two of the petals had turned brown. The carpet—a pattern of small squares inside larger ones. The light fixtures —blue glowing rocks sitting inside tulip-shaped glass tubes affixed to the walls.

The words from Rosa's journal echoed in my memory.

Time. Light. World.

If the objects were disguised as everyday knickknacks, something that resembled one of the three words, then I'd need to find the areas where those things were most common.

Time. A watch or a clock, maybe.

Light. A lamp. Could be a candle or something.

World. A globe, perhaps?

Most of the hallways were barren except for portraits. The rooms I snuck a glance inside were the same, some with only a table and chairs for furniture.

As I passed by a large doorway, a guard paused to stare at me.

Clearing my throat, I wandered away, looking intently ahead as if I had somewhere to be.

I made it to the foot of a wide staircase, and I decided to take Ivan's advice and check the second tier. I grabbed the mahogany banister and started up, the carpeted steps muffling my footfalls. As I ascended, I got a better view of the palace. Seeing it from this angle made a stone drop to the pit of my stomach.

How would I ever find the cerecite in such a vast place?

I wandered to the second floor, walking past wood-paneled walls and over slate-tiled floors, my bootsteps echoing.

"Are you lost?" someone asked.

Startled, I turned around. A man stood behind me. His eyes caught my attention—turquoise blue. Was it the light making them look so bright?

He smiled as he approached me, and it didn't escape my notice that he had perfectly placed dimples on either side of his well-proportioned mouth. I caught a glimpse of evenly spaced white teeth. He didn't dress like the others, as he wore brown leather pants and a white shirt with a leather vest atop it. The lighting gave his shortly cropped blond hair a bluish glow.

"You don't look familiar," he said, his voice softer than I expected and tinged with a Scottish accent.

"I just arrived today," I said. "I'm Sabine Harper, the prince's new caretaker."

"I see." He extended his hand. "I'm the gardener. Cade MacDougal."

I shook his hand. His grasp was firm but didn't linger.

"I'm pleased to meet you," I said.

His forehead scrunched. "Your accent is odd. Are you from one of the villages?"

"Yes." Ivan's words rang in my head. "I'm from Fable-march Vale."

"I see. I didn't realize they'd found a replacement so soon. Usually takes weeks to find someone the queen approves of."

"Yes, I got lucky, I suppose." I cleared my throat and glanced away. The intensity of his gaze unnerved me. "I'd like to get to work as soon as possible. I was told to find the kitchens. Do you know where they are?"

"Of course. I was just headed that way. Would you like to come with me?"

"Oh…" I glanced down the hall, to the rooms I hadn't checked. I'd have to find another time. "Sure," I answered. "That would be great. Thank you."

I followed him through the maze of hallways, our footsteps echoing through the corridors, until we ascended a staircase and stopped at the top where a plain wooden door barred our path. Cade pulled out a set of keys, then unlocked the door and led me inside.

I followed him into a narrow hall lined in wooden panels. Our footsteps creaked over hardwood floors until we reached a foyer. We passed a fireplace, its brief heat warming me.

Shouting and sounds of clanking pots came from the hall ahead. Cade led me under a red-bricked archway and into a sprawling room filled with cooking stoves and butcher blocks. The scent of warm bread made my mouth water.

Several cooks scurried throughout the room. Arguing came from the far side, where two serving girls wearing black dresses and green plaid aprons stood over a tray of food.

"I told you to serve him the haggis!"

"But I've already prepared the porridge."

"I don't care. He hates the porridge. And His Majesty asked for haggis."

A stout woman with heated red cheeks approached us, blocking us from the argument. She wiped her flour-covered hands on her apron.

"Aye, Cade, who've you got there?"

"The prince's new caretaker." Cade turned to me. "Sabine, meet Mrs. O'Connor. She's the head cook, among other titles. Housekeeper, too, I hear?"

She waved her hand. "Since the last one quit, aye. Until they find a replacement."

Cade nodded. "Mrs. O'Connor, this is Sabine Harper."

"New caretaker, eh?" A thick Scottish accent came through her words. She tucked a curl of wiry red hair under her bonnet. "She's come just in time. Justine and Abigail were bound to throw punches soon enough while his master's porridge grows cold." She turned to the girls. "Justine, His Majesty's caretaker will serve the porridge, thank you very much. And Abigail, quit your bellyaching over the haggis. The porridge is fine for His Highness." The girls pouted, but they turned away without another word.

Mrs. O'Connor rounded on me. "Well—" she placed her hands on her wide hips as she cast me a stern glare— "don't just stand there. Get to it."

"Don't I need a uniform?" I asked.

"To carry porridge across a room? I think not. You'll get your uniform soon enough. Now, there's no time to waste. His master's rooms are just out the way you came, past the foyer, and down the hallway on the left. I suppose he's quite anxious for his breakfast, so you'll want to hurry."

Wasn't it a little late for breakfast? "Okay…"

"Pardon? That's 'yes, Mrs. O'Connor' to you. I see you've got a few things to learn, haven't you?"

I stood stiffly with hands fisted at my sides. I might as well start playing the part. "Yes, Mrs. O'Connor." I strode away from her, her eyes boring a hole in my back as I passed by the bubbling cooking pots and fires crackling in enormous hearths.

The two serving girls looked up as I approached the food tray.

"Take this then." One of the girls picked up the tray and thrust it toward me. "I've had enough of his awful porridge." She cast a dark look at the other girl, who only crossed her arms and shot us a glare. I wasn't sure what to make of the look, but I took the tray and turned away from them.

"Good luck with him," one of the girls called after me, her tone sharp, as I carried the tray toward the exit. I searched for Cade, but he must've gone. The room felt emptier without him. I would have to find him again, if only for the reason of talking to someone halfway friendly.

I made my way out of the kitchens and back the way I'd come, past the fireplace in the foyer, and took the hall to the left.

Walking through the palace felt as if I'd entered a dream. I was too used to the metal walls of the facility, inhaling stale air, going from one training exercise to the next. Finally making it to this reality was surreal, and I couldn't stop gawking at the paintings on the wall, the rugs made of finely woven linen, the tapestries. So alien, yet so common.

I questioned how it all existed. Was this indeed an alternate reality? Or was there more to it? My only way to find out for sure was to locate the seven pieces of cerecite. I would have to be vigilant at examining everything.

When I reached an open alcove painted in soft grays, a white door with golden ivy leaves barred my way. Balancing the tray on one hand, I knocked with the other. Nerves twisted in my stomach.

As I waited, the image of his portrait formed in my mind with stunning clarity. Dark eyes that held a secret.

I knocked again. A muffled "come in" came from the other side, so I turned the knob and entered the room.

Darkness veiled my vision. I stumbled over thick carpet, almost dropping the porridge. The only light came through gaps in the heavy drapes. The shape of an enormous, canopied bed loomed across the room. I couldn't discern anything else, so I stepped to the window and pulled back the curtains.

The sound of a deep male voice moaning came from the bed. I turned and found a mop of black hair sticking up beneath the covers. I walked to the bed, placed the tray on the side table, and pulled back the blanket.

"Go away," he moaned, grabbing the covers, and attempting to pull them away from me.

"I've brought your breakfast."

"I don't care."

"But you need to eat."

"I don't care!" He yanked the blanket out of my hands. I lost my balance and fell on my backside. *Ouch.* As I sat on the floor, staring up at the lump beneath the blanket, my temper rose. I got to my feet, stood over him, and grabbed the covers off his face.

"What are you doing?" he demanded.

"Helping you wake up," I said as politely as I could muster. "It's nearly noon. I'm your new caretaker, and that's what I'll be doing if it's all the same to you."

He focused on me for the first time. The intensity in his eyes startled me. Pain and intelligence shone in the dark shade of his pupils. He had an angular face with flawless porcelain skin—his long eye lashes and thick, full lips bordered on pretty, but with the strong line of his jaw, he looked entirely masculine.

"Who the hell are you?" he demanded.

I sighed deeply to keep from saying something I'd regret. "I already told you," I said patiently. "My name is Sabine Harper. I'm from Fablemarch Vale, and I'm your new caretaker."

"Caretaker?"

"Yes."

"Why in the bloody hell did my aunt send another caretaker?"

"Because you needed to be cared for, I assume. If you're ill, please let me know and I'll fetch a doctor and let you rest. Otherwise, it's past time to wake up."

He scowled, and I got the impression of danger lurking behind his flawless facade. This was a person you didn't cross. "I didn't ask for your opinion, *Caretaker*."

I crossed my arms and bit my tongue. Mima June's knife weighed heavy in my boot. *Just be patient. You can't kill him, or you'll lose your job.*

He pushed into a sitting position. "Did you hear me?"

"I did."

"I don't want to hear your opinions. Got it?"

"Perfectly." I stood straight, hands behind my back, my days of being chewed out by Logan coming back to me.

"Do you want to keep this job?" he demanded.

"Yes."

He laughed, a mirthless sound without any hint of cheer. "Then you'd be the first. No one wants to stay here. Everyone quits eventually."

"I won't." Not yet. I picked up the tray and handed the porridge to him. "Eat, please." I commanded, placing the platter in his lap.

"I hate this stuff."

"I don't care. Please eat."

I spotted a chair beside the window, so I pushed it across the floor and sat. I gave him the sternest look I could muster. I wasn't backing down. I didn't care how stubborn he was because I was worse.

He must've seen the determination in my eyes because he took a small bite, made a face, then nibbled at another. As he ate, I glanced at the leather band encircling my wrist, wondering if communications would ever be restored, wondering why I was sitting in this bedroom with a thankless prince, wishing I could find the seven pieces of cerecite and figure out what was really going on in this place, and above all else, praying a second wave didn't hit before I had a chance to succeed..

The prince scooted the bowl of half-eaten food away from him.

"Are you finished?" I asked.

"Yes."

"But you hardly ate anything."

"Not hungry."

I rubbed my forehead where a headache pounded at my temples. "Fine." I gathered the bowl and tray. If he was done, then so was I.

I left the room, closing the door behind me, then headed for the kitchens. I had more important things to do, anyway.

7

I paced my room and repeatedly pressed the metal disc on my bracelet. Rosa's journal laid on my bed, the pages flipped open, and I'd scanned over every entry, looking for familiar words.

Some had stood out.

Cueva. Cave, maybe?

Estrella. Star.

Some of the drawings looked like rooms in the palace.

Sighing, I smoothed my new uniform—all black, with a dark green plaid sash and dragon pendant.

Pinewood-paneled walls and floors boxed me in. They must've put me in the smallest cubby hole in the palace. But I couldn't complain. The lavatory came with running water, and I had an armoire to store my things. At least I wasn't sleeping in my quarters at the Vortech facility, where the red lights of blinking cameras loomed in every corner—or camping out in the frozen tundra. Yeah, it could've been worse.

I pressed the bracelet's disc again.

A whisper of static buzzed.

"Agent Fifteen?" I asked. "Can you hear me?"

"...Harper? Are you there?" The sound of Fifteen's voice made excitement race through me.

"I'm here."

"How is our connection?" he asked.

"Fine. You're coming through clearly."

"That's a relief," he said. "I was worried my systems wouldn't calibrate on this side. I apologize for the loss in communications. How are you?"

"I'm okay," I answered. "I'm alive. The mission has been a success so far. I met Agent Nordgren and made it to the palace."

"Good. I'm glad you're there. Getting inside can be a bit tricky."

"I noticed." I glanced at my bed. No reason to waste time. "Fifteen, Nordgren gave me a journal. It's in Spanish. Can you help me translate it?"

"Of course. Do you have it handy?"

I sat on the bed and flipped to the first page, happy to finally make some progress in translating the journal. "What does the word mentiras mean?"

"Mentiras." He paused for a moment. "It means lie, as in a falsehood. Something that isn't true."

"Lie?" I questioned, confused. "You're sure about that?"

"Yes," he answered, his tone robotic.

Lie. Unease clawed at me. This couldn't be right. "Fifteen, why would Rosa call the seven objects lies?"

The line went silent for a moment. "I would suppose it's because the objects never stay in their true form. They're constantly changing, which would make them, in effect, be called false. Or lies."

I tapped my fingers on my lips as I pondered his words. "Is there any other reason?"

"Not to my knowledge."

"Fine," I said with a sigh. Another mystery to puzzle over. I'd lump it in the category with the unusual grass and the odd-smelling atmosphere. "Help me translate the rest of the words, please."

"Of course."

I read through Rosa's entries, translating as I went, until I came up with a list.

Sound is a lie.

Time is a lie.

Location is a lie.

Matter is a lie.

Light is a lie.

World is a lie.

Poison?

I read over the list until I'd memorized it.

"What do you make of it?" Fifteen asked.

"I'm not sure," I answered. "But I think Agent Rodriguez must've assigned specific tags to every object she found. It was something to correlate with the substance of the object, as giving a physical description would've been useless as they change shape so often. My guess is they stay in a certain category. For example, the first object will have something to do with sound. An instrument, a music box, anything that produces sound."

"Have you seen any instruments in the palace?" Fifteen asked.

I thought back to when I first entered the palace. "I saw some bagpipes earlier. That's all I've seen so far." I shook my head. "This won't be easy."

"Using your scanner on an object you suspect will make the task easier."

"The lightsaber. Right."

"Lightsaber?" he questioned.

"It's a joke, Fifteen. I've got to have little fun on this mission, right?"

I grabbed my bag off the floor, searching through the contents until I found the metal tube, about the size of a scroll. A horizontal gap bisected the tube. I pulled on the sides, and it opened to reveal a glass screen.

"How does this work?" I asked Fifteen.

"Accessing the file on function of Vortech Cerecite Scanner. One moment." A second ticked when he spoke again. "Once you think you've found an object, open the scanner, then hold it over the object. Click the button on the bottom right corner, and the device will image and transform it."

I touched each button, the metal casing chilly.

"The scanner was originally developed to detect the chemical makeup of any given substance," Fifteen continued. "But Vortech modified it to also detect cerecite—including white cerecite. You can use this device to scan an item, reveal its identity, and then catalog it."

"Got it." I pushed it back together with a click and carefully placed the device back in my pack.

"Best of luck, Agent Harper. I know this isn't an easy task."

"It's easier now that I know the journal's translation." I ran my fingers over the paper written by Rosa. Was she still alive? Had she died? Had someone killed her? "Fifteen, why didn't anyone besides Agent Nordgren look for her and the other lost agents?"

"Because Vortech refused to lose anyone else. They had to make sure whoever they sent next was not only capable of finding the hidden cerecite but physically and mentally stable. They had to make sure you would return."

"I see." I rapped my fingers on the journal. "Any idea how she went missing? Who might've done it?"

"I don't have a conclusive answer for you, Agent Harper. My programming is limited. I'm sorry."

"That's all right," I said with a sigh. "I suppose I should start my search for the objects."

"Where will you start?" he asked.

"The bagpipes," I answered. "They're the only tangible

thing I've seen so far that correlates with one of Agent Rodriguez's clues."

"I see. Best of luck, Agent Harper." Again, he repeated the phrase, reminding me this wasn't a person, but a computer, one programmed to be encouraging. "I'm sure Vortech is anxious for you to complete this mission."

"I am as well. Thank you."

The line silenced, and I sat alone in an empty room, with only the muffled sounds of voices outside my door. I hugged my knees to my chest. When I closed my eyes, I saw Dad hunched over the kitchen table with Mima's death certificate. Coming to this reality was worth it if I could stop a second flare. Queasiness filled me when I thought of Dad's cancer lying dormant, waiting to take him, just like it had taken my mom, just like it had taken Mima. He'd never survive the second flare, and that was something I wouldn't let happen.

No. I would fight to find the cerecite and save us from the flare—even if I had lingering doubts about Vortech.

Rubbing my eyes, I shook my head. Sitting and pondering gave me a headache. I would feel better if I went out searching. At least I'd be accomplishing something.

Plus, I had one clue to go on. Bagpipes. I'd look for them first.

Placing the book aside, I stood and smoothed my hand over my black leather vest and dark plaid shawl. Nerves flitted through my stomach. While this reality was strange to be sure, there was more going on here than I'd been told. I prayed I'd avoid being discovered as an agent of Vortech, or else I'd end up like the other missing agents.

Too many questions remained unanswered, and if I happened to find the answers while searching for the cerecite, then so be it.

After stepping into the hallway, I headed to the staircase leading to the main tier. With any luck, the musicians would still be playing outside.

My booted feet echoed on the stones until I reached the foyer I'd entered earlier. The expanse of marble tiles reflected the afternoon sunlight as it drifted through the tall windows.

A few people passed me, but most didn't glance my way. I entered a hallway lined with rooms on either side. Golden pinstriping lined the white-paneled walls. I didn't recognize this area. Had I taken a wrong turn?

Raised voices came from the room ahead. I stopped at the sound of the queen's voice. The deep male voice must've been the prince. Morven. Ugh. A real winner, that one.

"…not taking your role seriously."

"Why should I?" the prince demanded.

"Because you have to! Why am I having to explain this to you again? It makes us look weak and inept. No one wants to see that in a future ruler. You're bringing shame to our family and worse, disgrace to your parents' names."

"Do *not* bring them into this," he said.

"I'll do whatever I must," she yelled. "You will take your role seriously, or I'll see to it you're stripped of your title and thrown in the stocks."

He laughed, though it was a cheerless sound. "The stocks? I spend my life in the stocks. What do the stocks mean to a person who spends their life imprisoned?"

Imprisoned? What did he mean by that?

"You've got a new caretaker now. Heaven knows how horribly you treated the others. You're to show her respect."

"I don't need a caretaker."

"You absolutely do. I've asked her to help you in your studies as well. You're to attend your lessons and be respectful."

"My lessons?" he huffed. "I'm not in nursery school. If you haven't noticed, I'm about to take the throne."

"I will not tolerate your disobedience any longer," the queen seethed. "Attend your lessons and be respectful."

"And if I don't?"

"If you don't," she hissed, "then I shall remove every comfort you've got, including locking you in your room. Since you seem to enjoy spending so much time there, you can stay sealed inside for the next week."

"You can't do that."

"Yes, I can, Morven. I'm the queen regent, which means I can do whatever I want."

"Not for long," he mumbled.

I tiptoed past the room. There was certainly tension between the aunt and her nephew, but did it have anything to do with Rosa's disappearance or the missing cerecite? I'd have to keep my eyes on those two.

I left the hallway and entered another foyer, recognizing the bronze doors leading to the outside world. To a sense of freedom, if only imagined.

After exiting, I let the warm evening air wash over me, though it tasted a bit metallic.

I paced the portico, but the area was empty except for a few guards milling about. My shoulders sagged. Where were the men with the bagpipes?

"Miss Sabine." Someone panted behind me. I turned around to see Mrs. O'Connor hustling toward me, her arms laden with a canvas bag full of scrolls. "There you are. I've searched everywhere for you. What're you doing out here?"

"I just stepped outside for some fresh—um, fresh-*ish*, air."

"What're you going on about now? Talking about the air?"

"Oh, nothing." I waved my hand, hoping she would ignore my comment. "It's not important."

"No matter. I've come on behalf of the queen regent. She gave these to me hours ago and I've only now gotten the time to give them to you. Here, take these scrolls." She handed the bag to me.

"What are these for?" I hefted the bag.

"The scrolls are for his master, the prince. You're to instruct him from those. Queen regent's orders."

"Instruct him?" I wouldn't dare tell her what a lousy instructor I'd make, as I knew next to nothing about Ithical. But I had to play along. "When?"

"He'll be waiting for you in the solarium at four PM sharp. Don't be late. I doubt he'll wait long."

"I understand." Hesitating, I glanced at the empty portico without moving.

"You'd best be on your way," Mrs. O'Connor chided. "Start studying those scrolls. Honestly, Miss Sabine. You only just got this job. You wouldn't want to lose it now, would you?"

"No, of course not, but... would you mind telling me where to find the solarium?"

"It's just past the throne room and through the hallway to the right. Big domed glass thing. You can't miss it."

"Yes, thank you."

"Nothing to thank me for." She waved her hand and turned away, mumbling. "Hired me to cook in the kitchens and turned me into a common laborer instead," she muttered. "Honestly."

I took one last look at the empty portico where a quiet wind gusted. A few leaves blustered, but the men playing the bagpipes were nowhere to be seen, so I had no choice but to enter the palace. Maybe it didn't matter. I had a few hours before meeting with the prince, so I'd still get a chance to search the castle.

Hallways stretched, and I lost my way several times as I looked for anything having to do with the three clues—time, light, and world. Frustration built as I searched, and the overwhelming nature of the task weighed on me. How was I supposed to find anything in a place so immense? In one room, I found a broken violin, but it didn't shift appearance, and my scanner didn't register it as cerecite, so I continued my search. In another room, I found random objects: a china collection, some silverware, a few vases, and some pottery. But nothing shifted appearance, and nothing glowed under my scanner.

Footsteps echoed from the hallways from time to time. A few palace guards passed me. My pulse quickened every time someone came near. I couldn't let on I was searching for cerecite, and I was careful to keep my scanner hidden. I still didn't know what happened to the past agents, and I wasn't sure I wanted to find out.

As afternoon waned, I passed a large grandfather clock in a hallway. I stopped, my heart leaping as the clue *time* echoed in my memory. But when I scanned it, nothing happened, and my shoulders sagged.

The time read 3:45, so I abandoned my search for now and made my way to the solarium. Maybe some clue would be waiting for me there? I carried the bag of scrolls back the way I came, past the throne room, and to the hallway on the right.

Up ahead, dappled sunlight fell across the floor through a domed roof, revealing the solarium through a glass door on the left.

I opened the door and stepped inside. Sounds of trickling water filled the air. Pots holding trees with dark glossy leaves surrounded me. A narrow, stone-paved trail led through them, and I took the path as it wound around the solarium, past tropical plants with neon orange flowers, and banana trees with bunches of unripe fruit. The scent of greenery lingered in the air.

A wrought-iron table and chairs had been arranged near a glass wall. Morven sat by the window, his jaw clenched and face pensive as he stared outside.

He wore all black, and only now did I get a look at his full form—tall and lanky, all sinewy muscle and frailty. He sat with his hands in his lap, his palms upturned, as if he held something of substance and not of empty air.

He sat in a chair contrasting the others. One with wheels.

A wheelchair.

Is that what he'd meant about being a prisoner?

I approached him. "Prince Morven?"

He turned his gaze to meet mine. I was taken aback by the intensity in his eyes—the sadness and hunger, as if some pent-up demon lived inside him, ready to break free at any moment. Desperate loneliness shone in his eyes. It hit me so suddenly that I stopped walking, as if I felt his pain through that one glance.

I shook off the uneasy feeling, finished crossing the distance between us, and sat in the wrought iron chair across from him. The chair's cushion didn't help with the discomfort I felt while in his presence, as if he were a taut violin string waiting to snap.

He frowned. "You're late."

"Beg your pardon, I'm early." I placed the bag of scrolls on the ground beside me, then picked up a random one and placed it on the table.

As I unrolled the scroll, glowing letters appeared.

A map formed beneath the word *Ithical Island*.

Holding the scroll, I sat straight, as if I'd held something like this plenty of times. I'd studied the map Ivan had shown me, and I'd luckily stored it all in my memory. I could wing it.

"What do you know about the island?" I asked.

He crossed his arms. "You're really doing this?"

"Doing what?"

"Teaching me," he said.

"That is what I was hired to do."

"But was I hired to sit here and listen to this drivel?"

I cleared my throat, deciding to ignore him, and read the text below the map. "'The main city takes up the majority of the central island, and the outlying villages Harpinsger, Eden-brooke, Grimwillow Grove, and Fablemarch Vale, surround it. The geography varies, as there are mountains in the north-western portion of the island, lakes at the southern point, and plains to the east. Each of these areas are suited for particular industries. Fablemarch Vale specializes in the fishing industry, the mines lie to the north, where there are ample sources of raw cerecite ore, and the cattle and sheep herds are perfectly suited for the plains of the—'"

Morven placed his hand atop the map, stopping me.

"Sabine, that's your name, right?"

"I think you should refer to me as Miss Harper."

He smirked. "That's ridiculous. I'm nearly twenty-three. I don't need a primary school teacher."

"That may be so, but your aunt says your education is lacking, and I'm also your caretaker—"

"I don't need a caretaker. Nor do I need an instructor."

"Is that so?" I asked.

"It is."

I decided to take his challenge. "All right, prove it then. What do you know of the island?"

He kept his hand over the map. "Fine. There are five specialized industries on this god-forsaken rock—ranching, farming, fishing, manufacturing, and mining. Each village was specifically designed for a certain industry, and the capital receives and manufactures from each of those industries. None of this would exist if it weren't for the cerecite ore, which makes it possible to create the grass for the herds to feed on, the water for the fish to survive. We create wheat and oat seeds directly from green cerecite. Our rails run on yellow cerecite. Our lights burn blue cerecite.

"The mines are indisputably the most vital industry on Ithical Island. Without them, we die, and we're taking them for granted. We don't pay the miners enough to feed their families. They're sick from their contact with yellow cerecite, yet we turn a blind eye and do nothing to help them. There's a revolution coming, and when it happens, we'll have no one to blame but ourselves.

"There," he said with a fake smile. "Happy?"

I didn't know what to say. "Oh."

"What else do you have in there?" he said, gesturing to the bag of scrolls.

"Um…" I glanced at the bag. "Honestly, I have no idea."

"Because I already know it all. What else is a person supposed to do when they're bedridden except read? I've studied the educational scrolls so many times, I can recite them. Every. Single. One."

"Then why did the queen regent hire me to instruct you?" I asked.

He shrugged. "You tell me."

I swallowed, my stomach fluttering uncomfortably as I sat in his presence. I wasn't sure what to expect from him, and that bothered me. "I don't know."

"She wanted someone to keep an eye on me," he answered, his tone dark. "To make sure I was doing what she wanted."

"Which is?"

"Becoming her pawn." He crossed his arms. "Bending to her will so that when they give me the crown, it means nothing, and she keeps her place as Ithical's only true ruler."

"I see." I glanced at the windows. "I'm assuming that bothers you?"

He shrugged, staring out through the glass, past the wall surrounding the palace to the terra cotta tiled roofs crowding beneath the palace. But his gaze went farther than that. It seemed to go to the sky and peer straight through the shield, to the world outside—to a life beyond the dome.

"What are we studying next?" he asked, his tone flat as he kept his gaze on the window.

He wanted to keep going? I removed the first scroll from the table, placed it aside, and unrolled another. *A History of the Royal Lineage* was printed in ornate calligraphy across the top.

"The royal family," I said.

"Hmm." He pursed his lips.

I narrowed my eyes. "You know it already?"

He nodded.

I leaned forward. "You're being honest?"

He sighed. "'William Alexander Tremayne was named as the first ruler of Ithical Island after our people survived the shipwreck and came to live on this island in the year of our Lord 1887. He was the first to discover the properties of cerecite and utilize it for our survival. With the aid of a creature some called The Green Dragon, he created the dome that sheltered our people from the harsh Arctic winters, established a system for providing equal hours of day and night, and was the first to find the original seven cerecite orbs—'"

"Wait," I stopped him. The cerecite orbs? Not only had he quoted the text word-for-word, but the mention of the cerecite piqued my curiosity. "He found the seven orbs?"

"Yes," he answered with a nod. "They were a big deal back then. But they soon learned the stuff was too volatile. Changed its form so often they couldn't keep up with it. Even tried locking it up, but it wouldn't stay put."

"I see." I tapped my fingers on the table. Asking him if he knew where the cerecite was now seemed a pointless question. Not only would I arouse his suspicions that I was looking for cerecite, but I doubted he'd know the answer. "Tell me." I pointed to the scroll, which he'd quoted to me, and I was seriously reconsidering my purpose here. "Is there anything you don't know?"

"Yes." He met my gaze again, his eyes burning with passion. "There's so much I don't know. Will you help me?"

I hesitated before answering. "Help you with what?"

"Everything." He leaned closer, the scent of his cologne— wild forests and burnt amber—wafting toward me. "There are so many concepts we accept as truth when we've never researched a thing. We believe in fairy stories to explain what we don't understand—magic dragons and myths. I want to know the science. The truth. Will you help me?"

"How do you want me to do that?"

His eyes shifted before he spoke. "Take me to the observatory."

"The observatory?" I questioned. "Why?"

He clasped his hands atop the table. Tendons made strong from wheeling his chair stood out beneath his pale skin. "It's the room at the topmost tower of the third tier. No one goes there anymore except for me."

"What would your aunt say?" I asked.

A half-smile lit his face. "She doesn't have to know."

I frowned. "You want me to sneak you up to the observatory?"

He nodded.

Part of me wanted to know what was up there, but what about the consequences? "I can't do that. If your aunt finds out, I'll lose my job."

"Then I'll pay," he offered. "Double whatever my aunt's giving you."

"I can't."

"Triple it."

I shook my head. "No. I don't even care about money, so stop trying to bribe me. It won't work."

"Then what do you care about?"

I pursed my lips before answering. "It's complicated."

He eyed me, sizing me up, as if trying to see what motivated me. "I'll show you what I've discovered. There's more out there than we've been told, and I'm going to find it. If you've any interest in truth or science, you'll want to know, too."

Truth. That was an interesting word to use, as I was searching for seven lies. Wouldn't taking him up to the observatory be in my best interest? It would at least give me a chance to search for cerecite. "I'll consider it under one circumstance. How much junk is stored in the observatory?"

His eyebrows rose. "Junk?"

"Yes," I answered. "Humor me. I like antiques."

He leaned forward, his eyes dark and wide. "If you take me up to that tower, I'll give you every piece of junk in this palace."

I hesitated before answering, fairly sure I was going to regret my decision. But I'd never been one for caution. Besides, it wouldn't hurt to find out what he knew, and what he'd meant about the truth.

"All right," I said. "We have a deal."

8

P rince Morven's wheelchair rolled over the marble as I pushed him through the hallway. If anyone asked, I was taking him to study someplace quieter. I wouldn't mention the place happened to be the observatory.

I quelled my unease by gripping the wheelchair's wooden handles. Why I'd gone along with him was a mystery. I could only blame my curiosity at Morven's hint of learning the truth, my nagging suspicions that there was more to this world than I'd been told, and the chance that I'd find a musical *something*, or any of the cerecite, along the way.

We reached a hall that branched in either direction.

"Left," he said.

I turned, the long corridor ending at a copper elevator, its gears exposed, with an ornate gate partitioning the front.

"I didn't realize the palace had elevators," I said.

"Lifts, you mean?"

"Yes, lifts. Right." These speech nuances were going to get me in trouble.

He gave me an odd glance but didn't question me. "There are only a few. They built them years ago, and they try to keep them as inconspicuous as possible. Wouldn't want to give anyone the wrong impression."

"What do you mean by that?" I asked.

"The commoners. They don't know I'm like this. If they saw the lifts, they might believe our monarchy to be weak." He spoke with a high-pitched voice, as if he were quoting something his aunt had said.

I grasped the metal latch and pulled the gate open, then I rolled Morven inside and shut it behind us.

"The top tier," he said. The gears rotated, pulling us upward through a narrow tube lined in stone. The *click-click-click* filled the silence. The only light came from a single fixture above us, glowing in the familiar blue.

I studied the prince sitting in front of me. What was his story? Ivan's conversation came back to me—about the king's and queen's deaths, Rosa's disappearance, and Morven's illness. How were they connected? Would the prince flip if I asked what had caused him to be in the chair? I supposed it wouldn't hurt to ask.

"Morven, may I ask you a question?"

"That depends." He looked up at me. "What kind of question?"

"I'm curious. What happened to your legs?"

His brows knit with confusion, and he pursed his lips.

"You don't have to answer if you don't want to."

"No. It's not that. No one's ever asked me." He tapped his fingers on his knee. "Most people think it's taboo to question me."

"Is it?" I asked.

"I suppose not," he answered.

I tilted my head. "Then will you tell me?"

The elevator moved with echoing clicks as I waited for his answer. "It was the yellow sickness," he said. "It took my parents when I was ten, then I contracted it. I survived, but it left me like this."

"Yellow sickness?" I asked.

He nodded. "From the yellow cerecite during the outbreak. Surely you remember the outbreak?"

"Yes. The outbreak," I fudged. "Hard to forget." A line of text jumped out at me from one of the books I'd read in Ivan's hut. "I thought the royals had been quarantined when the sickness broke out."

"Yes. They were," he explained. "But my parents and I managed to catch the sickness anyway. Not many people knew about it."

"That's odd." I tapped my fingers on the wheelchair's handle. "Did anyone else in the castle contract it?"

He shook his head. "Only us." He locked his gaze on me. "You ask a lot of questions, *Miss* Harper."

"Oh." I answered too quickly. "Well, as I said. I'm curious." I glanced away and straightened the dragon pendant on my plaid sash. "I'm sorry about your parents," I added. "And about your illness."

"Don't be." He shrugged. "It doesn't bother me so much anymore. Besides, I'm alive, and I'm better off than others who've been paralyzed. I can walk when I'm feeling up to it."

"Really?" I questioned him.

"Sure. It's never easy, but I can do it when I have the strength."

Hmm. If there were any link between the royals and Agent Rodriguez's disappearance, I couldn't be sure. Not yet, anyway. Morven had been young at the time. Maybe he'd never known the last agent. But his aunt... that was another story.

The elevator stopped with a jolt. Beyond us stretched a hallway with a wooden door at its end. I opened the gate, the clanking metal echoing, then wheeled Morven down the hall to the door.

As I opened it, I revealed a room that reminded me of a domed cathedral. A telescope made of gleaming copper sat at the center, taking up half the floor space, its metal tube extending through a gap in the ceiling, past the glass tiles, pointing at the sky.

"A telescope?" My voice echoed as I wheeled Morven toward it. "You're studying astronomy?"

He laughed. "I thought that was obvious when I asked you to take me to an *observatory*." He drew out the last word.

I ground my teeth to keep from smarting off. "There's no need to be rude," I said as politely as possible.

"Why not?" he challenged. "It's not like anyone's ever polite around this place. Especially to me."

"Just because people treat you badly doesn't give you permission to do the same."

His eyes narrowed once again. I was beginning to hate that look. "I don't believe anyone has ever spoken to me so candidly."

"Really?" I bit my tongue to keep from laughing. "No wonder you have such trouble with manners."

He kept his gaze pinned on me. "Where did you say you were from?"

"Fablemarch Vale," I answered, speaking clearly. "The fishing village."

"Really?" His eyes didn't flinch.

I nodded.

He pursed his lips. "Interesting," he mumbled to himself.

I sniffed, looking away from him, pretending to act nonchalantly. The last thing I needed were his suspicions. I decided to direct our conversation in a different direction. "So, tell me about the telescope. Why are you so interested in astronomy?"

His gaze turned wistful as he stared up at the gleaming copper contraption. "Because no one else is. Because no one else cares. There's so much up there, but we only ever focus on the mundane things that surround us when there are planets and galaxies, life possibly, out there waiting to be discovered."

I wanted so much to tell him about the world outside the dome—everything he was missing—the beaches, and deserts, and all the cultures he'd only read about. But all I could do was play along and pretend I knew nothing. "Hmm. Fascinating."

He gave me a stern glare. "If you're not interested you can leave."

He must've mistaken my tone for boredom.

"No, I'll stay." Around the room, tables and shelves lined the walls. Clutter sat on every surface—an ideal place to store the cerecite. I picked up a vase. "Do you mind if I look around?"

"Go ahead." He waved me away. "Just be sure to stay out of my way." Gripping the wheels, he rolled his chair to the eyepiece.

Ignoring him, I circled the room and focused on every sight and sound, cataloguing each one as I went:

The telescope, the stacks of scrolls, the musty smell coming from the animal pelts—orange and white—from foxes, perhaps? The layer of dust covering the inkwell, brown with a golden rim, the compass—the spindle pointing north, and the broken gears. More vases, a horseshoe, a seashell—purple and white, the sound of Morven's wheelchair moving across the room, the chilly temperature raising goose bumps on my arms. A wooden chair with a missing spindle, the sextant, the star charts—*so many star charts*. They were all written in the same script. Had Morven created them all?

On and on I walked, running my fingers over some of the objects, until I was able to make a complete mental picture of everything in the room. I would be able to recall each piece with exact clarity for years to come. Not that such a talent had ever done me much good except for finding random objects—Mom's lost phone or Dad's truck keys that he'd dropped at the state fair. I'd found them near the Tilt-a-Whirl. He'd rewarded me with fried Oreos, and I'd been certain they'd tasted better than anything I'd eaten in my life, but maybe that was because Dad had smiled—*really* smiled—as he'd given them to me.

I must be the luckiest dad on the planet to have you.

Shaking my head, I pushed my memories aside.

I stood at the room's center near the telescope. Morven had moved away from it and sat at a table, scribbling away at another star chart.

Nothing had shifted appearance so far, but I needed to remember the clues.

Sound, time, world, matter…

I paced the room again, looking for anything that might have shifted shape or changed color. As I passed the compass, I noticed the needle pointed south. Picking it up, I looked at it more closely. It was definitely pointing south now. Plus, it fit the clue for world. Still, I couldn't scan it here, and what if it were merely broken?

I went to where Morven sat scribbling on his star charts. "Is this compass broken?"

He looked up. "What?"

"Is it broken?" I repeated.

He blinked. "It's not broken, but it doesn't work, either. Compasses are unreliable this far north."

"Oh." My shoulders sagged. I suspected as much.

He gave me a second glance, and his narrow-eyed gaze was far too discerning for comfort. Did he suspect I was here for the cerecite?

He placed his pen atop the scroll, sitting up straight and pinning me with that dark glare. I stiffened under his gaze, a tingle of anxiety racing down my spine.

"What's your game?" he asked, motioning to the compass.

I raised an eyebrow. "Excuse me?"

"What are you doing here?" he clarified. "You don't want the money. You're searching for antiques and concerned about compasses. Why are you *really* here?"

I scrambled for an answer. It had to be something believable. "Isn't it obvious? I needed a job and I had to escape my village. I was stuck fishing at the docks all day. I hated it there." I did my best to speak with confidence. "None of this is any of your business, by the way."

"It is if I make it. I'm the crown prince, after all. I'm in the habit of getting what I want." He had the audacity to wink.

I clenched my fists and turned away from him, a retort on the tip of my tongue. My cheeks burned, and my heart was beating too fast. This new fire in me was something I didn't expect, part anger, part attraction, which completely baffled me.

Placing the compass aside, I continued searching.

"I will figure you out, *Miss* Harper," he said.

I ignored him, reminding myself that I had to keep this job, and mouthing off wouldn't do any good except to get me fired.

A blur of white and pink caught my attention. I stopped, focusing on the seashell. Hadn't it been purple earlier? And now it looked lighter—more pink lining the outer edges, no purple at all.

I grabbed the shell and cradled it in my hands. Memories came to me, a vacation to Myrtle Beach with my mom and dad, building crumbling sandcastles that fell apart to be reclaimed by the surging tides. As I held the seashell to my ear, the nostalgic sound of the ocean overwhelmed me. The beach. It was one of my only memories of Mom bright and happy, her bronze skin warmed by the sun, unaware of the first flare that would hit us a week later. She'd been one of the first to die of the cancer caused by radiation.

I couldn't swallow the lump in my throat, so I closed my eyes, forcing the memories away, and snuck the seashell in my vest's inner pocket. I would scan it as soon as I got back to my room, and I would pray that I'd found the first piece of white cerecite.

When I wandered back to Morven, he drew a razor straight line across the parchment. The tendons in his hands moved in a mesmerizing way. The powerful strength of his fingers gripped the ink pen, creating a tapestry of stars and galaxies on the scroll.

He looked up, and our gazes locked. His eyes held such depth and intelligence. A spark connected between us, stuttering my breathing.

"Is something the matter?" he asked.

"No," I said, attempting a casual tone while my pulse thrummed. "Just wondering when you'll be done."

He placed the pen on the table. "Don't you have anything better to do than interrupt me?"

I crossed my arms. "Yes, actually. Sorry for the interruption. If it's fine with you, I'll leave you to work in peace." I spun on my heel and headed for the door.

"Sabine... wait," he called, his tone unusually subdued.

I glanced over my shoulder. "Yes?"

"Please don't leave yet. I... I need your help getting back to my room. The lifts don't go to my floor from here, and I can't navigate stairs in this chair."

I narrowed my eyes at him. "You're telling the truth?"

"Yes, the liftline from this tower to my room is broken, and my aunt doesn't want me up here, so she hasn't seen fit to fix it. Please..." he begged. "Don't go yet."

I bit my lip, tempted to tell him to find his own way back. Then again, he had said please, which must've taken an extreme amount of effort. Plus, if he called for help, his aunt would learn where I'd taken him.

"It'll only take a minute," he said. "I can explain what I'm doing if you'd like."

I frowned. "I thought you didn't want me to interrupt you. But... if you'd like me to stay, I will."

He gave me a tight-lipped smile, and I crossed the room and stood next to him, looking at his star chart. Lines and dots filled the parchment, with names written in tiny letters above each of the small circles.

"So…" I asked. "What is all this?"

"A partial map of our galaxy," he explained. "This star is Proxima Centauri, the nearest to us, although that's a relative term. Even if we could travel at speeds of more than a thousand kilometers per hour, it would take over a hundred thousand years to get there."

"A hundred *thousand* years?" I asked, surprised.

He nodded. "Incredible, isn't it? Did you know there are actually three stars in the Alpha Centauri system?" He pulled out another chart, with three circles inked in the center, labeled as Alpha Centauri A, Alpha Centauri B, and Proxima Centauri. "These are the stars in the system. If my calculations of their gravitational fields are correct, there should be planets orbiting them. Could you imagine?" He motioned to the dome, his eyes glinting with excitement. "What would it be like to look into the sky and see three suns?"

"Pretty bright?" I suggested. "Like blindingly bright?"

"No." He laughed. "These suns are dimmer than ours. And one is tinted blue. Can you imagine what the sky would look like? Beautiful."

I scooted a chair close to him and sat. "It seems like this really interests you?"

He hesitated before answering, as if he'd never told anyone about this—anyone except me. "Yes, but not only this. All of it. The planets, moons, galaxies, and the edge of space, as far as my telescope can see. Everything."

"Why does it fascinate you so much?" I asked, my voice soft.

He shrugged. "I guess I'd like to imagine there's more out there than just this." He tapped his wheelchair. "It's not always easy tracking their movements. The shield is hard to see through, but some nights are better than others. Plus, I've created something to help. He moved the papers aside and picked up a telescope. The long bronze tube had a set of gears attached to the eyepiece. "I've modified this to see through the shield, but it only works on clear nights, and it works best from someplace higher in altitude than here, like the mountains.

"Anyway." He placed the telescope back on the table. "Now you know." He arranged the papers back on top, hiding the metallic instrument.

It was good to see him so interested in something. He'd obviously put a lot of work into creating the charts, and I had to admire him for his dedication. Most losers I'd known back home only cared about their next high or who'd sleep with them. But Morven was different, and part of me was curious to know more about him.

"You like to know things, don't you?" My quiet voice carried through the dome.

He gave me a pointed stare, one that made heat rise to my cheeks. "I think everyone should be educated. We haven't had a proper university in more than a century. It's our complacency that's leading us to our downfall." He shrugged, as if trying to downplay the perceptiveness of his words, but I'd seen the intensity in his eyes. He cared more about his people than he let on, something I doubted his aunt realized.

Morven pulled a pocket watch from his vest. "Dinner is in a few hours, and I'd like to rest before then. Take me back to my room, then I'll expect you to join me for the evening meal."

"Join you?" I asked, my voice sharper than I intended. He was back to his usual demanding self. His moment of humanity had ended. I shouldn't have been surprised. "Why?"

"Aunt Tremayne expects all the upper staff members to be present during dinner."

"Really?" I questioned. "To serve you, you mean?"

"No, the lower caste staff members do that. Upper staff members are expected to sit at the table. We used to invite other noble families, but my aunt offended them all, so now she demands the staff join us." He gave me his stern glare. "And you'd better not treat her the way you do me, or else she'll put you out of more than just a job. You should be glad I'm so forgiving."

"Forgiving, huh?" I couldn't help but laugh, though it was a cheerless sound.

"Yes," he answered sternly.

I had to bite my lip to keep from smarting off as I pulled his chair away from the table, then wheeled him out of the observatory, the shell tucked inside my pocket.

When we arrived back at his room, I stopped the wheelchair beside his bed. A stripe of evening sunlight entered through the half-closed curtains. Dust motes drifted, and a ray of light fell over him, highlighting the exhaustion in his eyes. I reached to help him from the chair, but he held up his hand, stopping me.

"You don't want my help?" I asked.

He only shook his head, gripping the armrests as he stood, then sat on the bed. He hunched his shoulders, his breathing heavy.

A pang of sympathy gripped me. "Do you need anything before I go?"

"No, but... thank you."

I gave him a questioning glance. "For what?"

"For listening to me."

"Oh." I fidgeted as I straightened my pendant. "You're welcome."

He nodded, rubbing his eyes as he looked with a vacant expression to the window. I turned and left the room, closing the door quietly behind me. As I made my way down the hall, the fluttering in my stomach confused me. *Morven* confused me. I had to admit, something drew me to him.

I entered my room and flicked on the lamp beside the table, filling the space in hues of soft blue. With no windows and wood paneling surrounding me, I had to inhale and exhale deeply to suppress the claustrophobia.

After sitting on my bed, I removed the scanner from my bag and slid the tube apart to reveal the screen. I placed the shell on the bedcover, the purple deepencd a shade along the edges.

My hands shook as I held the scanner.

Please work.

I pushed the button. A laser beam moved horizontally over the shell, and a 3-D image of it appeared on the screen. A light on the scanner turned green, and then the actual shell morphed. The ridges and bumps melted into an iridescent sphere.

I placed the scanner aside, then picked up the baseball-sized orb, the colors like opal, the smooth surface warming my skin.

My heart leapt.

I'd done it. I'd found the first lie.

I pressed the metal disc on my bracelet.

"Agent Harper?" Fifteen's voice came through.

"I got it. The first piece of cerecite."

"Did you scan it already?"

"Yes." I held the orb carefully, as if it were made of glass.

"It transformed?"

I nodded. "Yes. Into a glowing white ball."

"Good," he said in his mechanical tone. "I knew you'd do it."

"That's one of us."

"You doubted your abilities, Agent Harper?"

"Not my abilities, per se, but even you have to admit the difficulty level of this mission is extreme. Thankfully, Vortech gave me an awesome pep-talk before I left. Warning me about a second flare worse than the first, seeing my mom and grand-mother die, and worrying my dad will go the same way is great motivation to walk through a gateway to an alternate dimension you may not return from."

"Is that a joke, Agent Harper?" he asked.

"Not really." I sighed. "But if it makes you laugh, you can do so."

"I'm not programmed to laugh."

No kidding. "Then by all means, don't try. Now, about this cerecite. How long will it stay in its original form?"

"A few weeks if you keep it in your bag. It's lined with lead to protect you from the radiation. Do *not* remove it. All the glowing spheres on the island are emitting radiation to a lesser degree, though this type can't be picked up on traditional measuring instruments."

"I understand." I placed the cerecite in my bag. Rosa's journal sat on the nightstand, and though I didn't open it, the pages opened in my mind's eye. I searched through the next entries.

The word *time* jumped out at me.

Morven had been using a pocket watch. Could it be cerecite? I couldn't recall seeing his pocket watch change its appearance, which meant I'd have to give it a closer look. He'd be at dinner in a few hours.

Until then, I decided that wandering the palace from one room to another could take me years to find anything, so I grabbed the bag of scrolls Mrs. O'Connor had given me, searched through them until I found what I was looking for, and spread it out over my bed.

A map of the palace, complete with every room drawn onto it, covered the parchment. I found a block of black chalk in a drawer and began the task of labeling each room. After searching a room, I would write a list of the items I found, then check off each space one by one. I'd search through the night if I had to.

I would find that cerecite or die trying.

9

I worked on the map until my fingers cramped, but at least I'd made some progress. I put an X on the observatory where I'd found the shell, and I'd made a grid of the other rooms in the castle. Two-hundred and forty-two to be exact.

Ticking came from a clock on the nightstand, and I placed the chalk aside as I read the time.

It was nearly time for dinner, so I stood, my muscles sore and protesting as I made my way into the hall.

As I wandered the castle, it helped to have the castle's map in my head. Even so, seeing rooms on a map and wandering the passageways were two different things, and I stopped, turning to glance from one hallway to another. Gray stones and green banners blended together.

"Lost again?" a male voice said behind me.

I turned around to see Cade leaning against a door frame, a smile creasing his mouth. "I was looking for the dining room."

"Ah! Well, I can tell you that you're heading toward the gardens, not the dining hall. And you're also on the wrong floor."

I sighed. Of course, I was. "Can you help me again, please? If it's no trouble?"

His face lit up with a smile, revealing his dazzling white teeth. He walked toward me, then held out his arm. He'd spiked his blond hair, and I had the urge to run my hands through it. He also wore a different shirt and pants, not the standard affair of black and green plaid, but a simple white shirt and blue pants. His lanky frame moved fluidly under the layer of clothes.

"It's no trouble at all," he said. "I'm on my way there myself, and I would be honored if you joined me."

I took his arm. "Thank you," I said, relief in my voice.

He nodded. "You're quite welcome."

As we walked, the tension in my shoulders relaxed. I could get used to Cade escorting me through the castle.

"What exactly do you do here?" I asked, trying to think of something to say to fill the silence.

"Work in the greenhouse. I cultivate green cerecite and create all sorts of seeds for plants—most of them are shipped out to the fields to be grown as wheat or barley, but others stay here in the castle. I make more than just vegetables, too. I create flowers and herbs. I've even been experimenting and making some hybrid species. You should come by the green-house sometime. I could show you what I do."

"That would be nice." *Especially if there's a hidden object inside.*

We turned down a broad hallway that led to a staircase.

"Have you been able to see much of the city yet?" he asked.

I nodded. "A little. I saw some of it before I started working for the prince."

The muscles in his arm tensed. "How do you like working for him?"

"*Like* it? That's a strong word." I laughed as we climbed

the stairs. "I'm tolerating it. And I'm still here. That's good, isn't it?"

"I guess that depends on who you ask." Genuine warmth spread from his smile—not at all the shrewd, calculating looks the prince gave me, as if he were trying to figure out my deepest secrets.

After walking up three flights of stairs, we turned down a hall, then entered a broad foyer. A jutting, curved balcony overlooked the floors beneath us. On the opposite end, a wide set of marble stairs led up to a pair of ornately carved doors

"Impressive," I said as we climbed.

"Yes, you're lucky you get to see it. Most people never get access to anything but the queen's audience chamber." We reached the doors and Cade pulled them open, revealing an enormous dining hall with tall ceilings, dramatic stone pillars, and flowing green banners Our echoing footsteps mingled with the sounds of chatter as we crossed through the room, past rows of long, empty tables, and to the very back, where only one table was filled with people.

I spotted Morven and the queen regent at the head of the table. The queen's eyes met mine, and she motioned me toward her.

"I guess this is where we'll part," Cade said.

I gave him a brief smile. "I guess so."

"Would you like to meet me tonight after dinner at the main gates?" he asked. "I can show you around the city if you'd like."

"That would be nice. Thank you."

He gave a slight nod, then released me to sit at the end of the table, opposite the queen and Morven.

I paced to the head of the table, spotting an empty space beside Morven.

"Sit," the queen regent commanded. I took a seat beside Morven. He eyed me, but he didn't speak as servers arrived from the side doors, carrying platters of seared beef, stewed vegetables, soups, bread, and mounds of fresh fruit. After arranging the platters on the table, they spooned the food on our plates. Steam rose from the food, warming me, its scent making my empty stomach rumble.

The protein drinks and nutrition bars I'd eaten at Vortech's facility, and the TV dinners I'd shared with Mima June and Dad, paled to the exquisite heaps of food here. Knot-shaped rolls glistened with a buttery sheen, smelling of freshly baked bread, tender grilled meat fell apart on my fork, and the fruit burst with flavor as I chewed, savoring each bite.

The queen thrummed her fingers on the table as she focused on me, her gaze overcritical. She nibbled her food, but still she eyed me. I took a bite of the roll, though my appetite escaped me. Replacing the half-eaten bread on the table, I couldn't find it in me to finish it. What was it about the Tremayne family that completely intimidated me?

"You took Prince Morven to the tower today, didn't you?" she asked.

What? How had she found out?

"I—"

"He's not to go there. I don't care what he tells you. He needs to focus on his studies and nothing else. I don't know why he has such a fascination with the observatory, but it must end. In no way does such an obsession prepare him to become king, which is happening much sooner than anyone would like." She sighed, thrumming her fingers on the table. "Me included."

I glanced at Morven, but he sat unspeaking, staring straight ahead, the muscles in his jaw locked.

"I would like him to continue to study from the materials I provided you," the queen continued, her voice heated. "There will be no more excursions up to the observatory. Is that understood?"

"Yes," I answered. But why was she so determined to keep us out of the observatory? Was she perhaps protecting the cerecite from being found? If so, what else was she trying to keep a secret?

"Well then." She spoke with forced cheerfulness. "Let's enjoy our food before it grows cold, shall we?"

"Of course," I said, taking another bite of meat, though its flavor had grown bland, and I had a sudden longing for a frozen microwave dinner, Dad at my side, as we watched a *Star Trek* rerun.

A knot lodged in my throat, and I had to fight back a sudden pricking of tears. I'd see him again, and he'd be okay. We'd both be okay, especially after I found the cerecite and kept us safe during the second flare.

Morven stirred the gravy, though didn't take a bite, his gaze distant. His watch's chain dangled from his vest pocket.

I pressed my fisted hands into my lap to keep from grabbing it.

"Morven," I said as politely as possible. "Do you have the time?"

He gave me a sullen glare but didn't speak as he pulled out his watch, clicked open the lid, and checked the time. "Six-thirty-seven." He closed the lid with a snap, then stuffed it back in his pocket.

A brief glance was enough. The etching on the back had been silver-plated, with ornate curlicues creating three-leafed clover patterns. In the tower, the pattern had consisted of four leaves.

Prince Morven had white cerecite, and now, I only needed to steal it.

10

Chilly night-time air drifted as I walked through the streets with Cade at my side. After dinner, Morven went back to his room without speaking a word to anyone, and I hadn't gotten a chance to observe his watch again. My next option was to wait until he'd gone to sleep, slip inside his room, and take it, but that would have to wait.

As we entered a narrow street, Cade's fingertips brushed mine. My stomach flipped at the touch of his skin. Did he expect to hold my hand? But he only smiled, blue lamplight cast over his eyes of the same color, and he stepped away from me. Emptiness tugged at me at the distance between us. I folded my arms over my chest, my fingertips cold.

We entered a town square where vendors set up carts. Pastel bunches of roses and lilies filled vases or hung from strings along the vendor's awnings, swaying in the brisk breeze. Other carts held trays of pies—meat, lemon curd, or haggis—their sweet and savory scents wafting. In other places, the aroma of citrus drifted from the oranges and other unfamiliar fruit.

Music played with a staccato tempo, and couples and children danced. The rich sounds of the banjos and lutes mingled and echoed off the tall buildings.

"Is this a festival?" I asked.

"Not exactly." Cade smiled. "They're celebrating the prince's coronation."

"His coronation? Already?"

"They've been celebrating for years now." He laughed. "The prince was supposed to take the throne on his eighteenth birthday. Then his twenty-first. Now it's his twenty-third, and for whatever reason, the townspeople are convinced this time, it'll happen." He held out his hand. "Would you like to dance?"

My mouth gaped. "Dance?"

"Yeah." His smile showed his dimples. "You know how to dance, don't you?"

"I don't really dance."

"Don't dance?" he questioned with mock surprise. "Nonsense."

I glanced back at the castle, a looming structure that stood dark against the sky. I should've been at the palace searching for the timepiece.

Without warning, Cade grabbed my arm and pulled me toward the crowd. When he placed his hand on my waist, I stiffened. The buildings surrounding us closed in on me the same way the walls had trapped me at Vortech.

"Is something the matter?" Cade asked.

I steadied my breathing. "I'm fine."

His forehead creased. "You're sure?"

"Positive. Just thinking about the prince."

His grin faded. "What about him?"

"You don't like him, either, huh?" I asked.

He shrugged. "He's not the easiest to get along with."

"Agreed, and I get to be his caretaker." I hoped he heard my sarcasm.

"Yes, but you know why you got the job, don't you?"

"I've heard rumors," I answered. "It seems the last person quit."

His gaze darkened. "There's more to it than that. His aunt needs extra eyes on him."

I nodded. "I gathered that."

The violin strings and flutes harmonized, creating a lively tune. Cade gripped my cold hand in his warm one, a steady anchor. His other hand he kept on my waist, his warmth helping to melt the chill in the air. We moved in a square pattern over the cobblestones, the soles of our shoes ringing out, echoing around the stone and mortar buildings, resonating with the music.

The song ended, and the crowd broke apart until a slower song started. The musicians played softly, a melody that conjured a mournful sound. A hulking man wearing furs stalked along the edge of the crowd. A glowing wolf stood by him.

Ivan?

What was he doing here?

The light of the streetlamps didn't penetrate far into the lane, even so, a glint came from the man's machete strapped to his side.

Was Ivan watching me? Cade held my hand and led me away from the man in the shadows. When I glanced back, he'd disappeared, and I stared into an empty lane.

"Do you see something?" Cade asked.

I shook my head, trying to erase the image of Ivan stalking me. "I'm not sure."

"What do you mean?"

Once again, I looked over my shoulder, only to find an empty street.

"I thought I saw someone I knew. But he's gone now."

Cade nodded. "Then let's dance."

"Okay," I said with a smile, attempting to put Ivan out of my mind. But what was he doing?

I tried to match my steps to Cade's. My fingers warmed where he clutched them. I hadn't touched a person in so long, the sensation caught me by surprise. I could get used to this.

When the music stopped, several guards moved toward us. "Curfew in thirty minutes," they yelled.

"Curfew?" I asked as the square emptied. "What for?"

"The miners are threatening revolution, so the queen regent is doing everything to make sure that doesn't happen."

The crowd scattered, awnings and food carts taken down for the night. We followed a group of people away from the square, then took a copper-paved road away from the others. We stopped at the center of a stone bridge. Below us, the roar of the river filled the silence, its dark surface creating swirling eddies.

"It's so different here." I stopped, realizing my slip-up. "Different from Fablemarch."

"I agree." His smile returned. "I came from a small village also. The city never fails to impress."

His casual attitude made me hope he hadn't noticed my mistake. "How long have you lived here?" I asked, leaning against the railing.

"Half my life. My da died working in the mines. Mother was able to get work as a seamstress in the palace, so we came here. I haven't left since then."

"I'm sorry for your loss."

He shrugged. "It was a long time ago."

Blue lights softened the towering buildings, a wonder that such a place could exist without the whole world knowing. A civilization silenced under a dome.

"Cade, how did our ancestors build the dome?"

He cocked his head. "You don't know?"

"I know what's in the books. But you'll have to forgive me. I spent most of my time helping my da with his fishing business. We never had much time for history lessons. He cared more about nets and hooks than my education." I was scaring myself at how easy I spoke these lies.

Cade leaned his lanky frame against the rail, his elbows propped behind him. "Well, doesn't really matter anyway, because no one knows much about the dome or how our ancestors created it. Legend says that after our ancestors washed ashore, they got sick, cold and exposure, you know. But then the green dragon magically swooped in and saved them. Helped them mine cerecite. Build the dome and all that."

I eyed him. His skeptical tone made me curious. "Do you think that's what happened?"

He kicked a pebble that skittered over the bridge and fell in the river with a splash. "There's more to the story."

He piqued my curiosity. "You say that as if you're sure?"

"I have my reasons." He glanced away, as if putting an end to the discussion, but I wasn't giving up that easily.

"Has anyone ever seen the green dragon?" I asked.

"Sure. Plenty of people have seen it. It's a creation of the green cerecite, just like any other Mystik creature. The answer most people want to know is where does it come from? If it was once the spirit of a person, then whose? How did it become a Mystik? They say we become them because we ingest green cerecite all our lives, then after we die, our essence changes into the form of a Mystik creature."

"Right," I said, processing his story, what had really happened on the island, how the dome had apparently been built by a dragon. "Do you think someone lived on the island before us?"

"Maybe." He crossed his arms. "If so, they would've lived here long enough to mine cerecite, long enough to ingest it. That takes effort. Mining cerecite isn't easy. I don't know if you've ever been out to the mines, but they're a major operation. No one could mine cerecite on their own. Not for an entire lifetime, which basically means that for the green dragon to exist in a scientific sense, *someone* had to've been here before us."

"More than just someone," I said. "A group of people. A civilization."

"Exactly." His eyes grew dark. "The problem is, our island oasis was thought to be uninhabitable before we came here."

Yeah. I'd heard the same thing about Champ Island on my side of reality, so where did the supposed green dragon come from?

Was it a green *alien* dragon, maybe? Seriously. I'd been watching too much *Star Trek*.

"Keep in mind," Cade said. "This is the theory of yours truly. Not a very popular one, especially with the queen and other nobles, who don't like to question the existence of the green dragon. But..." he leaned closer, speaking quietly. "I have proof."

"What kind of proof?"

"This." He pulled at a chain around his neck, untucking a pendant from beneath his shirt. A black, pyramid-shaped stone hung from the bottom of a silver necklace. Golden ribbons danced through it, moving like wisps of smoke.

I caught my breath. "What's that?"

"Da found it in the mines, along with other things that don't belong here. Super-advanced tools, things like that."

I held out my hand. "May I look at your pendant?"

"Sure." He took off the necklace and handed it to me. His fingers brushed my open palm, and my heart fluttered. Was I attracted to him?

The weight of the pyramid pendant distracted me from reading too much into his touch. I held the stone in my hand. Under the streetlamp, the golden ribbons shimmered with crystal flecks.

"I've never seen anything like it." I looked up at him. "Where do you think it comes from?"

A knowing smile tugged the corners of his mouth. He

placed his hand over mine, trapping the pyramid inside. "It's a mystery, Sabine." He said my name softly, his gaze lingering on my lips.

Calloused fingertips covered my fisted hand, the pyramid pendant pressed between our palms. With a stuttered breath, I pushed the pendant toward him, then unthreaded my fingers from his.

Swallowing, I crossed my arms over my chest, glancing away, needing to look at anything but him and his devilish sapphire eyes.

Without speaking, he put the chain over his head and tucked the pendant under his shirt.

He placed his hand at the curve of my back. "We'll have to get back to the palace soon," he spoke quietly, his breath tickling my ear. "I'm sorry we couldn't stay out longer. Hopefully, this business with the miners will get cleared up, and we can stay out dancing all night."

He flashed his charming smile, bringing out the dimples around his shapely lips.

I held his arm as he escorted me back through the city, walking nonchalantly, not commenting when we passed by the vehicles glowing with blue lights, the domed carriages, and the ornate architecture, a stark contrast to my rundown farmhouse and Vortech's lifeless, sterile facility.

By the time we made it back to the palace, darkness veiled the courtyard. An eeriness came with the silence of the night —a hushed, mysteriousness that rested in the stone steps and towering pillars.

Cade's words came back to me, as if whispered on the wind. Vortech hadn't mentioned anything about a civilization living here before the immigrant ship crashed. If it was true, then who was it?

The vestibule and palace doors rose before us, glowing white in the moonlight. Cade stopped me.

"My room is in the outer building near the gardens. I'll have to say goodbye for now. I enjoyed our visit."

"So did I."

He smiled. "I hope we can do this again."

"Yes, me too."

"Good. Then I'll leave you with this." He held up his hand, his pointer finger and thumb pressed together, and moved it down through the air, until a flower appeared—a lavender-colored rose.

I cocked my head, unable to hide my smile. "You didn't tell me you were a magician."

"I prefer the term illusionist." He handed the rose to me, and I took it from him. Its soft floral fragrance tickled my nose.

"Goodnight, Sabine."

"Goodnight to you, too."

He turned away and left me alone on the veranda. When his body blended in with the shadows until he disappeared, I opened the doors and entered the palace. None of the guards questioned me as I passed by them on my way up. Snooping wasn't my first choice, but I didn't want to waste time before finding the second object.

There were things going on in this place that I didn't understand, and I needed to find the answers.

A warning niggled at the back of my mind.

Rosa had also looked for answers, and she'd never been seen again. But I had to find the seven pieces of cerecite, and if I happened to stumble upon solving the mysteries of this place while I did it, then so be it.

11

My footsteps echoed through the empty hallway as I made my way to the prince's bedroom. I tiptoed over the rug-strewn hallway, my gaze darting as I searched for guards. Lights burned behind glass sconces, their glows pooling on the floor.

The door to the prince's room loomed ahead.

My training kicked in, and I tucked my fear away in a remote corner of my brain, thinking only of the mission. Recovering the watch. Nothing else mattered.

I grabbed the doorknob and turned it slowly, then snuck a glance inside. Silence shrouded the room, and the moonlight shone over an empty bed with rumpled sheets.

I tiptoed to Morven's bed, listening for his breathing, searching for his form hidden under his covers, but only an empty mattress greeted me.

Either I was incredibly lucky, or the complete opposite. If he happened to walk in while I was searching, I was screwed.

As I spun around, the cavernous room surrounded me.

My mind went into overdrive as I started looking.

An armoire, desk, and a nightstand…

I paced to his nightstand, running my fingers over the

marble top. A yellowed, tatty copy of *From the Earth to the Moon* by Jules Verne sat beside a lamp. I flipped it open. The copyright date read 1865.

On quiet feet, I went to his armoire and rifled through his suits, which all smelled faintly of a woodsy, cedar scent. Not something I'd expect from someone who spent all his days indoors. Glass knobs of a drawer gleamed in the faint light coming from the hallway. I knelt and opened it, blindly feeling the contents. Leather shoes, lined up in a neat row, smelling of polish.

After closing the drawer, I stood. Through the half-opened door, I listened for rolling wheels or sounds of any kind.

A faint *tick-tick-tick* came from the full-length mirror on the wall. Curious, I stepped to the mirror, and the ticking grew louder. I ran my fingers over the ornate frame, then grasped one edge and tugged on it.

It opened on hinges, like a door, revealing a row of shallow shelves. In the light shining through the door glinted a pocket watch. With a sigh of relief, I grabbed it and tried inspecting it, but the dimness made it impossible. Instead, I stuffed the watch into my vest, carefully closed the mirror, and walked back to the door, thankful for the thick carpet muffling my footsteps.

I glanced back at the empty bed before closing the door behind me. Adrenaline fueled my blood, demanding I run, though I slowed my pace. Now was no time to cause suspicion, and I couldn't risk anyone finding me with the prince's watch.

As soon as I locked myself inside my own room, I sank against the door, the wood cool behind my back, and took a moment to exhale.

Nice work back there, I could hear Logan saying. I pulled out the scanner, sat on the bed, and repeated the process I'd done with the shell.

When I pushed the button, the beam moved from top to

bottom, scanning the watch. I held my breath as I waited for the light to turn green.

"Please work," I whispered as the seconds ticked by, and then, the light changed to green. The pocket watch morphed, opalescent colors shining from a smooth, spherical surface.

Relief washed through me, and I slumped on my bed. Without wasting time, I pushed the disc on my bracelet.

"Fifteen?" I asked.

"Agent Harper," he answered in his robotic tone. "It's good to hear from you. Have you found the second object?"

"Yes, I stole the prince's pocket watch. I'm becoming a regular thief. You know, I might become a professional burglar and drop this Vortech gig. What do you think?"

"I would advise against such a lifestyle."

"Well, it was worth a shot."

"Be sure to store it in your bag," he said. "Just like the first object."

"I will." The sphere painted refracted rainbows on my walls. "Fifteen, I need to ask you a serious question."

"Go ahead."

"Okay." I folded my legs under me, the mattress springs creaking. "What if I were to tell you there's evidence this island was inhabited before the immigrants built the shield?"

"What sort of evidence?" he asked.

"A triangular shaped stone that has bands of gold moving through it."

"May I ask where you encountered such an object?"

I picked at the lint on the blanket. "From one of the palace staff. The gardener. He was wearing it, and he said his father found it in a mine."

"A mine, you say?" he questioned.

"Yes."

"Well, it's possible the object is a form of cerecite. The mineral is known to combine to create unusual colorings."

"So, you think it was made of cerecite?" I asked.

"Quite possible."

"The gardener seemed to think it came from another civilization entirely. Is there any evidence for that?"

"No. But I have heard the rumors before. The locals hold superstitious beliefs. You must question anything they tell you. Keep in mind that the island was uninhabited until they arrived. Without the dome, the island is inhospitable. There's no way anyone could survive, especially an entire civilization."

"But you're thinking of our side of the dimension. On this side, couldn't it be possible if such a civilization used the cerecite to help them?"

"No, Agent Harper. I'm afraid it just isn't possible. Imagine terraforming Mars with technology from the middle ages."

"Then how do you explain the dome? The immigrants couldn't have built that by themselves. They say a green dragon helped them."

"Yes, I know the story."

"But what was the green dragon really?"

"I don't know, Harper. What do you suppose it was?"

I rubbed the tension knot in my neck. It was late and thinking at this hour was like slogging through wet sand. "An alien. That's all I've got." I sighed. "I know, there's no evidence for that either. Maybe I'm overthinking this. Cade's pendant probably was made of cerecite. Sorry to have bothered you, Fifteen."

"It's not a bother, Harper. Helping you is what I'm programmed to do."

The sphere refracted rainbows on the ceiling, as if taunting me with the secrets of this reality.

"Do you have any other questions?" he asked.

"Yes, what do I do when the prince finds out his pocket watch is missing?"

"I wouldn't worry too much."

"Why?"

"Because you didn't steal the actual watch. You stole a cerecite mimicry of it. The real watch will appear back in the last place it was removed from."

"How does that work?"

"Do you have the cerecite handy? I'll show you."

"Yes, it's sitting on my bed."

"Good. Now find something in your room that represents time."

I glanced at the nightstand and grabbed the clock. "I've got a clock."

"Good, perfect. Place it beside the orb, then use the scanner on the cerecite. Scan it as you did earlier to reverse the process."

I picked up the clock and placed it on the bed. With a click, I opened the scanner, and held it over the glowing orb. After I pressed the button, the laser scanner slid from top to bottom.

The cerecite disappeared. Only the ticking clock remained on my bed cover.

I gasped. "Where did it go?"

"You restored its normal levels of radiation. It's what usually happens in nature when the cerecite is left untouched, so it took the appearance of the clock. Scan it again."

I pressed the button, squinting my eyes against the light. When the brightness dimmed, an orb replaced the clock.

The actual clock sat on my nightstand once again, *tick-tick-ticking*, as if it had never been interrupted.

"That's so weird." I placed the scanner aside and cupped the orb, the feel of curving glass warm in my hands. "So, the prince's watch—his real watch—will have appeared back in his dresser by now."

"That's right," Agent Fifteen said. "I doubt he'll realize it was ever missing."

"So weird," I repeated. "What *is* this stuff?"

"Good question. Once you bring our scientists a sample, we may be able to answer it."

I held the orb a moment longer, its warmth glowing around me. Was it a new undiscovered element? If so, why didn't it exist in our reality?

Sighing, I placed it in my bag. So many questions.

"Excellent work on finding the second object," Fifteen said. "I dare say you've located the first two in record time. I don't believe any other agent has found the first two as quickly as you. Keep it up."

"I'll do my best. Right now, all I want to do is sleep."

"That's reasonable."

"I'll be in contact," I said with a yawn, then disconnected our conversation and laid on the bed. Questions nagged me. Cade's pendant. The cerecite. The green dragon. How did they connect?

Shaking my head, I stood and washed up, then settled in for the night.

Scratchy fabric against my skin, I closed my eyes. An image of Morven's empty bed formed in my imagination as my conversation with Fifteen echoed.

What is the green dragon really?

What do you believe it is?

I carried the tray of porridge to Morven's room, my head pounding with a dull ache, and my eyes bleary. Nagging thoughts had kept me awake most of the night. At some point during my restlessness, I'd decided I was stuck in a giant virtual reality dome created by Vortech who was sending me through a series of experiments for nefarious purposes.

When I'd woken this morning, I'd decided I may've gone too far with my theory, and I'd decided to stick to finding cerecite.

I reached Morven's room, and I rapped on the door. A quiet "Come in" came from the other side.

Balancing the tray on one hand, I entered the room. Morven sat on the edge of his mattress, fully dressed, his bed made.

"You're awake?" I asked.

He clasped his hands. "Does that surprise you?"

"Yes, I thought you'd still be asleep." Especially after he'd been gone last night. I placed the tray on his nightstand.

He eyed the porridge and frowned. "I won't eat that."

"Sorry, but you don't have a choice."

He crossed his arms. "Says who?"

"Says me. My job is to tutor you, and I won't do it unless you're mentally fit, which means you need to eat a healthy breakfast."

"*That* is not healthy. It tastes like dirt or mold. Sewage, perhaps."

"I have trouble believing it tastes that bad. I think you're not being grateful for what you've got. There are some people who have no food whatsoever. Now, please eat."

He motioned to the bowl. "You eat it, then."

"I've already eaten my breakfast in the kitchen. I ate the same thing, and it tastes fine."

He clenched his jaw but still didn't move. Had I actually thought of this person as attractive? A strong jaw line and feathery lashes could only get a person so far.

"You. First," he enunciated.

"Fine," I muttered, grabbing the spoon, and shoving a bite in my mouth. It tasted no different from the food I'd eaten in the kitchen, except when I swallowed, it had a gritty aftertaste, like swallowing grains of sand with the flavor of dirt. I did my best to make a pleasant face.

"It tastes fine," I lied.

"No, it doesn't." He knit his dark eyebrows. "I saw you grimace."

I eyed the bowl. Hadn't it come from the same cooking pot?

My stomach churned, and I felt I might be sick. I placed my hand on my abdomen, pretending to smooth my vest, hoping the food stayed down.

It bothered me that Price Morven was right. But what caused it to taste so horrible? I had an idea, and it wasn't good.

"Morven, how long has the porridge tasted like this?"

He shook his head. "As long as I can remember."

"Have you always eaten it?" I questioned.

"Not all the time." He sniffed. "Only when Aunt Tremayne demands I eat it before I can leave my room."

I narrowed my eyes with suspicion. "Your aunt demands it?"

He nodded, then fixed his gaze on the window. "She thinks it'll help with my strength. Better for my health."

"I see," I answered to myself, wheels spinning in my head as the word *poison* teased me.

He looked at me with shrewd, dark eyes. "Are we getting started with my lessons or what?"

"Ready so soon?" I smiled. "That's wonderful, Morven. I see you'll be a model pupil after all."

He gave me a bemused laugh. "Don't push it that far, *Miss* Harper. Anything beats being locked in this room, even studying things I can recite in my sleep." His gaze went to the window again, the look of an animal longing to break free of its cage.

Pity tugged at me. I didn't wish imprisonment on anyone, not even someone as bad-mannered as Morven.

"I'll have to bring your bowl back to the kitchen. Will you be able to meet me in the conservatory?"

"Yes." He clasped his hands, then nodded to a bell attached to his wall. "I'll ring for a servant to wheel me there."

I nodded, then I walked to the door, bowl in hand. The cinnamon scent of the porridge wafted. Before exiting, I turned to him.

"Morven," I said hesitantly. "Is there a chance your aunt could be poisoning your food?"

He gave me a sharp glance. "Poison? That's a bit farfetched, isn't it? No, I don't believe she would do that."

"Well," I mumbled. "It was only a theory. We'll start our lessons in the conservatory in half an hour."

I turned away from him and left the room, shutting the door behind me, keeping the bowl held close. What had caused the food to taste so awful? If someone had tampered with it, then who?

The bowl grew cold in my hands. I had to stop thinking about it. Chances were, it was completely fine. But it hadn't tasted fine. Could it really be poisoned?

Even more alarming were the implications between poison and the lost cerecite. Someone in the royal family had taken the cerecite back to the palace after the other agents' disappearances. Could that same person have something to do with the poisoned porridge? It was a longshot, and maybe nothing, but a person capable of stealing cerecite was also capable of poisoning the prince. Maybe the two were connected.

Which led me back to the queen.

If Morven died, she kept the throne. She'd also been present ten years ago when the last agent had disappeared, and she was trying to keep us out of the observatory where I'd found the first object. But what motivation did she have to keep us from the cerecite? Maybe Morven would know more. I'd heard them arguing. I had trouble believing she cared for him, yet for whatever reason, Morven didn't believe me.

Was there some way to prove there was poison in his food?

I stopped walking and tightened my grip on the bowl.

If it was poisoned, I had the evidence right here in my hands. And it just so happened that I had a scanner in my room that could show the colors of elemental substances.

Including poison.

I hesitated for only a moment before turning away from the kitchen and heading back to my room. When I reached it, I entered and shut the door behind me, then placed the bowl on my nightstand.

I'd have to do this quickly.

I sat on the bed and removed the scanner from my bag. As I pulled apart the two rounded ends, the mechanical hiss echoed through the small space. Holding the scanner over the porridge, I wasn't exactly sure how this would work as I pressed the button.

The scanner beam moved from top to bottom, then stopped. As it finished, bright yellow spots glowed in the porridge.

Weird.

What were the yellow spots? I had my suspicions, but I didn't know anything for sure. I did, however, know who to ask.

After pressing the disc on my leather band, I waited.

"Harper?" Fifteen asked.

"Yes, hi," I answered quickly.

"You've found the next object so soon?"

"No, sorry. I'm communicating for something else." I took a deep breath. "I think I found poison, and I need to know for sure. When I scanned the prince's porridge, it turned yellow. Is there any chance it could be yellow cerecite?"

"Yellow cerecite?" He paused. The line crackled. "That's a possibility. However, there are other substances that would appear yellow—sulphur or lead iodide, for example."

I eyed the bowl. "But why would anything of that nature be in the prince's food?"

"I don't have an answer, Agent Harper."

"Then it's probably poison." My stomach roiled. I placed a hand on my abdomen, imagining the yellow cerecite inside my own system. I groaned. Why had I thought eating it was a good idea?

"Is he experiencing any unusual symptoms?" he asked. "Memory loss or severe weakness to the lower extremities?"

I thought about the question before answering. "He's in a wheelchair. He can't walk most of the time. I don't know about memory loss. He seems smart enough. Too smart for his own good, most of the time." I tapped my knee as I pieced together the information. "But the question is, who put the poison there? His aunt?"

"Possibly. As I said, the noble family has a poor reputation. Poisoning wouldn't surprise me in the least. However, I'll warn you not to get involved. Whatever is happening with the nobles doesn't involve you."

I stiffened. "Actually, I think it does. Agent Nordgren told me when the last agents disappeared, someone took their cerecite and brought it back here. To the palace. It doesn't take a giant leap to think that someone capable of possible murder and theft is also capable of poisoning. Fifteen, if I find the one poisoning the prince, I may find the lost cerecite in the process."

"No," he said sharply. "I'm sorry, Agent Harper, but trust me when I say your logic is flawed. Becoming the prince's caretaker is a ploy to get you inside the palace. Nothing more. Don't concern yourself with him. Your priority is to find the cerecite. Might I remind you that we're on the verge of experiencing another flare? One that will destroy every grid on the planet if you're unsuccessful?"

We were back to the flare again. Why did it seem any time I questioned Vortech's motives, the flare was conveniently brought up? Yet they failed to provide me with any proof of it. Something wasn't sitting well with me. He was distracting me, and I wouldn't allow it.

"Agent Fifteen," I said sternly. "I'm sorry, but I refuse to sit back while someone poisons the prince."

"Agent Harper," he answered with equal sternness. "Be reasonable. If you get involved, something worse could happen to you."

Rosa came to mind—and the word *poison* written in her journal.

"Fine." I sighed, unclenching my hands fisting the blanket, only now realizing I was doing it. "I'll keep my distance, but I won't allow him to keep ingesting poison."

"How do you plan to do that?" he asked.

"I'll start by preparing his food myself."

The line went silent for a moment. "Will you continue searching for the cerecite?"

I almost agreed, but I stopped myself. Too many suspicions were making it hard for me to trust my employer. *What happens if I don't?* I wanted to ask, but I knew the answer. I would never go home, never see Dad. He'd lose a daughter, the last of his family.

"Yes, of course I'll keep searching," I answered. "You know I don't have a choice."

"I understand," he said gently. "I understand completely, Sabine." He'd used my given name, which surprised me. "What are the next clues?"

Rosa's journal sat on my nightstand, but I didn't pick it up. I tried to refocus on my mission, grounding myself in time and place—in the palace, on Ithical Island.

I could do this. I *had* to do this.

The journal entry came to me in perfect clarity, as if I held it open on my lap. "I've found sound and time. Location, matter, light, world, and poison are left." I thrummed my fingers on my bedside table as I thought through the clues.

I stood, pacing my room. "Location. That could be a map, right? What about a star chart?"

"Yes," he conceded. "That could very well be it. Have you seen a star chart?"

I stopped, staring at my nightstand where I'd placed the porridge. "I've seen quite a few."

"Then I suggest finding them be your priority. Good luck, Harper. We're counting on you." His voice had an uncharacteristic edge of sharpness, a warning.

"Yeah," I answered drily. "Thanks."

The line went silent, and I was left to stare at a bowl of cold porridge. My stomach still roiled from the single bite I'd eaten. I was starting to understand Prince Morven's unpleasant attitude—and I couldn't blame him.

Someone was poisoning him, and despite Fifteen's warning, I would find out who it was *and* discover the location of the third object.

Crossing my arms, I tapped my fingers on my elbow. Had any of the charts changed appearance? I couldn't answer conclusively because I hadn't checked. Going through them individually was the only way to know for sure.

For now, I had to make an appearance and pretend to tutor Morven, although why his aunt demanded he learn things he already knew was a mystery to me. His aunt did many things that bothered me, and if I could prove she was the one responsible for poisoning him, it would do more than benefit the kingdom. It would save Morven's life, and possibly reveal the truth behind Agent Rodriguez's disappearance.

I would also have to tell Morven what I'd discovered, and I wasn't sure how to approach the subject. I put it on my list of things to figure out later.

After leaving my room, I returned the bowl and tray to the kitchen, then wandered through the palace, searching for the stairs to the bottom floor. I passed the dining hall. Inside, servants hung long tapestries embroidered with the image of the dragon from the ceiling, and they draped banners and garlands over the balconies.

The symbol of the green dragon taunted me. Its presence was a mystery—one that made no logical sense in a scientific way of thinking.

Shaking my head, I turned away from the dining hall, then I took the staircase to the bottom floor. When I reached the conservatory, Prince Morven sat at the wrought-iron table, hands clasped on its surface. He looked pensively out the windows—the same gaze I'd seen yesterday—past the city and its bustling life, to the dome, and into the stars beyond, though none of them were visible.

He didn't smile as I sat across from him, merely gave me his penetrating gaze that seemed entirely too intelligent. I had the urge to shudder under that dark glance, but I sat tall instead.

The bag of scrolls remained near my chair, and I dumped the entire thing on the table.

"Today," I said, "you teach me."

He raised an eyebrow. "What?"

I motioned to the scrolls. "Your aunt demanded I teach you, but you know more about this world than anyone else—and more about what's beyond the dome. You've made hundreds of star charts. Do you keep them all upstairs in the observatory?"

He scrunched his brow. "Why do you want to know about the star charts?"

I shrugged. "Because I have a sudden interest in astronomy."

"Really?" He laughed, leaning forward, his mouth quirked at the edges. "That can't possibly be true." He spoke with a deep, quiet voice. "I nearly bored you to tears when you joined me in the observatory yesterday. What's the real reason?"

"Fine." I crossed my arms. "My da and I used to go stargazing. It's one of the only things we enjoyed doing together. I'd like to know more about what's out there." If stargazing translated to watching *Star Trek* reruns, then I wasn't far from the truth.

He leaned back, his eyes wide, as if I'd surprised him. "You're curious about astronomy?"

"Yes," I said firmly.

"You know we're not allowed in the observatory."

"I know. Can't we sneak up again?"

He exhaled a heavy sigh. "Unfortunately, no. Since our last visit, my aunt disabled the lifts. She also decided to lock the tower."

"*Lock* it?" I questioned, not terribly surprised.

He shrugged. "That's the way she is. I've learned to deal with her."

I stood, pressing my palms to the table. "That will change after your coronation, won't it?"

He nodded. "She'll have less power over me. It eats her up."

Which was a perfect motive to poison him, and to keep the hidden cerecite away from him. "Morven, have you considered that she has motivation to harm you?"

He shook his head. "Are we back to the poison thing again?"

"Yes," I said firmly. "We're back to the poison thing again. I tested your porridge. It was positive for yellow cerecite."

He gave me a shrewd glance. "How did you do that?"

"I—" I stopped myself. I'd almost said, *I used my scanner.* I'd have to lie now. Darn it all. Why'd I open my big mouth? Now I had to come up with a story.

Keeping my composure, I sat down and threaded my fingers on the table. "It was easy. I just compared its taste to yellow cerecite."

He frowned. "You've tasted yellow cerecite?"

"Yes." I silently thanked Ivan for his story. "When I was a child, I was walking along the rails with my parents. I thought they looked so pretty and yellow, like candy, and for whatever reason, I decided to lick them. Don't judge me."

His frown deepened. "You licked the rails?"

I held up a finger. "I was four, mind you."

"You *licked* the rails?" he repeated.

"Yes, but that's not the point." I waved my hand in a dismissive gesture. "I can't forget that aftertaste. It was just like your porridge."

His mouth quirked into a half-teasing grin. "Sorry, I'm still focused on the image of four-year-old you hunched over and licking the rails. It's hilarious, actually."

Crossing my arms, I gave him a smug glare. "I'm glad my humiliation is entertaining you."

"It is." His smile showed his perfect teeth. "Very much."

I snapped my fingers at him. "Will you focus? Don't you see what this proves? There's yellow cerecite in your porridge. Someone is poisoning you."

"Sorry, but it doesn't prove anything." He folded his arms over his chest. "You were four. Children of that age are known for their idiocy. Case in point, you licking the rails. You probably don't remember correctly. Plus, there are any number of substances that taste like cerecite."

"No there aren't. Name one."

"Dirt, mold. I could go on."

"Fine. But what about the symptoms? It can cause debilitating weakness to the lower extremities."

"I've heard all that before, but I still don't believe my aunt would be responsible."

"Is that because she's family?"

"Partially, yes. It also doesn't make sense because I've been this way since my parents died. I don't think she would've been poisoning me for ten years. If she wanted me dead, there are easier ways to do it. Why would she bother? Why not sneak into my room at night and stab me?"

"I don't know." I drummed my fingers on the table. "Maybe she's trying to control you more easily. If you're stuck in that chair, you're forced to remain under her power."

"Let's get one thing straight," he said darkly. "She does not control me. It doesn't matter if I'm in a chair. She has no power over me. She never will."

I disagreed, but I wouldn't tell him that.

"Can we drop the poison thing now?" he asked. "I think there may be a way to get up to the star charts."

I sighed. "Fine. I'm listening."

"The celebration ball for my birthday is happening soon. She's posting all the guards on the two bottom tiers, which will

CHAPTER 12 119

leave the observatory unguarded. It's the *only* time it will be unguarded, mind you."

"But what about the locked tower?" I asked.

"We'll have to get the key."

I tilted my head. "Where's the key?"

He thrummed his fingers on his knee. "She's wearing it."

My eyes widened. "Wearing it?"

"Yes, and I doubt anyone will be able to get close enough to her to remove it."

I massaged my throbbing temples. "That's a problem."

"Yeah, a big one." His shoulders sagged. "We would need a magician to get that key off my aunt's neck."

"A magician?" That gave me an idea. "Morven." I leaned forward, whispering. "Are servants allowed to attend the ball?"

"The upper-level servants, yes."

Excitement quickened my pulse. "Is the gardener an upper-level servant?"

"Yes." He nodded, drumming his fingers on the table. "What are you getting at?"

"Would she ever dance with the gardener at the ball?"

"Possibly. It depends on how many nobles attend. Usually there aren't many. I suppose if the gardener asked her to dance, she'd do it. She wouldn't want to make herself look like more of a snob than she already is."

"Good." I smiled inwardly at my scheme. Thievery was becoming a viable career path for me. "I know someone who can help us steal the key. Where are the gardens?"

13

I left Morven behind as I walked to the gardens. He said he wasn't feeling well, so he'd gone back to his room. When the last of the yellow cerecite left his body, he'd start to feel normal again. At least, I hoped so.

After pacing through the sunlit hallways, I passed through a doorway leading outside. The wind blustered, its hint of a mechanical smell reminding me of the exhaust from Dad's tractor the first time he'd cranked it after a long winter.

Shaking my head, I didn't know what to make of the unusual odor. Maybe it came from an enormous VR facility created by Vortech. Yes, and an alien green dragon had helped them engineer it.

I bit my lip to keep from laughing at the absurdity. I'd really have to start coming up with better theories.

The glass dome of a greenhouse rose beyond the trimmed trees, and I strolled down a cobbled path toward it, my boots crunching loose stones. Uniform grass grew on either side of the winding trail. The palace walls—gray cinder stones—blocked out half the sky.

The path ended at the greenhouse door. I hefted the wooden latch. Metal hinges squeaked as I entered. The scent of fresh-cut greenery drenched the room. My boots splashed through puddles as I walked past tables lined with rows of planters, my arms brushing trailing vines. Sweat beaded on my skin from the damp humidity weighing heavy in the air.

Past the tables, a set of steps led down to an open circle. Tropical trees laden with bananas and lemons dotted the perimeter. I inhaled the scents of ripening fruit. Other trees stood tall enough to reach the glass-paned ceiling. Trickling came from watering cans as a few gardeners poured liquid into planters. I straightened my dragon pendant as the gardeners' eyes wandered to me, as if to remind them—and myself—that I belonged here.

Cade stood at the back wall. His shears clicked every time he cut a branch from a tree. Dirt smudged his brown leather pants and his wrinkled white shirt, and sweat clung to his forehead, making clumps of blond hair stick to his brow.

His eyes widened as he took me in. He placed the shears aside.

"Sabine!" Dirt smudged as he attempted to wipe it off his clothes. "I wasn't expecting to see you here."

"What can I say?" I raised both hands in a questioning gesture. "I was hoping you loved surprises."

"I guess so." His smiled showed his dimples. "What brings you here?"

Nervousness fluttered in my stomach. Could I really just ask him? What if he said no or turned us in? I clasped my hands behind my back and cleared my throat.

"Cade, I need your help." I spoke as firmly as possible. "Please."

"Of course," he agreed. "Anything."

I glanced at the workers behind us, who cast curious stares in my direction. "I'd prefer if we speak outside."

He narrowed his eyes at my unusual request.

"If it's no trouble," I added.

He shrugged. "Sure, it's no problem." He led me back the

way I'd come. When we stepped to the path, he shut the door behind us. His cobalt eyes met mine, made brighter in the sunshine. I caught my stuttering breath. No need to let him distract me.

"What's on your mind?" he asked.

A breeze stirred the trees lining the path. "Do you remember that rose you gave me when you did the magic trick?"

He smiled. "It was an illusion, but yes."

"Are you good at sleight of hand?"

"I'm okay, I guess."

"Then…" I pushed a strand of hair behind my ear. "How are you at taking things from people? Things like necklaces?"

"Necklaces?" He cocked his head, curiosity written on his face. "Miss Sabine, what's this about?"

I squared my shoulders. "I need the queen regent's necklace. Her key, actually. She'll be wearing it at the ball, and I thought maybe you could ask her to dance—that is, if you're planning to attend."

He crossed his arms. "You want me to steal her key?"

"Not *steal*, exactly…"

He gave me a sidelong glance. "What for?"

I debated on coming up with a story but thought it best to be honest. "It's a key to the observatory. She banned the prince from going up there, and I don't think it's right. I'm his instructor, and he shouldn't be banned from learning something he's interested in."

"I see."

"Will you help?" I asked.

He shook his head. "I wish I could, but I don't know if you understand how hard it is to get into the queen regent's good graces. If she found out I'd stolen her key, she'd have no problem sending me away from the palace. I'd be out of a job."

I sighed. I should've known.

"But…" he said. "That's only if she finds out, and I have ways of returning objects to people without causing suspicion. Mind you, I've only done this sort of thing during magic shows, and only my nieces were in attendance. I'm afraid they're very gullible, too. Are you sure you want my help?"

"Absolutely."

"Fine." He sighed. "But I have a small favor of my own to ask."

"All right, what is it?"

He took my hands. "Will you dance with me at the ball?"

His dirt-smudged fingers felt cold in mine, and I attempted to smile back. "That shouldn't be too difficult."

He tucked my hair behind my ear, his fingers trailing down my cheeks. I flinched, forcing my feet to hold their ground. *It's okay. He's just touching you. It's what normal people do.*

He released my hands. "You okay?"

I sighed to hide my nervousness. "Fine. I just have this thing. Sometimes when people touch me…" Too much time without human contact in Vortech's facility, plus side effects of being EPC, I could've added, but didn't. "It's okay."

He gave me a concerned glance, but he didn't press the issue. "I look forward to seeing you at the ball," he said, smiling as he straightened his shirt. "Let's hope I scrounge up something a little better than this to wear."

I cast him a curious glance. "Wear?"

"Yes. It's a formal ball, after all."

Darn it all. What was *I* supposed to wear?

"What's the matter?" Cade asked.

"The ball," I sighed. "I've got exactly two uniforms, one pair of street clothes, and a nightdress to my name. Do you think I could get away with this?" I tugged at my vest.

"You want to wear your servant's uniform?"

"I don't *want* to wear it. But I don't have anything else."

"Well, I have good news," he said. "It just so happens that

the greatest seamstress in Ithical resides at our palace. Her name is Mrs. Jennings. My mother used to work for her."

"Really?" I questioned. "How long ago was that?"

Cade gave a casual shrug. "Twenty years ago, at least, although Mrs. Jennings has been here forever. Her room is on the second floor. Little gray door near the kitchens. You can't miss it."

"Second floor. Gray door. Got it." I glanced back at the palace. If Mrs. Jennings had been here that long, would she have known Rosa? And possibly several other agents before her? "I guess I'd better pay a visit to the seamstress. Thank you, Cade."

"Sure, no problem." He smiled warmly. "I suppose I'll see you at the ball, then?"

"Yes, at the ball." I left him standing on the path as I returned to the palace. I tried to shrug off the feeling of his eyes following me, relieved when I heard his footsteps retuning to the greenhouse. At least he'd agreed to help. But how could I be certain he wouldn't betray me and tell the Queen regent? Then again, perhaps I was worrying too much.

When I made it back up to the second floor, I spotted the gray door near the kitchens, so I knocked lightly.

After a moment, the door opened, and a slight woman stood inside. Wisps of white hair framed her wrinkled face, a few loose strands falling from her bun. She stared unfocused at the wall behind me. The grayish-blue hue of one of her irises was too cloudy to be a natural eye. Was it made of glass?

"Hello," I said politely. "I'm looking for the seamstress. Is she here?"

"I'm Mrs. Jennings, the seamstress." She spoke with a voice that would have once commanded attention yet had grown shaky with age. "Who are you?"

"My name is Sabine Harper." I stood tall. "I'm the prince's new caretaker. Would you have time to help me? I need a dress for the ball."

"A dress?" She shuffled back, rustling the layers of her black gown. "But the ball is in less than a fortnight."

"I know, but I've only just arrived at the palace. I didn't know there was a ball until yesterday. Could you please help me?" I hoped she heard the desperation in my voice.

"I'm afraid I won't have time," she said. "I'm already behind schedule making gowns for the ball as it is. If you'd given me a month, perhaps I could. But with such little notice…" She shook her head.

"I understand," I said patiently. "But you don't have to *make* anything. Do you have anything hanging around? Anything other than servant's clothes? They're all I've got."

Her brow creased. "You've only got servant's clothes?"

"Sadly, yes," I answered.

"Well then," she said with a sigh. "We can't very well leave you in that, can we? Come inside."

I stepped inside and she closed the door. Bolts of fabric in rich colors surrounded me, and the scent of clean linen filled the air. An arched window allowed sunlight to stream into the room. Dust motes floated as Mrs. Jennings led me to an area with a full-length mirror. Suits and dresses in various stages of completion hung in open armoires. High frilly collars and long rows of pearls beaded the gowns' bodices.

Mrs. Jennings stood at the long line of gowns. Her crooked fingers grasped each piece, feeling the fabric of each one, as if she could divine some inner message from the touch of the velvet and satin. Dark colors—deep plums and reds, comprised the collection.

"Nothing, nothing, nothing," she muttered, moving down the row. After tugging on each piece, the dusky velvet heavy in her hands, she turned to me. "I've got nothing."

"Nothing?" I pointed. "What about that burgundy one?"

"Burgundy?" she chuckled. "Too dark. It hardly suits a girl with a free spirit like yours."

Free spirit? How could she know a thing like that? "Honestly, I don't care about the color."

"You should." She stepped toward me, reaching out and grasping my face between her hands. Her rice paper skin reminded me so much of Mima June. A deep pang of nostalgia tugged at me.

Mrs. Jennings ran her hands down my arms, to my hands, then back to my face again.

"Beautiful bone structure," she said. "Very different. I've never seen anything like it before." She cocked her head. "Are you not from the island?"

Panic quickened my pulse. "Of course, I'm from here. Where else would I be from?"

"I'm sorry." She smiled and patted my cheek. "I'm an old woman. You'll have to forgive me. Must've been nearly a decade ago when there was someone here who reminded me of you. Unusual bone structure. I have an eye for these things." She pointed to her glass eye and chuckled.

She knew Rosa? "What happened to the girl you knew?"

"Ah, a very good question. She worked as a maid for the queen, I believe. After the queen's death, I never saw her again. Rose was her name. Smart girl, though she seemed a little fearful. She asked me about the Spirit Caves."

"Spirit Caves?" I questioned, my heart thudding.

"Yes, the ones out past the canyons," she explained in a hushed tone. "I told her I didn't go there. No one does."

"Why?" I asked.

"Haunted, they say."

Haunted? Interesting. "Where are they exactly?"

"Near Edenbrooke. Out past the canyons, though I do hope you're not planning to go out there." She shook her head. "Those who do never come back. At least, that's what the old stories say, and who knows how reliable those are." She chuckled. "Well." She clasped her hands. "Let's stop this talk of spirits and find a dress for you. I imagine it will need to be something unique." She tapped her lips. "I think I might have an old gown that might work. Follow me."

She led me past the mirror and into a smaller room. A stained-glass window painted red and purple squares on the rug. After Mrs. Jennings's revelation about Rosa and the caves, I had trouble focusing on clothing.

A cave near Edenbrooke. Hadn't Ivan mentioned he'd found Rosa's things near a cave?

Mrs. Jennings grasped the edge of a table, feeling her way to an open armoire filled with gowns. When she faced it, she grasped a gown, running her fingers over shimmering silk. Lighter colors and simpler designs contrasted those in the other room. Storing away the puzzle pieces of Rosa's disappearance, I did my best to focus on the dresses.

"Why do these dresses look so different from the others?" I asked.

She chuckled. "Because they're out of style, that's why."

"But they're beautiful." I smoothed my hand over a lilac-colored gown.

"I don't make the styles, just the dresses. Here." She pulled a sea-green gown from the armoire. "What color is this one?"

"Green."

"Hmm." She frowned.

"It's fine," I argued.

She clucked her tongue. "No, it won't do." With a sigh, she hung it on the rod.

"How about this one?" I suggested, holding out the lilac gown. She felt for my arm, then clutched the gown.

"Is this the lavender one?" she asked.

"Yes," I said.

"Bah." She made a face. "It's not right. Something more stunning for you, I think."

"Stunning?" I questioned impatiently. "Honestly. I only need a dress. It doesn't have to be anything special."

"Nonsense." She reached the end of the row and stopped

at a silver gown, running her fingers over the light, shimmery fabric. Tiny crystals had been sewn in an ivy-vine pattern that covered the long, sheer sleeves.

Mrs. Jennings pulled it off the rod but held it to her chest.

"What's the matter?" I asked.

She frowned. "It's a very old dress. If you wear this, you must take care."

"Do you trust me with it?"

"We'll see, won't we? Let's try it on, then." She led me to a small changing room, and as I dressed, the shimmery fabric felt light against my skin. When I stepped out, Mrs. Jennings walked to me. Her hands grasped my arms. She knit her eyebrows.

"Is it okay?" I asked.

She didn't answer, only ran her fingers over the sleeves, then tugged on the skirt. I scanned the gown, the tiny crystals sewn into the bodice on the sheer overlay, and ran my hands down the long sleeves, wondering if I looked hideous. With Mrs. Jennings's dour expression, I couldn't be sure.

"Well, the hem will have to be taken up a bit. The bust and waistline will have to be taken in a bit as well…"

"But how do I look?" I asked.

"I can't tell." She laughed. "I'm blind in one eye, nearly blind in the other. You'll have to see for yourself."

She led me back to the first room where we stopped in front of the mirror. If it weren't for my hair worn in a loose ponytail, strands sticking out sloppily, I might not have recognized my own reflection. The person in the glass didn't look like the disheveled person I'd become so accustomed to seeing in the mirror. She was a vision of flowing cloth and soft curves.

The silver fabric contrasted the dark undertones of my olive-brown skin and brought out the gray flecks in my eyes. My collar bones still protruded more than I would've liked, thanks to Vortech, but I'd filled in a little. Was it possible I could be attractive?

Thinking of Morven's and Cade's reactions when they saw me wearing this made my stomach twist uncomfortably. Heat rushed through me, and I wasn't sure I could go through with attending the ball and drawing attention to myself. Maybe I'd just wear my servant's uniform after all.

"Well?" Mrs. Jennings asked. "How is it?"

"I think it works," I said, clearly understating, yet not sure how else to describe it.

"Then it's yours." Mrs. Jennings finally smiled, and I couldn't help but smile back. When the time for the ball arrived, I would be ready.

14

I cracked an egg and emptied it into a skillet. Popping grease mingled with shouted orders. Steam rose from the pots surrounding me, holding the scent of poached pears. Stifling a yawn, I tried to focus on the task of cooking His Royal Majesty's breakfast.

Bodies scurried around me. Maids carrying jugs of cider, servants with baskets of lemons or pears, and trays of porridge being carried to the nobles. None carried yellow cerecite with them. Not in plain view, at least.

The queen regent wasn't in the kitchen, of course, but I doubted she would've been doing the deed herself. Most likely she'd hired someone to do it for her. But who?

I'd had two weeks to ponder the question as I waited for the ball. In the last fourteen days, I'd taken the opportunity to work on my map. I'd checked off nearly all two-hundred-and-forty-two rooms. So far, I'd found nothing, although I had heard some strange knocking in the dungeon and chalked it up to rats. Or ghosts. Still, I wasn't giving up hope. It was now more likely than ever that at least one of the objects was locked in the tower.

I'd spent most of my free time in the greenhouse with

Cade. I was fascinated by the flowers and plants created from the green cerecite, and it felt nice to spend time with someone who I could laugh with. We also traveled to the surrounding city often enough, and I was learning to navigate the streets myself.

I'd also fallen into a rhythm of teaching the prince, although he'd taught me more than I'd taught him. I'd prodded him to tell me as much as he knew about the white cerecite, and he'd taken me to a room where the seven orbs had once been kept in ornate glass boxes designed to keep them in their primary state for several weeks, though they were all missing now. In the time I'd spent with him, I'd come to grow fond of him despite his seemingly rude exterior, which I was now starting to see as a mask.

However, the past two weeks hadn't gone without trouble. More often than not, I'd found myself looking over my shoulder, feeling as if I were being watched. I'd spotted a tall hulking figure on more than one occasion, and my suspicions of why Ivan needed to follow me didn't lead to any satisfactory conclusions.

In the kitchen, I'd begun the task of cooking the prince's breakfast, which I'd accomplished quietly so far.

I jumped as stomping footsteps approached behind me. Spinning around, I faced Mrs. O'Connor. She stood over me, her cheeks blotchy and lips pinched, a wooden spoon clutched in her fist. She wiped the sweat beading on her forehead.

"Don't think I haven't noticed you in my kitchen. For the past fortnight at least!" Mrs. O'Connor shook the spoon in my face. "I've ignored you until now, but not today when we're all about to lose our minds preparing for the feast. What are you doing here, Miss Sabine?"

I stood straight. "I've been making the prince's food. He refused to eat the porridge."

"Why?" she snapped.

I sidestepped a maid who rushed past me and grabbed an

empty tray. "Because he didn't like it, I assume." I spoke over the clanking silverware. "I told him I would make it."

"He doesn't like my cooking?" she challenged.

"He didn't like the ingredients that were being added." And that was the total truth. "I haven't gotten in your way yet, have I? I can make eggs."

She huffed. "Go on, then." She waved her wooden spoon. "I hated cooking for that spoiled mutton head anyway. But I'll not be helping you, and you'd better not expect it of me."

"Fine." I'd gotten along just fine without her anyway.

I turned to the skillet as she marched away. Eggs popped and sizzled, the rich scent curling into the air on puffs of steam.

"Are you going to let them burn or what?" a maid said as she rushed past me. I'd seen her before. Justine, wasn't it?

I turned back to the eggs. The edges were curling and beginning to brown. Sighing, I picked up the skillet and slid them on a plate.

Justine eyed the platter. "You've been preparing the food for the prince, haven't you?"

I added a pinch of salt and pepper. "Yes," I answered.

"I'm sorry you're stuck tending to him." She smoothed her blonde braid that hung to her waist. "We all know how he is."

I grabbed a few slices of rye from a basket and placed it on the plate. "He's not so bad sometimes."

She laughed mockingly. "You must be joking. He's horrible. You are funny, Miss Sabine."

"I think he's only rude because he feels trapped here. If you get to know him, he's not so bad."

Her eyes widened. "Not so bad?"

"He's nice, actually," I explained. "And he's exceptionally intelligent."

"Careful, Miss Sabine." She narrowed her eyes. "It almost sounds as if you fancy him. The queen regent wouldn't take kindly to such a thing—what with you as his tutor."

"Justine," I said confidently. "I promise, I would never fancy him."

Her lips protruded in a sulky pout. "Then I suppose we've nothing to worry about." She sniffed before turning away, her shapely hips swishing as she pushed her way through the crowd of servants.

"Not that it's your business anyway," I mumbled.

I turned away from her. On my way out, I grabbed an apple from a basket and a jug of cider, then escaped the kitchens as Mrs. O'Connor gave me an evil glare. I exhaled a sigh of relief as I paced through the cool air in the hallways. It was no wonder Mrs. O'Connor was constantly barking at everyone and being sour. I wasn't sure I would've been much kinder if I'd been stuck in that hellish place all day.

When I got to the prince's doorway, I went through the usual motions of knocking and entering, then balancing the tray as I crossed into the room.

An empty bed greeted me. The blankets were tucked neatly, and pillows were arranged. As I scanned the room, I spotted Prince Morven's tall frame by the window. He'd dressed in his usual all-black attire as he stood with his arms folded across his chest.

Standing.

I almost dropped the tray.

"Morven?"

He turned around and looked at me, his face revealing no emotion.

"You're standing?" I said, shocked.

He gave a slight nod, but he offered no further explanation. I placed the tray on the bedside table.

"Eggs today?" His face brightened as he focused on the food.

"Yes." I motioned to the food. "I also grabbed some bread, an apple, and cider. No porridge ever again, thankfully."

His wheelchair was arranged next to him, and he sat, his movements cautious.

"You must be feeling better?" I asked as he wheeled up to the food.

"It's hard to tell. As I said before, some days are better than others."

"Let's hope you keep improving—which, you now will, because I've been making sure you're not eating poisoned porridge."

He gave me a slight smile. "You still believe it was poisoned?"

"No. I know it was. But the eggs are safe, so you should eat them."

He poked them with the fork. "They look… delicious?"

I laughed. "They're only burnt a little around the edges. I thought you wouldn't mind."

He shoveled in a bite, and finished them off in less than a minute, then ate the bread before taking a long drink from the mug of cider.

As he took a bite of the apple, he nodded at me. "Delicious. When I'm King, I'll replace Cook with you."

"Thanks." I shrugged. "But I think I'll pass."

"I'm serious. The food is amazing. You really are a talented chef."

I couldn't hide my smile. "You think so?"

"Absolutely." He motioned to me with his apple. "Where were you yesterday?"

I gave him a quizzical glance. "Yesterday?"

"During dinner?" he clarified.

"Oh…" I answered. "Mrs. Jennings was putting the finishing touches on a dress for me."

He cocked his head. "What for?"

"What for?" I placed my hands on my hips. "You seriously don't know? It's for the ball, you idiot," I said teasingly.

He placed the apple on his lap, eyeing me with his calculated gaze, which seemed no less menacing than when I'd first met him. "You're going to the ball?"

"Yes, that was the plan, wasn't it? We're going to steal your aunt's key and all. By the way, I found someone to do it for us."

"Who?" he asked.

"Cade."

He knit his brow. "The gardener?"

"Yes. He's talented at sleight of hand, so I asked for his help. He only asked for me to dance with him, and he agreed to do it."

His eyes narrowed. "You agreed to dance with him?"

I nodded. "Is something wrong with that?"

He gazed out the window. "Nothing," he muttered.

"You don't like the gardener?" I prodded.

He shrugged, then took another bite of the apple. "I don't like anyone."

"Not even me?" I winked.

"Of course, not you." He smirked. "You just called me an idiot. Do you enjoy calling me names?"

"Yes, I do—which is why I do it. Now." I sighed. "With all those pleasantries out of the way, what's on the schedule for today? More lessons?"

"No, thankfully." He took another bite of the apple, and I supposed he'd let the whole being-offended-that-I'd-called-him-an-idiot thing slide. I didn't know why it stung when he'd said he didn't like me. He was teasing about that anyway, right?

"My aunt wants me in the ballroom to discuss the night's schedule. She's domineering when it comes to this sort of thing—wants everything to be perfect, so she demands I be there all day."

"All day?" I asked, stunned.

"Yes, unfortunately." He placed the apple core on the tray. "And she wanted me there five minutes ago."

"Fine." I crossed my arms, annoyance clawing at me. "But I don't like how she controls your life. What is she planning to do with herself once you're king?"

"To be honest, I don't think much will change."

"What do you mean by that?" I asked.

"She'll still be my advisor," he answered. "Depending on how capable I am, she could retain most of her power."

Meaning Morven's handicap would allow her to keep her control over him.

I went to the back of his chair, grabbed the handles, and pushed him out of his room and down the hall. As we walked, with no one passing us by, I decided now was a good time to question him about his nightly activities. I'd found him missing from his room more than once in the last two weeks I'd been here, and I couldn't ignore it any longer.

"Morven, I came to your room a few nights ago to check on you, but you were gone. Where were you?"

He glanced back at me. "You came to check on me?"

"Yes." I nodded.

"Why on Earth would you do a thing like that?" he asked sharply.

"Because I'm your caretaker," I said matter-of-factly. "It's my job."

"First, you're not my caretaker," he explained. "That may be your title, but I'm a grown man, and, not to be offensive, but I have more than enough servants to push my chair around. I have no need for you. Second, what I do at night is my business."

"You really won't tell me?" I asked. "I thought we were getting to be friends."

He glanced up at me, dark eyes narrowed with confusion. "Friends?" he said the word as if it were something foreign.

"Yes, friends," I repeated. "I thought we could be honest with each other. Why won't you tell me where you go?"

He crossed his arms. "No," he muttered. "That's not something I care to tell you."

"Fine," I murmured.

He remained quiet, and I pushed him toward the ball-room in silence.

When we entered, servants bustled around the enormous room, carrying armloads of green and gold streamers or vases of flowers. Tables had been arranged and were in various stages of being decorated. Shuffling feet and hurried voices echoed through the domed space.

Queen Regent Tremayne stood talking to a group of servants near a cluttered table at the back. Her eyes snagged on me and Morven. She dismissed her servants and stalked toward us, her wide skirt rustling, her gown's dark hue contrasting her chalky skin.

"Morven," she snapped. "I told you to arrive ten minutes ago."

"Yes." He motioned to his legs. "But as you see, I'm incapable of walking."

She held up a bony finger. "Don't be high-spirited with me," she argued. "I've had enough of that from the servants." She pursed her lips, eyes narrowed. "They've brought in the wrong flowers. White roses when I ordered red tulips. I had to have them tossed out. Now I don't know if we'll get the arrangements set up in time."

"Would you like me to help?" I didn't know why I offered. Getting into her good graces seemed a pointless goal, but it was the only thing I could think to say.

"No." She shook her head. "You're to help Morven learn his place." She crossed to the table and rifled through a pile of scrolls, then handed one to me. "This is tonight's program. You're to make sure Morven is where he needs to be at certain times, and at those times only. He can only be seen when necessary. Do you understand what I'm saying?" she asked, her voice sharp. "His appearances are to be closely monitored, and I need you to make sure that happens. Read through the instructions carefully. There can be no missteps. Do *not* fail at this."

I stood tall. "I understand."

"Good." She clasped her hands. "Now, go over the program as many times as possible so there aren't any slip-ups."

She bustled away.

"I don't like her," I mumbled.

Morven sighed. "She's family."

I opened the scroll and scanned the schedule. *Queen Regent's entrance. Queen Regent's welcome. Royal dinner. (Morven to sit at the end table near the doors. Must be able to enter and exit room without aid of the chair.)* I skipped ahead. *Introduction of Prince Morven. (MUST BE ABLE TO STAND while being announced, then return to chair where HE WILL SIT for the rest of the evening!!)*

"Well, it looks like your aunt is expecting a miracle." I rolled up the scroll. "Any idea how you're supposed to walk across a room when you can't even stand up most of the time?"

"She expects me to walk?" he questioned.

"Yes, I believe so." I thumped the scroll. "There's the whole must-be-standing thing. And the two exclamation points at the end."

"If I fall, she'll blame me." He heaved a deep sigh. "It's happened before."

"That's ridiculous."

"Yes, but I expected it." He gripped his chair's armrests. "Wheel me to the dining table. I might as well start practicing now."

I tucked the scroll under my arm, then pushed him over the marble floor to the end of the row of heavy oaken tables. I stopped when the archway overshadowed us.

"I'm assuming this is where we'll put your chair. You'll only have to walk from here to the table, then back again."

He tapped his fingers on his knee. "Shouldn't be too hard."

I stepped to his side, then held out my hand. He eyed it. "What are you doing?"

"Helping you stand up," I explained.

He paused, observing me cautiously, as if not sure he could trust me. Did he have the same problem with touching people as me? But he clenched his jaw. Determination shone in his eyes, and he didn't argue as he put his hand in mine. As we touched, his firm grip made me catch my breath, shattering my urge to push him away. That had never happened before, and I was left bewildered and exhilarated. Usually my extra perception made it hard to touch anyone. But now...

Our eyes locked.

Words escaped me as I looked into dark, knowing eyes. I could've gotten lost in their depths.

Keeping his hand in mine, Morven stood up straight.

"You're doing it," I said encouragingly.

"I stood up, yes. Wow," he answered with sarcasm. "Now comes the part where I have to actually try."

Holding my arm, he shuffled one foot forward, then the other. He made it halfway to the table when his legs buckled. He fell, pulling me down with him. My tailbone took the brunt of the impact on the stone floor.

Ouch.

I sat up, looking at Morven who lay on the floor. "Are you okay?"

"Fine." His chest rose and fell. "I'm used to it." He sat up. "How about you?"

I rubbed my back. "Just a bruise. I've had worse."

He nodded. "Shall we try again?"

"Are you sure you want to?" I asked.

"Yes," he said with determination.

"Okay, then." I stood, then helped him do the same. He held tightly to my arm as we walked, one step in front of the other, the warmth of his body near mine, though only our arms touched. I inhaled the scent of his cologne—of spiced amber and mountain forests, reminding me of the wilderness.

With one final step, we made it to the dining table. He collapsed in the chair.

"You did it." I sat next to him.

"No." His shoulders slumped. "I did what everyone else does all day without even thinking. It's nothing you should congratulate me for."

"Morven, you *should* be proud. Just because everyone else can walk without thinking doesn't diminish your achievement. You did something that was challenging for you. Don't compare it to what everyone else does."

He gave me a curious glance. "You really believe that? All I did was walk a few steps."

"Yes, I do believe it." I sat tall. "And it is worth congratulating. Once you figure that out, this will get easier."

He sighed, not meeting my gaze, perhaps pondering my words.

"Fine," he said. "Let's walk back to my chair."

"Are you sure?" I questioned. "You don't want to rest a moment?"

"Yes." He took a deep breath. "I'm sure."

"All right." I stood, then helped him do the same, his hand gripping my forearm. He shuffled forward, moving with slow, deliberate actions. When we reached the halfway point, he stopped.

"I think I'll try it by myself." He straightened his back.

I raised an eyebrow. "Really?"

"Yes," he answered with a determined nod. "I need to do this."

"Okay." I released his arm, then took a step away from him.

His chest rose. He took one step, then another. As he walked, he glanced at me. A smile stretched his lips.

"You're doing it!"

He nodded. His face filled with concentration as he finally made it to the chair.

I walked back to him. "That was amazing!"

He nodded. "I think that's it for today."

"You're sure?"

"Yes." He rubbed his thighs. "I don't think I could make it again. I should probably save my strength."

"All right. If that's what you want. Good job, by the way."

He hesitated before answering, as if he were ready to downplay his accomplishment and tell me it wasn't a big deal. Instead, he gave me a slight smile. "Thank you," he answered, sincerity in his voice.

When our gazes connected, his eyes softened, and I wondered if anyone had ever genuinely praised him. With the way he'd reacted, I doubted it.

Standing behind his chair, I grabbed the handles and pushed him away from the table. As we crossed through the room, Cade entered. He carried a box of tulips in crystal vases. He smiled when he saw me, pausing to place the flowers on a table.

Morven stiffened. "What's *he* doing here?"

"He's the gardener," I answered. "I'm sure he's got plenty of chores to do with getting all the flowers arranged."

Morven snorted. "Flower arrangements. Right. Why's he coming over when he's obviously got such a huge blunder to fix?"

"Maybe he wants to talk to us," I offered.

"Talk to *you*, more likely." He crossed his arms. "That man doesn't give one whit about me. He's always pretended I don't exist, like I have the plague. Won't even acknowledge me half the time."

"Really?" I asked. "That doesn't seem right. That's certainly not the attitude of the gardener I know."

"Well… I can only assume he hates people in wheelchairs."

"Really Morven, I think you're reading too much into it." Morven was probably just sensitive about being in the chair, but I decided not to mention it.

Cade shot me his rakish grin as he stopped near us. "Prince Morven, Sabine," he said with a nod. "I'm glad I've found you here."

"Still working on fixing your mistake with the flowers, I see," Morven said in a bored tone. "Too bad you can't tell red tulips from white roses. Have you ever been tested for color blindness?"

His smile faltered.

"Cade," I said as politely as possible. "We were just headed outside, but I'm glad you've found us. Morven, Cade's helping us with tonight's task, remember?"

"How generous of him. But he wasn't doing it for nothing, was he? What did he want in return?" He brushed his hand through the air. "Oh, yes. A dance. With you. Perhaps if he'd been concentrating on his work instead of ogling you, he wouldn't have made such a blunder with the flowers."

Embarrassment heated my cheeks. "He wasn't ogling me," I hissed through gritted teeth for only him to hear. The idea of Morven suggesting such a thing made me unbearably uncomfortable. Why couldn't he keep his mouth shut?

"Sure, he wasn't. Well—" Morven sat straight— "it looks like Mr. MacDougal is swamped with all these flower arrangements he needs to fix before the ball. It's a shame he couldn't get them right the first time. Maybe someday my aunt will fire the idiot who makes such reckless mistakes. Oh, wait, she won't have to." His voice held an edge of warning. "Because in three days, I will."

I tightened my hands around the wheelchair's handles.

"Fire me?" Cade asked, aghast. "You've got to be joking. It wasn't even my fault. Your aunt placed the wrong order."

"Now you're blaming someone else?" Morven shook his head. "Something like this had better not happen when I'm king, or I won't hesitate to send you away."

"Well, then." Cade frowned. "I won't waste any more of your time. I'd best get back to work."

"Excellent idea." Morven tapped his fingers on the wheelchair's armrest. "You should've been doing that in the first place."

Cade flexed his jaw. "Sabine, Prince Morven, good day." He turned and marched away, back to the flowers he'd left on the table.

Why did it seem every time I made progress with getting Morven to act like a decent human being, he turned into the rude, selfish prince once again?

"You're an ass," I hissed through clenched teeth as I pushed Morven to the doors leading out of the room.

"He deserved it." He clenched his armrests. "He shouldn't make such careless mistakes. Once I'm king, he'll be the first to go."

"Once you're king, I won't care, because I'll be gone too."

He tilted his head. "What do you mean by that?"

"Nothing," I grumbled. "Where are we going now? Back to your room so you can sleep the day away? So you can mysteriously escape the palace tonight while you're well-rested?"

"Where I go at night is none of your business," he snapped. "And I don't want to go back to my room. I hate that place. Take me outside. I need some air."

"Can you go outside?" I questioned. "What would your aunt say?"

"I don't care," he bit out.

"Do you care about anything?" I huffed, anger rising, making my blood turn hot.

"No," he answered. "Not really."

Well, at least he was honest. I turned down the hallway.

"You had no right to treat Cade so coldly," I said. "He's helping us tonight. With the way you acted, I wouldn't be surprised if he decides not to."

"I don't care. He's overpaid and arrogant."

"*He's* arrogant? What world do you live in, Morven?"

"Ha." He laughed to himself. "Good question."

We made it outside the main doors and to the veranda, then onto a cobbled path. Wheels bumped on the uneven surface. A chill wind smelling of rain rushed past, battering my hair against my cheeks. Goosebumps prickled my skin. The wall loomed before us, and I steered us toward a gate.

"Not that gate," he said. "Turn right, follow the wall until we reach a wooden door."

"Where are we going?" I asked.

"Outside the gate."

"Yes, I got that. But where?"

"You'll see. Just find the door first."

I glanced back at the castle, its tall spire reaching up to the sky. As I wheeled him away from the main entrance, we rounded the palace. I didn't speak to him. In truth, I was too transfixed as I stared up at the enormous structure—its three tiers pyramid-like in their construction.

How did a group of nineteenth-century immigrants manage to build such a thing? And more confusing than that, how had they managed to create a shield that separated them from the rest of the world—complete with weather patterns and everything? It boggled my mind, and so far, I hadn't been given a good explanation.

15

"There." Morven pointed to a wooden door hidden by ivy in the wall's shadow. "That's it. Take me through there."

I glanced back at the palace before continuing through the castle's courtyard. When we reached the door leading outside the castle grounds, I lifted the latch. It swung on rusty hinges as the wind gusted it open. After steering Morven's wheelchair onto a gravel path, we hiked the trail leading toward a dark forest.

Spruces and oaks stood out against soupy gray clouds. The path sloped and curved around a bend. My hands burned as I gripped the handles. When we reached level ground, we made it to the shade of the trees, the branches covered in verdant leaves—all uniformity, no brown spots or decay.

As we continued, creaking came from up ahead, though the thick branches obscured the source of the sound, until we entered a clearing. A wooden swing—like a porch swing—swayed in the wind, taut ropes groaning around the tree branch high above.

"Why'd you want to come here?"

"Because once I'm king, I doubt I'll get another chance." He motioned to the chair. "Will you help me into the swing?"

"No." I stepped in front of him and crossed my arms. "I'm not taking another step until you explain why you acted so rudely to Cade."

He crossed his arms, mimicking me. "Why do you think?"

I sighed in frustration. "I really don't understand you sometimes."

"Good. Then you fit in with the rest of the staff," he said, eyes dark and piercing.

"Do you *want* people to hate you?"

His gaze didn't flinch. "What if I do?"

I stood facing him, my heart racing with the tiniest drop of pity, though he deserved none of it. "I'm taking you back to the palace." I walked to the chair's handles and wheeled him around.

"Sabine, no." His voice held an edge of desperation. "Please, let me stay." Pleading replaced his scornful tone.

I stopped pushing him. Closing my eyes, I heaved a long sigh. "Fine," I bit out. "We'll stay for a minute."

After wheeling his chair to the swing, I grabbed his arm and helped him sit. I slid beside him, wooden slats beneath me, and used my feet to push off the ground, allowing us to sway gently, the air rushing against our faces.

Something about swinging made a flash of memories burst to life. Dad pushing me on the swings in the park. I'd laughed as he'd pushed me higher and higher. He'd said I could touch the moon. I'd looked at the white orb glowing in the sky on a darkening evening, wondering if I really could swing high enough to reach out and touch it. *Dad said I could, so it must be true,* I'd thought at the time.

What was he doing now? He was probably riding his tractor through the field, endless amounts of labor that never paid enough to support us. Was he thinking of me?

"Thank you," Morven said, bringing me out of my thoughts. "For letting me stay."

I laughed quietly. "You're welcome. I guess. I'm not sure you deserve it."

He looked at his hands clasped in his lap. "You're right," he mumbled. "I shouldn't have acted that way to the gardener."

"You were awful to him," I said sharply. "Why would you think it's okay to treat someone that way?"

"If you really want to know, I'm jealous of him." His Adam's apple bobbed as he swallowed. "He can dance with you. I can't."

Surprise struck me, though I should've expected as much. "You would want to dance with me?"

He gave me a sidelong glance. "Do you have to ask?"

I studied him. He made no sense at all. "I…"

"Would you dance with me if I asked you?"

Not sure how to answer, I dug my toes into the dirt. "Does it matter what I want? If the crowned prince asked me to dance, I'd do it because it was expected. Not because I wanted to. Otherwise, I'd risk losing my job."

He only nodded, studying his hands. "And if I wasn't the crowned prince?"

"Maybe. If you acted the way you do when we're alone."

"That's a lie. I'm never nice to anyone. I only do things for myself. I'm surprised you haven't figured that out by now." He focused straight ahead, revealing the ridge of his forehead, the straight line of his nose, and his full lips, pinched with worry, and perhaps regret.

"Why do you act like that, Morven?" I asked softly. "Are you hiding from something? Are you trying to protect yourself?"

He shrugged. "Why do you care?"

"I don't. It's just curiosity."

He sighed. The ropes creaked rhythmically.

"You said you're leaving after I become king. Where are you going?" he asked.

"Back home, hopefully. My family needs me. My da doesn't make a lot of money with his... fishing." I'd almost slipped and said farming. "He works a lot. I don't see him much." The wind carried my sigh. "I just lost my grandma, and I know it's hard for him without her. She did a lot for our family..."

I tried to swallow that great lump in my throat, the way I always felt whenever I thought about losing Mima—which was why I tried never to think about it.

"I understand," Morven said, his voice distant. "My parents are gone too. All I have now is my aunt, and you know what she's like."

"Yeah."

"She'll be looking for us soon," he said.

"Okay." But I didn't move from my spot on the swing. I hadn't told anyone about my family since I'd gotten here. Talking about them now lifted a weight from my shoulders. It was the one thing I truly cared about, and I didn't want to go back to the place where I'd have to pretend they didn't exist. Maybe I'd told Morven too much, but talking to him came easily, and I needed someone to talk to—I needed a friend. But had I made a mistake in telling him?

Someone in the castle was responsible for Agent Rodriguez's disappearance. How did I know he wasn't involved? Except he would've been a kid at the time.

A bird's call came from the forest. I glanced up, spotting shimmering blue-green feathers. A falcon dove from overhead, skimmed the forest floor, then soared back up.

"Mystik falcon," Morven said. "I wondered if we'd see her."

I gave him a curious glance. "*Her?* You know that bird?"

He nodded. "She visits me sometimes when I come out here. Likes to bring me rats or snakes."

I bit my lip. "Lovely."

Morven held out his leather-clad arm, and the bird landed on it. I sat transfixed as she fluttered her wings. Pale turquoise light shimmered from her feathers. Though I'd seen Ivan's wolf in the tundra, I had trouble accepting what I saw wasn't some sort of technological trick.

"Can I pet her?" I asked.

"Yes. Just here." He smoothed the feathers along her neck, and I did the same. They held the same softness of Ivan's wolf.

"Our people like to think the Mystik creatures come from the souls of the reborn, but I see them as something else," Morven said.

"What do you see?" I asked.

"I see the byproduct of cerecite—a meld of chemistry and biology. The building blocks of all life."

I tilted my head. "What do you mean by that?"

"I mean there's nothing else like cerecite on Earth," he explained. "It's been frozen at the top of the world and never studied by science. No one can say how our ancestors took the leap from chemicals in a lakebed to living creatures, but that's because they never studied cerecite. One day, I hope to convince our people to believe in more than myths—to study the truth around us instead. Cerecite is the link between living and non-living."

"Do you really think so?" I asked, his theory piquing my curiosity.

The falcon ruffled her feathers, then started preening, just like an ordinary bird.

"Yes, and I wish our people would study it, would care more about knowledge and break free from the mundane, but that will only happen if something drastic changes their minds."

Drastic like what? I wanted to ask, but the bird flapped her wings, then screeched before leaping off Morven's arm. She circled upward until she soared over the treetops and disappeared.

"We should go." Morven moved to stand. I rushed to grab his arm, but he made it to his chair without my help.

"You did it by yourself," I said. "That's progress."

"Yes." He sat up straight, his gaze roving over the rustling tree limbs. "I think I'm getting stronger."

"You do?"

"I think so, but I always feel stronger when I'm away from the palace."

"Are you sure you're ready to go back?" I asked.

"Yes," he said. "I, for one, would like to get this ball over with."

"I agree." I didn't find it necessary to tell him why.

16

Violin strings carried a harmonized melody through the ballroom as the orchestra warmed up. Goosebumps prickled my arms covered in sheer sleeves as the chilly air came from the enormous chamber. I stood in a shadowed hallway, watching as servants bustled around tables, arranged chairs, and straightened stalks of red tulips. The queen regent clasped a scroll as she paced on the dais, overlooking them with drawn lips and narrowed eyes.

This had better be perfect, I imagined her saying.

I tried inhaling, but the tight bodice compressed my lungs. Standing straight helped a little. I ran my hands over the silk. I'd gotten accustomed to functional clothing: the stiff bleached cotton of my Vortech uniform, the supple leather of my bomber jacket, and the threaded wool of my palace uniform. The shimmering beads felt foreign. I picked at the crystals, as if I wore something that didn't belong on me.

Beyond the shadows of the hallway, the queen stepped off the dais.

"One minute," she shouted. The harsh timbre of her voice carried through the domed chamber. Anxiety quickened my pulse.

When Vortech had recruited me to go on a mission to a remote island north of Russia, I'd been expecting wilderness survival and frostbite. I preferred that to this. Dancing? Interacting with actual people? Clearly Vortech had pegged me for someone I wasn't.

But I had to get the next objects. I'd spent nearly two weeks looking through the palace. If the next objects weren't in the tower, I didn't know where else they could be.

I pressed my hand to the wall—rough, unyielding cinder blocks.

A man approached the queen regent, his embroidered green robes moving fluidly as he walked. The chandelier's light made his bald head glisten. He spoke quietly to her, his words drowned out by the violins.

She nodded, then clapped her hands twice. The doors on the far side swung open. A line of people entered. Heavy fabric draped the women who treaded through the room beside men wearing fitted black suits and tall boots. They stopped at the edge of the ballroom.

The man on the dais unrolled a scroll and announced the names of the noble houses. A blonde woman with a stacked bun strode forward. Behind her, the other nobles paced inside. The women's dresses matched, with lacy collars and puffy sleeves, only varying in color. They all wore their hair up with copious amounts of jewels and combs.

I brushed my fingers through my long strands. My hair fell down my back in a dark wave without so much as a barrette to decorate it. But I'd brushed it until it shone, and it wasn't in its usual messy ponytail.

Baby steps.

When the nobles began eating, I glanced behind me. Where was Morven?

Laughter and soft voices drifted from the dining hall. Floral scents of women's perfume combined with the succulent aroma of the food. Waiting was killing me. Where was he?

Rolling wheels caught my attention. I turned around. A male servant pushed Morven through the dark corridor.

Finally.

Only a little light seeped into the hallway. In the bluish glow of the lamps, Morven neared me.

"Stop here," Morven said to the man. "Then leave me."

The servant nodded and marched back the way he'd come.

Morven grasped the wheels. His broad shoulders flexed under a black suit fitted to his lean, corded muscles. A silver dragon-shaped brooch held his plaid in place, which he wore over his shoulder. His hair had been combed, though a small clump fell across his forehead. I clasped my hands, quelling the compulsion to smooth it back.

My heart fluttered at the sight of him. When Morven's eyes met mine, my breath caught in my throat. The now familiar scent of his cologne washed over me, conjuring images of wild forests and the heady scent of spruce.

He stopped beside me, his eyes fixed on me as he cocked his head. "Sabine?"

"Yes?" I answered, my voice pitched too high.

He laughed quietly. "I wasn't sure it was you. You look different."

"Different?" I questioned.

"Yes," he said, smiling, and I couldn't ignore the dark glitter to his eyes. "In a good way."

The deep tone of his voice made a warm shiver course from the top of my head straight to the tips of my toes.

I pressed my hands to my stomach, my insides on fire.

"Are you okay?" he asked.

"Fine." *Just a little breathless.* "The nobles are eating. We should hurry." I hoped he didn't hear the quiver in my voice. "Are you ready to walk to the table?"

His eyes were set with determination. "Yes."

"Don't worry." I rested my hand on his shoulder. "I'll be right by you."

"Good." He sat tall. "Don't help me unless it looks like I'll fall."

"You're sure?" I asked, butterflies dancing in my stomach at being so near him.

He nodded, and I took a step back. He locked his jaw as he pushed off from the seat. He wobbled, but he managed to gain his balance. I walked beside him out of the shadow of the hallway.

The man standing atop the dais looked in our direction. "Prince Morven Alexander Tremayne, son of the late king and queen, crown prince of Ithical Island," he announced in a booming voice.

Every eye in the room locked on him.

Morven walked steadily, as if he'd done this a thousand times before, yet I kept my fingers flexed, expecting to grab his arm if I had to.

His aunt sat at a table by herself, not far from us, a few empty chairs arranged by her. Her shrewd gaze stayed fixed on her nephew.

Do not fall, she seemed to say.

One step after another, he crossed the distance, my heart pounding with every footfall. After one last step, he sat in the chair by his aunt. I took a seat beside him, my stomach still twisting with nervousness, allowing my hands to rest on my lap without feeling I had to catch him. He'd done it. Now he only had to make it to another chair, sit through the dance, and that would be it.

Once Cade got the key, we'd find a way to sneak out and unlock the tower. *If* Cade saw fit to help. One thing at a time. First, we had to sit and make small talk.

"You're late," his aunt hissed through a forced smile, whispering so only we could hear.

"Aren't I always?" He mindlessly tapped his fork on his plate. "I hate to break habits, Aunt Tremayne. You know that."

She pressed her lips to form a thin line. "Where were you?"

"I'd rather not answer." He took a sip from his goblet. "It's so much better to have mysteries to solve in life, isn't it?"

"You're wearing down my patience," she seethed. "If you're not careful, I'll have to demand you leave the ball early."

"Oh no. How horrible," he said in a mocking tone. "Please don't do such a dreadful thing. Leave the ball early? Whatever will I do?"

I nearly choked while trying not to laugh. I grabbed a yeasted bun from a basket and took a bite to hide my smile.

With a sigh, his aunt turned her sharp gaze on me. "Miss Harper, I see you've done nothing to teach him his place. It seems his attitude is growing worse."

"I didn't realize I was supposed to be teaching him his place."

She huffed. "I hope you do realize it, or your time here will be cut short."

"I understand. He's a stubborn student, but I'm trying my best."

Morven and I traded glances, sharing a secretive smile.

"At least you made it to the table," she whispered. "There are more nobles here tonight than I expected. I'd hate for them to see your chair, or else we'd be ruined forever."

"I fail to see how the sight of my chair would ruin us," Morven said with a yawn.

"You don't?" Her eyes narrowed. "Well, that's easy to understand. You don't give one whit about procedure and propriety. How we're to survive your reign is a frightening thought."

"I think it will turn out just fine." He smiled reassuringly.

"Besides, you've taught me everything you know. Just today I was threatening to fire the gardener. As you see, I catch on quickly. Fire the staff, and you'll never have to worry about them."

"You're mocking me," she said through gritted teeth. "I won't tolerate it."

I speared a roasted potato, then stuffed it in my mouth, chewing so I wouldn't have to contribute to the conversation.

As I ate, I watched her closely. If she were slipping poison into her nephew's food, would she try to do it now?

But if she had realized Morven was no longer eating his porridge, would she try to come at him in another way? If so, I would be watching.

As the queen regent slowly chewed her food, I focused on the silver chain hanging around her neck, a key dangling from it. My stomach twisted in a nervous knot. No longer hungry, I placed my fork aside and scanned the room, searching for Cade. I didn't spot him.

When the meal ended, the man wearing the green robes stood on the dais once again.

"Prepare for the dance." His voice boomed through the chamber. After the servants cleared the food, they opened the doors to let in the other guests.

More men and women wearing suits and dresses entered the ballroom.

I self-consciously combed my fingers through my hair as the crowd grew, and I moved away from the table, choosing to stand by the wall and watch the dance from a distance.

With the aid of a servant, Prince Morven strategically made it to a chair near the front. His aunt remained at his side. She kept her eyes on him, as if warning him not to move from where he sat. A group of people gathered around them and blocked my view.

Chills prickled my skin as I lost sight of Morven. Why did it seem so much colder without him close?

The queen regent moved to stand on the dais. Her voice carried as she gave a lengthy speech. I didn't pay attention. Something about the green dragon, the monarchy, and copious amounts of her own achievements.

My gaze wandered. The crowd gathered around Morven. What would it be like to go home and leave him behind? Emptiness tugged at me, a sensation that sent a chill down my spine. I'd never found anyone like him before. He was intelligent beyond his years, and he cared for his people more than he let on. Leaving him was something I didn't want to ponder. I hugged my arms around me, trying to stop the loneliness from settling like a dark shadow.

When the queen finished her speech, she sat beside Morven. Violins started playing a light tune. Near the orchestra stood men with bagpipes. As they played, the sound carried, a rich melody that stirred the soul.

Dancers whirled in a blur of jewels and vibrant colors. Laughter and conversations echoed. I didn't recognize any of the smiling men and women as they danced past me.

Where was Cade? With any luck, he'd go without dancing and decide to get the queen regent's key anyway. One could wish. It wasn't that I didn't want to dance with him, but I hated social gatherings. In high school, I'd always ended up standing alone and pretending to be okay with it—and here, halfway around the world, on a foreign island in the frozen Russian tundra, was no different.

People brushed by on their way to the dance floor. Most songs were played with a lively beat, but others were slower, and partners danced closely. I paid attention to each dancer, at the way their bodies swayed with the music, the pattern their feet created, hoping I'd be able to copy the steps. Her right hand clasped to his left, his hand wrapping her waist, hers placed on his forearm. They moved in a square pattern, side to side, then a step back, then side to side in the opposite direction, and then forward again.

Through the crowd, Cade appeared, grinning at me as he always did—showing the dimples around his mouth. I smiled back, but the fluttering butterflies were absent, a stark contrast to being with Morven.

"Hello, Miss Sabine." He bowed slightly, blending in with the other men in the room, dark suit, and a white shirt underneath with a raised, stiff collar.

"Hello, Cade," I answered with a smile. "I suppose you've come for your dance?"

"I have." He held out his hand. I hesitated, then I placed my hand in his, and we walked onto the floor.

No problem. I could do this.

Cade kept my hand in his, and he placed his other hand on my waist. I tensed, shocked by his closeness. With a forced smile, I placed my hand on his forearm. I was supposed to rest it on his forearm, right? Why had my mind blanked?

He gently guided my hand to his arm. "You look nervous."

"I'm... just not used to dancing in a place this big. It's overwhelming."

"I see." He nodded. "What are the dances like in Fablemarch?"

I shrugged, not wanting to say much. "Smaller."

"I would imagine they're a bit livelier than this."

"Sometimes." I smiled, trying to come up with something to change the subject. "I see the flowers were arranged in time."

"Yes." He sighed. "I don't want to look at another tulip for the rest of my life. Sometimes I wish I could have a simpler life. I wouldn't mind living in a place like Fablemarch, to be honest. Do you think anyone in your village needs a gardener?"

I cleared my throat. "Maybe." We were on the subject of my pretend village again. How'd that happen?

"I've been at the palace too long." His eyes roved the

room. "Sometimes it seems impossible to leave. Don't get me wrong, I like it well enough, but I think I need a change of scenery from time to time."

"Yeah, I guess so."

He went on about his duties as gardener—specific details of watering schedules and shipment arrivals. I only half-listened, preferring instead to gawk at the couples surrounding us. I spotted Morven sitting smugly next to his aunt, arms crossed in his usual defensive position, his eyes boring into mine. Did he have to look so completely hateful? He'd known I was going to dance with Cade. Maybe he didn't like it, but he didn't have to stare daggers at me. What did he expect me to do anyway? Cade was getting his aunt's key for us. He'd asked for a dance, and I'd agreed.

"What do you think?" Cade asked, breaking my attention away from the prince.

"Sorry." I blinked. "About what?"

He only shook his head. "Nothing. It wasn't important. It seems your attention is somewhere else." He glanced at the prince.

"Oh, well, maybe a little."

He raised an eyebrow.

I sighed. "It's just that I'm his caretaker, you know. I worry about him, even though he doesn't deserve it. You know how rude he is."

Cade shrugged. "But he seems to have taken up with you. If I didn't know any better, I'd say he's attracted to you."

Heat rushed to my cheeks. "That can't possibly be true. He treats me just as rudely as he does everyone else."

"No. He doesn't. For one thing, he acknowledges you exist. For another thing, he can't take his eyes off you. I can't blame him really. You're different from most young ladies in the city —or anywhere, to be honest."

Panic made my throat tighten. "I'm not all that different."

"Aren't you? You speak differently, dress differently." He

reached out and ran his fingers through my hair, his hands trailing down my cheek, brushing my skin and the top of my exposed collar bone. Such an intimate expression unnerved me, and I had the urge to push him away, as if he were doing something I hadn't given him permission to do. Maybe I should have been flattered. Truthfully, the opposite sex had avoided me for most of my life. Cade was attractive and sweet, but his touch didn't make butterflies dance through my stomach. Not the way Morven did with only a look.

The song ended. I breathed a sigh of relief as he walked me off the dance floor.

"I'll be asking the queen regent for a dance now," he said, leaning so he had to whisper in my ear. "When the next song ends, I'll hand the key off to you. But you'll have to hurry and unlock the door, then return it to me. When I give it back to her, I'll say I found it on the dance floor, and she must've dropped it. Hopefully, it won't make her too suspicious."

"I understand," I whispered back.

His body heat warmed me. With the close contact and whispering, it was a wonder people didn't get the wrong impression about us.

He brushed a kiss across my cheek, then turned and strode straight for the queen regent who sat at her post beside Morven. I rubbed my cheek where he'd kissed me, my fingertips cold on the warm, tingling spot.

When he reached the queen regent, Cade dipped into a deep bow. Although I couldn't hear his words over the music, she replied with a strained smile, gave Morven a dark look, then accepted Cade's hand and stood.

At least he'd gotten her to dance. With any luck, taking the key would go just as smoothly.

Morven sat alone. He kept his gaze pinned straight ahead and locked his jaw. I decided now was a good time to humor His Majesty and let him know my true feelings for Cade. He was getting worked up for nothing.

"Hello, Morven," I said as I wandered near him.

"Hmm," he grunted, hands clasped in front of him, tendons straining beneath his skin.

I stood by him. "You could at least say hello."

He didn't reply.

"Why are you frowning?" I asked. "It doesn't suit you."

"You sound like my aunt."

"I'm trying to cheer you up."

"Good luck with that," he muttered, then clenched his jaw once again, the way he did when he was annoyed with something. Why did I find it attractive? The strong line of his jaw and the firm resolve. The righteous anger. Obviously, something was wrong with me.

I knelt to be eye-level, resting my hand on his. "Are you jealous?" I asked quietly.

"I'm not jealous," he answered too quickly.

"Then what's the matter?" I spoke with a soft voice, hoping he heard my sincerity.

"I hate dances, that's all."

"Really?"

"Yes. I would much rather be up in the tower with my charts."

I'd much rather be in the tower with the charts too, but for different reasons. "Is that the only reason? I think you're upset because Cade danced with me."

He narrowed his eyes.

"Don't let it get to you. It was a dance. It didn't mean anything."

He glanced at me.

"I'd rather spend time with you."

His brow scrunched in confusion. "Are you toying with me?"

"I'm being honest. I like being with you more than him."

"Why?" he asked, as if I'd just admitted something untrue —like I enjoyed getting sunburns.

"Because you're more intelligent than most people," I said honestly. "I think education is important."

"But I insult you every chance I get."

I stood, sighing. "Then it's a good thing I'm skilled at ignoring you."

He gave me an odd expression, as if he couldn't decide if I told the truth. He turned away from me to focus on his aunt dancing with Cade. The key reflected the chandelier's light, still hanging around her neck. Cade spoke animatedly, and she smiled, a half-quirking of her lips, so odd-looking on her usually stoic face.

Beside me, Morven's chair scooted. He grabbed the armrests and pushed up to stand.

"What are you doing?" I asked, surprised.

"I have to do this," he answered with purpose.

My eyes widened. "Do what?"

"You're going to dance with me."

"What?" I gasped. "Morven, you can't."

"Actually, I can."

He grabbed my arm to steady himself. I looked up into his eyes, realizing how much taller he was than me, wondering why I'd just now noticed it. Was he really so jealous of Cade that he felt he needed to prove himself?

"Will you dance with me, Sabine?" His deep voice resonated from his broad chest, and I reminded myself to breathe.

"I—yes, but will you be okay?"

He shrugged. "Doesn't matter. Plus, this way, my aunt will be distracted, won't she?"

Ah, this made sense now. He didn't actually *want* to dance with me. This was a ruse to distract his aunt, and by the way she looked at him, her smile gone, fire in her eyes, I'd say it was working.

He led me to the dance floor. Everyone stopped dancing to watch us walk to the center. Embarrassment rushed through me. I glanced at the hallway, to the shadows where I could hide. But Morven held my hand, and if I let go, he might fall. When we walked past his aunt, her seething, hate-filled expression focused on us.

The bagpipes and violins combined to create a stirring, haunting symphony. Morven held my waist in a firm grip as we began dancing. Surprisingly, I didn't stumble as he led the dance, and neither did he. With his hand gripping mine, and my stomach fluttering, I reminded myself to keep breathing. Worries nagged at me. What if he fell? What if his aunt fired me over this?

But those worries melted away as the music played and we swayed to its beat, our feet working in square patterns across the floor.

Morven moved fluidly, as if he'd never been paralyzed. He grasped my hand with firmness, his skin warm, the pads of his fingers callused from gripping the wheels of his chair.

I became aware of every place he touched my body—the heat of his flesh on my hand, warmth spreading through the layer of silk to the place where he touched my waist. Butterflies fluttered uncontrollably through my stomach.

His presence barraged my senses, overwhelming me. Instinctively, I reacted by picturing the pages of a book to calm my hypersensitivity, to dull the sensations that struck me like bolts of lightning.

But what would happen if I didn't? What if I allowed myself to experience everything about him?

Letting go of my defenses, I allowed myself to exhale, releasing my inhibitions. Instead, the scent of his cologne— seductive, wild, and mysterious—enveloped me. His eyes— dark, intelligent depths that held me motionless in the web of his spell. The firm strength of his hand placed on my waist, making my skin tingle at his closeness through the thin layer of silk.

A twinkle lit his eyes as he focused on me. "You're a good dancer."

"Thank you," I answered, lightheaded.

His thumb slowly moved over the back of my hand, caressing my skin. My stomach twisted into impossible knots. The sensations overwhelmed me until I couldn't hear the music, couldn't see anything but the darkness of his pupils drinking me in, couldn't feel anything except his skin.

"Are you all right?" he asked.

"Fine." It was the only reply I could make.

I stayed focused on him. Everything about him enchanted me. How would it feel to kiss him?

As we danced past the other couples, their eyes locked on us. Shocked expressions filled their faces.

"They all think I don't dance," he explained, as if reading my thoughts. "Not because I couldn't, but because I chose not to. Because I was too proud to dance with anyone."

"Because they didn't know you were in the chair?"

He nodded. "We've had these balls for as long as I can remember."

"And you've never danced?" I questioned.

He shook his head. "Not after my parents died."

Some of the guests whispered to one another as they watched us, no doubt wondering who I was—this girl who dressed in the outdated gown, with the loose hair, the only person the prince deemed worthy to dance with.

But the glances in our direction didn't bother me. Morven's strength held me, helping me dismiss their glares. I'd thought I kept him from falling, but I was wrong. It was the other way around.

There was so much more to him than I knew. He used his pride as a mask, but I'd seen through it.

The song ended. He slowly led me off the floor, keeping my hand clasped in a possessive grip. I shuddered to think what would happen when he let go. He walked with a straight back, not stumbling once, until we arrived back at his chair. I expected him to sit as soon as we arrived, but he remained standing.

His aunt and Cade approached us, her cheeks red. She huffed as she faced her nephew, though he stood a head taller than her. She pointed her finger in his face.

"What is the meaning of this?" she seethed.

"It's a dance, isn't it?" Morven answered, his voice conversational. "Shouldn't I dance?"

"You were under strict orders to remain seated in that chair."

"Because you didn't want me to fall," he answered. "And I didn't. I don't see why you're upset. Besides, that's the most fun I've had in… well, my entire life." He glanced at me, our hands still clasped.

Don't let go. I wanted to say.

"You've made a spectacle of yourself. Go." She pointed at the hallway under the alcove where we'd entered. "Go now."

He arched a dark eyebrow. "You want me to leave?"

"I want you both to leave. Miss Harper, you've failed me miserably." Her chin jutted. "You're both to leave the dance this instant. Do *not* return."

He eyed her shrewdly. "Yes, Aunt Tremayne. But know that in three days, you'll no longer have the power to control me."

She crossed her arms, returning an equally spiteful glance. "We'll see about that, won't we?"

I couldn't take it any longer. She'd gone too far, and I could no longer stand aside and watch her belittle her nephew. "Are you threatening him?"

She turned her hate-filled look on me. "This is none of your concern. You are no longer welcomed in this ballroom. If you push me, you'll no longer be welcomed in this castle. Have I made myself clear?"

I fisted my free hand, ready to tell her how I really felt. But getting thrown out of the castle now would mean I never found the rest of the objects. It meant I failed my mission, let down myself and my dad, and it meant I doomed the world to suffer through a second flare.

Biting my tongue, I pushed down my urge to argue with her.

"I understand," I conceded.

Morven and I turned away. He walked with a straight back, focused ahead as we made it across the floor. Every pair of eyes in the room fixated on us. If Queen Regent Tremayne was worried about making a spectacle, she'd done it now.

We stepped under the shadow of the alcove with Cade following us. When we stopped at the end of the hallway, we faced him. Cade smiled, glancing briefly at mine and Morven's entwined hands before he cleared his throat. He clutched a chain that glinted silver in the dim light.

"Is that the key?" I whispered.

He nodded, opening his fist to reveal a small silver key sitting atop his palm, then handed it to me. "It wasn't too hard. As soon as she saw you two dancing, she didn't pay me any attention. Thanks for the distraction, by the way."

"It wasn't a distraction," Morven said coolly, then turned to me. "Let's go. We've got to unlock the observatory's door then return the key before she finds out. Meet us here," he said to Cade.

We brushed past the gardener. I turned and gave him a brief "thank-you," which didn't seem like nearly enough gratitude as we made our way out of the hallway and back into the foyer. We walked past Morven's chair, but he ignored it.

"You're not going to use your chair?"

He shook his head. "It would take too much time."

I gripped his hand tighter. "But what if you fall?"

"I won't."

I rushed to keep up with him. "You're awfully confident."

He turned, smiling as his gaze lingered on me. "Is there anything wrong with that?"

My mouth grew dry at the look he gave me, dark and intimate, laced with excitement. I cleared my throat to break up the tension. "We should hurry."

"Fine. Try to keep up with me." Grinning, he led me down the back hallways where we only passed a few people, wobbling only a little. When we reached a staircase, he stopped, holding to the banister as he exhaled.

I glanced back the way we'd come. "Should I get the chair?"

"No." He waved his hand. "I'm just not used to walking this much. I'll make it." His chest rose and fell with a deep inhale. He held to the banister but managed to make every step.

When we finally walked down the hallway leading to the observatory, I eyed him.

"What's your trick?" I asked.

He cocked his head. "Trick?"

"How can you suddenly walk so well?"

He shrugged, then removed a flask from his coat pocket where green liquid swirled inside. "This helps."

I eyed the metal container. "You've been drinking green cerecite?"

He nodded. "Since I stopped eating the porridge, my strength came back, so I decided to speed up the process. Seems like it's working, too."

He didn't offer any further explanation as he tucked the container in his pocket. At least the mystery of his miraculous recovery was solved, but we had other problems. What if Morven's aunt discovered the key was gone? She was already mad that we'd danced. Discovering what we were doing now would send her over the edge.

But I had a mission to accomplish. I'd searched for two

weeks now. If the cerecite wasn't in the observatory, then I was out of options.

We stood in front of the door. I handed the key to Morven, and he stuck it in the lock. The mechanism clicked, and the door opened.

I followed Morven inside the observatory. Moonlight shone through the windows in the dome roof, casting everything in a silvery glow, illuminating the rolled star charts covering the table.

Excitement raced through me. *Finally.*

We stopped at the table. He shuffled through the scrolls until he found his telescope, then he picked up a bag and started stuffing maps inside.

"What are you doing?"

"Getting ready to make a huge discovery." He motioned to me with a scroll. "You're going to help me."

"*Me?* What are you talking about?"

"This." He held the slender metal tube. "Tonight's the perfect opportunity to escape. The queen regent banned us from the ball. She won't even be looking for us."

"Where are we going?"

"Outside the palace walls." He motioned to the door. "There's a mountaintop just north of here that will give us the perfect view. The shield will be easier to see through up there."

I glanced at the dark window. "We're escaping the palace?"

"Yes."

"But I can't leave."

"We'll only be gone a few hours." He hefted the bag. "We'll be back before anyone knows we left."

I eyed the bag of star charts as he slung a strap over his shoulder. "You're taking them all with you?"

"Yes. I have to. Is something wrong with that?"

"Nothing." I sighed, following him through the dark room

until we made it back to the hallway. "How do you expect to travel up to the mountains? You can't very well hike. And I'm *not* pushing you in your chair."

"We won't have to. We'll take the velocipedes. They're parked in the palace stalls. No one uses them at this time of night, so we'll be fine."

I had to stop myself before asking him to explain what a velocipede was, so I asked a different question instead. "What if the guards catch us?"

"They won't. They're all too preoccupied keeping watch at the ball." He stopped walking to face me. "Have you asked enough questions now?"

Butterflies fluttered wildly at his nearness. As I stood looking up at him, he dipped his head down slightly, drawing his lips near. The sudden urge to kiss him made my heart beat faster, if that were possible. What would it feel like? Would it be a guarded kiss? Or something more passionate.

I shook my head. What was I thinking? I couldn't kiss him. I had a mission. Plus, Fifteen would kill me.

"One more question," I asked softly as I held up the key. "What about this? Also, I refuse to go anywhere in this gown."

He slipped his hand around my back, drawing me closer, and my stomach did a complete one-hundred-and-eighty-degree somersault. "We'll pass the key back to Cade and then you can change." His voice was entirely too deep and seductive. Did he realize the effect he had on me? "Sound good?"

"I… umm…" How was a person supposed to have a single coherent thought at a moment like this? He kept his hand pressed to my back, and every thought in my head disappeared—every thought except one.

I had to physically force myself to grab his hand and push away from him. Nothing about getting close to him was a good idea. It wasn't even a semi-okay one.

"I think we should return the key," I said with forced calm.

"Then we'll leave." I took a step backward. "Also, we should probably keep our distance. I am your caretaker, after all."

Hurt shone in his eyes for half-a-second, then the look disappeared, and I realized I'd hurt him. I must've been the only person in his entire life he'd gotten close to since the death of his parents, and I just rejected him.

"I agree," he answered with equal dispassion, and he turned away. I followed behind him as he walked ahead, the light casting an eerie glow over his dark-clad frame. For the hundredth time since I'd arrived on this island, I wondered what I'd gotten myself into.

17

Humid nighttime air washed over me as I stood with Morven inside the palace stalls. We'd returned the key to Cade and hadn't heard anything since. I hoped he'd slipped it back to the queen regent without incident. We hadn't been caught. Yet.

Morven pulled two vehicles from their spots by the wall and stood them beside us. The aluminum frames held a single seat. Twenty wheels made of yellow cerecite lined in a row beneath the body. The machines reminded me of giant rollerblades—or perhaps caterpillars. Blue lanterns glowed from headlight-shaped lamps at the front of the engines. I tried not to gawk, reminding myself that I was supposed to be familiar with machines—*velocipedes*—like these.

Morven sat on the seat and buckled his legs to the sides. Interesting. He must've had this one custom made. How often had he gone out on it?

He pressed a button and a quiet engine purred to life. I sat on the vehicle next to his, scanning the rows of buttons. How many were there? I settled on a red one in the center and pressed it, but nothing happened.

"The blue one," Morven said, frowning. "Haven't you ridden a velocipede?"

"Of course, I have." I cleared my throat. "Just not one like this." I pushed the blue button and the engine rumbled to life, making my seat vibrate. I adjusted my bag's straps on my shoulders.

Morven wore the sack of maps on his back. The tops of the scrolls peeked at me, tempting me to check each one. But I couldn't do that yet. Not without causing suspicion.

"How far are the mountains?" I asked over the noise.

"Not far," he shouted back. "We'll make it there in less than an hour if all goes smoothly. Follow close behind me. Once we get out of the city, the roads get rougher."

He pushed the handlebars forward, revving the engine, then kicked the stand up and rode out of the stall. I did the same, though the velocipede lurched as I shoved the handles forward with too much force. Luckily, Morven didn't look back, and I followed closely behind him as we rode out of the palace, through the back courtyard, and toward the wall surrounding the castle.

Behind the palace, a delicate stillness draped the night, with a little light from streetlamps to illuminate our way. As we passed through the gate, Morven waved to the guards, who only nodded.

He must've done this before, which solved the mystery of where he went at night.

We rode into the city, and I stayed close behind Morven. We followed the curving road. Estate homes made of white limestones overshadowed us. Trailing vines cascaded from windows lit with soft blue light, and water trickled from fountains shaped as lotus flowers—such a contrast to my bunker in the frozen wastes of Champ Island.

We crested a bridge spanning over a churning river. A view of the mountains appeared—a dark block of jagged peaks against a star-filled sky. As we rode away from the city, the wind picked up. I'd changed into my standard shirt and pants, but the chilly wind cut through me.

Round, turquoise stones stood out against the black velvet night, highlighting the flat plains that stretched to the horizon. What *were* the boulders? Who created them? And not just those here, but the ones in my reality, as well.

Better yet, who created this island? Where did cerecite come from? I hadn't been given a good answer. Except aliens. At this point, I wouldn't exclude anything.

Maybe Morven's astronomy experiments would help solve the mystery. He'd been vague about what he'd been doing, but since I'd agreed to follow him all the way out here, maybe he'd be more forthcoming. Plus, I couldn't deny that being in his good graces was necessary to keeping the palace accessible. I also could no longer deny the powerful attraction between us. I'd never felt so strongly toward anyone before. The thought frightened and excited me at the same time.

The landscape turned to rolling hills. More boulders appeared, some taller than Morven. Their strange blue-green glows seemed to burn like fire, their light flickering over the too-even grass. We approached the mountains. A steep path wound up through the rocky cliffs. Our velocipedes' wheels crunched over the gravel road, engines growing louder as they strained to make it to the top.

When we crested the hill, we rode onto a flat plateau. The moonlight, coupled with the many boulders speckling the mountaintop, gave us enough light to see.

We stopped our velocipedes and turned off the engines. My ears buzzed at the sudden quietness, with only the swaying of the grass in the wind to break up the silence, strange without the chirping of insects. The air tasted crisp, though the metallic taste lingered.

Above us, stars crowded the sky, leaving hardly any black space between them. Some glittered in distinct shades of pink, green, and periwinkle blue—more contrast than I'd ever seen before, even on the farm without the glare of city lights.

"This is amazing," I said with awe.

"Yes," Morven answered. "That's why we came up here. This is the best view on the island." Kneeling, he took off his bag, then dumped out the scrolls and removed his telescope.

I knelt beside him and helped unroll the parchments. Words, bright lines, and dots lit up on the paper. I trained my eye for any inconsistencies.

"We need to arrange the charts in order," Morven said. "See the dates on the top? Start from those that begin three years ago, then arrange them up to the current date."

I gave him a sidelong glance. "What for?"

"Because that's how to see the stars moving. More importantly, how we're moving."

I stopped shuffling through the charts. "What do you mean by that?"

He gave me a pointed stare. "That's why we've come out here. That's why I've been doing this research." He shook his head. "I can't be sure of anything yet."

He shuffled through the scrolls until he pulled one out. "This is my most recent. As soon as I get it filled in, I'll know for sure."

"Know what for sure?"

Starlight twinkled in his dark eyes. "You'll see."

After picking up his telescope, he stood, doing it without any hesitation. He aimed the lens at a star cluster just above the horizon. I continued arranging the scrolls, from least to greatest, as if I were counting down the days to some unforeseen time—from three years past to the present.

I memorized the dates as I went…

The day of our Lourde, Seventeenth of May
Eighteenth of June
Eleventh of August…

Morven's words bugged me. *That's how to tell how we're moving.*

Shaking my head, I turned back to the charts, sorting them by date while looking for inconsistencies. Dots and lines connected. Labels on the more prominent stars were easy to memorize.

Big Dipper. Cassiopeia. The North Star. Betelgeuse. Planets were also labeled. *Mars. Jupiter. Mercury. Venus.*

I arranged one after another. A pattern emerged in the movement of the stars as they tracked across the night sky.

Morven walked past me, shifting his telescope, jotting things on his scroll. A breeze carried across the mountaintop, fluttering the glowing scrolls. I arranged the rest until they sat in a neat row atop the grass.

Thirty-seven scrolls in total. Two-hundred and seventy labeled stars. Seventeen labeled planets, including those in the Kuiper Belt. Each written in Morven's neat, precise script. The pattern of the stars' movements captured like a snapshot.

Morven clicked his telescope shut, then crossed back to me and placed the last star chart at the end of the row. The last piece of the puzzle.

"What are we looking at?" I asked.

He gave me a guarded, knowing smile. "I've found something no one else knows."

I couldn't hold back a grin. "Aliens exist?"

"Ha, funny Sabine." He scratched his chin. "The problem is, I'm not sure I should tell you."

"Why not?"

"I don't know if you'll believe me."

I frowned, then I sat back, the ground damp and slightly spongy, and patted the grass. "Tell me."

With a sigh, he sat beside me and looked up at the sky. "You really want to know?"

"Morven," I said sternly. "I didn't come all the way out here for nothing."

Eyes guarded, he looked at me as if trying to decide to trust me. "Fine." He pointed at the sky. "You see the stars there, just above the horizon?"

"Yes."

"That constellation is called Cassiopeia. I noticed it first. If you study the star charts from before our people ship-wrecked on the island, they look different. The shield is designed to be in harmony with our world. It's built to resemble our home in Scotland. Even the night sky was designed to look that way. That's why Cassiopeia looks like it has an extra star. The shield is filling in the blanks."

"So…" I studied the sky. "Are we even seeing the actual nighttime sky?"

He shook his head. "Not quite. Some parts of the shield are easier to see through, but you can only do that at night. That's why it seems like there are so many stars here. Some of them are the actual stars we see through the shield, and others aren't real—they're constructs—light glowing on the shield and nothing more. Even the moon is a construct."

"That's interesting." And confusing. It wasn't likely a group of 19th century shipwreck survivors could've created it. Not without help, at least. Aliens again. Why was that my only explanation?

He smiled. "It gets better. Three years ago, I started charting only the stars we can see through the shield. It was tedious to do. The stars were impossible to see most of the time. That's why I made this." He tapped his telescope sitting on his lap. "It lets me see only the actual nighttime sky. That's when I first discovered it."

I tilted my head. "Discovered what?"

He pulled a chart off the ground and showed it to me. "This planet." He pointed to a dot without a label. I looked from his chart to each map on the ground. The same unla-beled dot stood out on each one. I'd noticed it before, but since it had been unlabeled, I figured it hadn't been important.

I pointed to it. "What is it?"

"Good question," he answered. "That's what I've been trying to understand. I tracked the other stars and planets to see if I could get a better grasp. The weird thing is, some of this didn't add up. Jupiter, for example." He pointed up at the sky. "That bright star there. It's in the wrong spot."

"What do you mean?"

He handed his telescope to me. "Hold this to your eye. Look at Jupiter, then turn west by twenty degrees."

I did as he said, first focusing on the planet, then moving to the left. A bright glowing orb appeared through the lens. "I see something. Is that Jupiter? The actual Jupiter?"

"Yes."

I placed the telescope in my lap. "Why is it in a different position?"

He rested his hands on his knees. "I thought it was because the first settlers were constructing the sky to appear the way they would've seen it in Scotland. But now, I'm not so sure. It's not just Jupiter in the wrong place, but all the planets. Mars, that one there." He pointed south. "See how it appears red?"

The reddish orb glowed in the sky against the blackness. "Is that the real planet?"

"No, the actual Mars is somewhere on the eastern horizon, and it's significantly brighter."

"What causes it to look brighter?" I asked.

Wind gusted, tugging dark hair across his forehead. "I thought maybe it was because we're so far north, the stars appear brighter here," he said. "But now I realize that's not the case."

"Then what is the case?" I asked, confusion and curiosity making my heartrate quicken.

"You're not going to believe it." He shook his head, his eyes pensive. "No one is."

"Why?" I demanded.

"Because…" He pointed to the nameless dot on the chart. "I know which planet this is. It's Earth."

I blinked. Had I heard him correctly? "What?"

"It's Earth," he repeated.

"But… *what?*"

"See, I said you wouldn't believe me."

"I…" How was this possible? *Earth?* "Assuming for a moment that I did believe you, if that's Earth, then where are we?"

He shook his head. "I don't know."

"Another planet?"

"No. I've accounted for all the planets."

I almost suggested we could be on a spaceship but held my tongue. Girls from fishing villages couldn't possibly have known about those things. "Are you sure that planet you saw through your telescope is Earth?"

"Positive. I've been mapping it for three years. I also mapped Venus and Mars, and this planet—" he pointed to the dot— "is orbiting between them. I only know of one planet that does that. I don't know where we are, but we're not on Earth."

"Wow." Dizziness made my head swim. Did Vortech know what Morven had discovered? We weren't on Earth. But how could that possibly be true? I'd never boarded a spaceship. Not to my knowledge, anyway. However, this did explain a few things. The uniformity of the grass and plants, this place being so much larger than the actual Champ Island, and the mechanical smell in the air. We were under a dome, but it wasn't on Earth.

I had to contact Vortech. I had to know if they knew. And if they did—if they'd been lying to me all along, then what?

I didn't want to go there, but I couldn't ignore the

evidence. Vortech had most likely lied to me, or at the least, withheld the truth, which brought up another question. Did they know what had happened to Rosa?

Honesty shone in Morven's eyes, hitting me with the impression that no matter how callous and rude, he would never lie to me. At least there was one person I could trust—with some things.

"What are you thinking about?" Morven asked, his voice deep, yet soft, a sound that calmed me.

"I don't know. I suspected for some time that our world was different. Certain things existed that shouldn't have. I never realized we weren't on Earth. But now that I know, it makes sense."

"So, you believe me?"

"Yes."

He nodded, looking intently into my eyes, as if he'd half expected me to call him a liar—what his aunt would've most likely told him.

"Is this where you've been sneaking off to at night?" I asked.

He swallowed, looking away from me, clasping his hands in a nervous gesture. "Partially, yes."

"What do you mean partially?"

"There are things…" he started, then stopped.

"Go on," I said. "You can tell me."

"I don't know." He picked at the grass, not meeting my eyes.

"I believed you about Earth, didn't I?"

"Yes, I suppose so. But please don't repeat this to anyone. I could be imprisoned. Disowned, possibly."

"Disowned? For sneaking off? I know your aunt's harsh, but that's a bit much."

"No. Not for sneaking off." He looked at the stars. "For being who I am."

"What do you mean by that?"

"I... I've been coming out here at night, that's true. But then, sometimes, around midnight, I black out. I wake up in my room. It doesn't happen all the time, but frequently enough."

"That's it?" I asked.

"What do you mean *that's it?* Don't you see how bad this is?"

I shrugged. "Not really. I definitely don't see how it would get you disowned."

His eyes widened. "You seriously don't see why? Sabine, where have you been your entire life?"

Ha. Good question.

"Haven't you heard the legends?" he asked.

I shook my head. "I guess not."

"Sabine," he whispered my name. "There's a possibility that I'm a Cu Sith."

"A what?"

"Cu Sith. Don't you see how bad this is? It's possible that when I was born, a spirit creature inhabited my body. If so, it can control me. It can make me transform back into the animal it once was, making me a shape changer."

The wind picked up, an eerie wail that sent a shiver down my spine. "Shape changer?"

"Yes." His gaze didn't meet mine. "A wolf, actually."

My mouth gaped. "You can transform into a wolf?"

"I don't know for sure. But I think that's what happens when I black out. I turn into a Mystik wolf. As I get older, it gets stronger. Whenever I become king, it may learn to control me completely."

I pondered his words, not sure how to react. One thing I knew—none of this was normal. "That's not good."

"Yeah, that's an understatement."

"But I don't understand. I thought you didn't believe in legends."

"I don't, but I do believe in science. The Cu Sith came

from old Scottish folktales, that's true. Our ancestors thought they were hellhound harbingers of death. But when we came here, some of our people started to become possessed by the spirit animals. They called them the same name. They aren't mythological creatures. They're real."

I stared out over the mountaintop. What would it be like to encounter a spirit wolf—glowing turquoise fur and eyes burning in the darkness. "But you don't know that for sure. You've been blacking out, but you don't actually know what's happening."

"That's true, but…"

"But what?" I asked.

"Nothing." A haunted expression crossed his face.

I sat up straight. "What do you mean *nothing*? Do you know something else?"

"I don't want to discuss this, Sabine." The determination in his voice kept me from pressing the issue. He looked away from me to gaze at the stars. Away from the confines of the palace, I was finally seeing the real Prince Morven. I had to admit he wouldn't be a bad king. If he could learn to be tactful, he might even be a great one.

But that was assuming he became king.

"Morven, I know you don't like it when I talk about this, but I have to be completely honest. I still believe someone was poisoning your porridge. Since you've been growing stronger, and you stopped eating it, you have to admit I may be right."

He nodded. "I know."

"You do?" I asked, surprised.

"Yes. Whoever's doing it, they've been at it for a long time. Ever since my parents died. It's possible they also poisoned them, but I can't be sure."

"Was it your aunt?"

"Not necessarily. It could be the miners. They've wanted the royalty dead for a long time. Or…" Hurt shone in his eyes. "I won't exclude the possibility that it may be her."

"But why wouldn't she just kill you the way she did your parents?"

"I don't know. But I need to find out."

"What made you change your mind? The last time I talked to you, you didn't believe your aunt could have done it."

"Well, I suppose I thought about what you said. This may be hard to believe, but Aunt Tremayne wasn't always awful. Before my parents died, she was kind to me. We had fun together. She took me out to the city once, just me and her. She bought me a bag of candied nuts, even though my parents didn't allow me to eat sweets before dinner. She laughed back then. I don't know." His voice became wistful. "She was a different person. I suppose I still think of her that way sometimes, as fun-loving and happy. But after my parents died, she changed. I think the responsibility of taking care of me scared her. She'd never been a parent, and I think she was terrified of messing me up, especially as I was to become the king."

This came from nowhere. Imagining the queen regent as someone other than a bitter shrew was a difficult thing to do.

"I guess I still think of her that way sometimes," Morven continued. "As carefree and happy, as someone who looked out for me. Someone who loved me. But I know she's not that person anymore. Just because she loved me once doesn't make her innocent. Plus, she's the only person in the castle who would benefit from my death—or from my disability. She's been controlling me since I've been in the chair. I realized you may have been right."

I held back a laugh. "That would be a first."

He glanced at me. "No, it wouldn't. I always listen to you, Sabine."

Blood pulsed hot through my body as I sat transfixed by his gaze.

"So," he said, "now I believe you, and you believe me." A

mischievous grin lit his face, and he took my hand. The touch of his skin sent a jolt of warmth through me. "Does this mean we're getting along?"

I gave him a sidelong glance and returned his grin. "I wouldn't go that far."

He gently squeezed my fingers. "Then would you consider us friends, at least?"

"Friends?" My smile faltered. "I'm your caretaker, remember? I'm not sure we're supposed to be friends. Acquaintances, maybe."

"Acquaintances." He shook his head, dark hair blowing across his forehead, and I wanted nothing more than to reach out and smooth it back. "That's a stuffy word." He spoke with a deep bass, his words soft. He kissed the back of my hand, his lips pressing lightly. Warmth seeped through my entire body, making it impossible for me to concentrate on anything but him.

Morven wrapped his arm around me, and we gazed up at the sky.

With everything Morven had told me, my head spun. What was going on in this place? We weren't on Earth and people were being possessed by spirits? Now I was really believing in aliens.

I would have to ask Vortech, assuming they'd give me a straight answer. If they'd been lying to me all along, I doubted I'd get the truth.

18

Morven and I paced through the palace's dark, empty hallways, our footsteps reverberating like an alarm bell I feared would wake Morven's aunt. We made our way up the stairs and she didn't appear. Morven kept his bag of star charts strapped to his back.

My fingers itched to look at them again. I only needed one more chance and I was sure I would find cerecite.

Morven ambled slowly down the hallway leading to his rooms, then he stopped, propping his elbow against the wall. His face grew ashen, and he gasped for air.

"Can you make it?" I asked.

"Yes." His chest heaved. "Give me a minute. I haven't walked this much since... since I was a kid."

I rested my hand on his arm. "Do you need me to help you?"

"No. I can make it." He attempted a step forward when his knees buckled. I caught him, then slung his arm over my shoulders.

"You don't... have to help me," he wheezed.

"I'm doing it anyway." I tightened my arm around his chest, his muscles taut, his body heat surrounding me.

He didn't argue as we shuffled to his door, then opened it and entered his room. I helped him to his bed and, after removing his shoes, he collapsed. Breathing heavily, he stared at the canopy overhead.

"I hate being so weak," he said through clenched teeth.

"Weak?" I whispered so only he could hear, smoothing a hand over his forehead. "You walked more than you have in years. You're one of the strongest people I know."

His eyes met mine, dark, intelligent eyes that set my insides on fire. "You really think so?"

"Yes." I knelt beside him. "But tonight, you need to rest." I reached for his bag. "Let me take that."

He pulled it off his shoulders, then handed it to me. Guilt tugged at me as I took it from him.

"Get some rest, all right?" I said softly. "I'll take care of these."

He nodded, then pressed his eyes closed. The creased lines on his forehead and around his eyes revealed his exhaustion. "Thank you, Sabine."

"Of course." I carefully leaned forward, gently pressed a kiss to his forehead, and stepped away with the bag of scrolls. On the opposite side of the room, I spotted a writing desk.

I glanced at Morven, but he turned away from me, his form ghostly in the moonlight.

With the moonbeams drifting through the window, I crossed to his desk and slid a scroll from the bag. Guilt weighed heavier in my chest as I went through the scrolls. Morven had opened up to me, but I hadn't told him my secret. What would happen when he found out I was an imposter and a thief?

Shaking my head, I focused on the scrolls. I couldn't worry about this now.

Words and lines lit up as I unrolled it. Scanning it took seconds. No changes. Nothing out of the ordinary. After placing it aside, I pulled out the next, then the next. I got through more than a dozen scrolls with nothing to show for it.

I peeked back at Morven, his dark form hidden beneath the bed covers. Was he asleep? I couldn't be sure. But if I stood here any longer, he'd get suspicious.

I pulled out another scroll and unrolled it. The words on the top left corner caught my eye.

The day of our Lourde, Eighteenth of May.

That couldn't be right. None of the scrolls had been dated the eighteenth of May. I'd gone through each one of them while we'd been up on the mountain. No. I was positive. Not even one had had that date.

This had to be it. The third object. I hastily placed the scroll in my own bag, then left Morven's on the table. Pacing to the door, my feet quiet on the carpet, I kept my pack on my shoulder, intent on scanning the scroll as soon as I got to my room.

I glanced at Morven. He lay beneath the covers, his eyes closed. Even as he drifted off, it seemed as if he held some dark secret, the way his mouth parted slightly, and the hard set to his jaw. He'd said he was some sort of wolf shapeshifter possessed by a spirit, but I wasn't sure I agreed with him. Having a bad case of amnesia every now and then didn't make a person a shapeshifter.

Still, it was a curious story. I wished I could've gotten to the bottom of it. He hadn't told me everything. Part of me wanted to stay behind and see if I could get the truth from him. But I had work to do, so I stepped to the door and gripped the knob.

"Sabine." His whispered voice came from the bed. I turned around. He was looking at me with a penetrating gaze that set my insides on fire.

"What is it?" I whispered back.

"Don't leave," he said.

I adjusted the bag. "What?"

"Don't go yet," he repeated.

I walked back to his bed, then placed my pack on the floor. "Why not?"

He reached for me. "Stay with me. Just for a little while. Please."

I glanced at the door. Didn't I need to go? But I found myself kneeling by the bed, and I wasn't even sure how I'd gotten there. He reached for my hand, gently grasping my fingers. "I want you to stay with me."

"Morven—I can't do that. I... I have to get back to my own room."

"Why?" He smoothed his thumb over the back of my hand.

"Because... I just do."

"What's the rush?" He spoke softly. "Why are you always evading me? Looking for random things, pretending you know things about this world when you really don't."

I didn't know how to answer.

"Just lay beside me. I promise to be a gentleman." The intensity in his voice caught me off guard. The muted moonlight drifting through the curtains captured the passion in his eyes.

My heart pounded as I glanced down at my pack, the scroll hidden inside.

"I can't stay for long." I climbed into the bed and lay down beside him. The warmth of his body molded to my back, and he carefully wrapped his arm around me. My pulse thrummed. He ran his hand up my shoulder, to my hair, where he combed his fingers through the long strands.

"Tell me who you are," he whispered, his breath warm against the back of my neck.

Uh-oh. "You know who I am."

"Everything about you is a mystery to me." The hairs on the nape of my neck prickled as he spoke. "The way you talk, the way you look at things, the attention you give to details

when you think no one notices. Your hair—the smell. Intoxi-
cating. Like nothing I'm familiar with."

Heat swirled deep in my stomach as he spoke.

"I guess we're even," I whispered.

"What do you mean?"

I rolled to face him, then ran my fingers along his jawline,
his skin smooth with only a slight prickle of facial hair. "You're
a mystery to me, too."

"Why?" he asked.

I couldn't tell him my true feelings—how close I was
becoming to him, how I desperately wanted to know what it
would be like to kiss him. How I was a thief from another
reality. How I'd leave this existence when I found the seven
lies.

No, I couldn't tell him that.

I would *never* tell him, so I went with something else, something less personal. "When you told me about the Cu Sith.
You didn't tell me everything."

He moved his hand away from my hair. Though I couldn't
see his face, I imagined his jaw had gone rigid, the way it
always did when something bothered him.

"I can't tell you," he said.

"Why not?" I asked.

"I just can't," he answered, pleading.

Silence stretched between us.

"I can handle it," I said softly. "Whatever it is, I give you
my word I won't tell anyone."

"You promise?" he asked after a pause.

I nodded. "I promise."

Sighing, he stroked my hair again, his fingers light as they
brushed against my cheek.

"I told you I felt a Cu Sith had inhabited my body, but I
wasn't being completely honest," he explained, his voice
distant, as if he were reliving the past. "When I was a child, I
knew I'd lived another life before this one. I knew specific

details no one else would know. His name was Isaac. He had the same personality as me—stubborn and too proud for his own good." He chuckled quietly. "He looked like me, too. I think he was a miner, but I don't know much about his life. It got cloudy when I focused on it. When I got sick, the memories went away. I forgot about Isaac, to be honest. Decided I must've imagined it. That or I was schizophrenic. But a few days ago, the memories came back. When they did, I saw something happen to me—to *Isaac*—that I'd never seen before."

"What did you see?" I asked, my voice guarded.

"I saw someone murder him—murder me."

My stomach lurched. "Murder you?"

He gave a single nod. "I know it's a lot to take in, especially after I told you what I discovered about our world."

"It's pretty unbelievable. You were reincarnated?"

"No. Not exactly. You see, when Isaac died, his soul became a spirit animal—a wolf, actually, it lived that way for a long time."

"How long?" I asked.

"I don't know for sure. But it felt like hundreds of years until I was born, and then, Isaac's soul merged with mine. I know that's all truly incredible. I won't blame you one bit for thinking I'm crazy."

"Morven." I squeezed his hand, his fingers cold against my warm ones. "I don't think you're crazy. Rude, maybe. Self-absorbed, absolutely. But not crazy."

A half-smile lit his face. The moonlight painted interesting shadows on the smooth plane of his forehead, the curve of his nose, the smoothness of his pale skin, and the depth of his eyes. He seemed so much wiser than his almost-twenty-three years.

He smoothed his thumb over my cheek. "I've never told anyone except my parents, and they took my secret to the grave with them. Do you believe me?"

I pressed his hand to my face, cupping it there, as if willing him to know that I understood. How could I tell him that he wasn't the only one who felt that way—who felt isolated from the rest of humanity? Losing my mom and Mima, being separated from Dad, and spending too long in the frozen tundra had taken something from me. Plus, with my ECP, I'd wondered if I would ever be able to make human connections. But saying words like that out loud didn't come easily.

"It's hard to believe," I said, "but I think we can both agree that this world isn't what it appears. There's something going on beyond our comprehension. You're a part of it."

"I agree. And I think Isaac was part of the civilization who came before ours."

"But how would we find out something like that?"

He hesitated, his lips pursed, before answering. "There may be a place we can go, but I haven't been there in years."

"Where?" I asked.

"The Spirit Caves."

I sat up. "Spirit Caves?"

"Yes. It's where Isaac—where I—was murdered. It's also where he lived and worked."

Everything led to the Spirit Caves. It's where Rosa had gone. It's where Ivan had found her things. "What do you know about the caves?"

"My da and I went exploring there when I was younger. He'd never believed it was haunted, although most people avoid the place like the plague. While we were inside, I remember feeling as if I'd been there before, like Déjà-vu but more intense. Now I know why. I lived there. I died there." He released a shuddering sigh. "There's more, too. Whoever murdered me then, I think they're still after me."

I laid down as I pondered his words. Why was everything so difficult to believe in this place, wherever we were? "But how is that possible? That would've been an awfully long time ago. Wouldn't they be dead?"

"Not necessarily." His voice held an edge of fear. "Not if they were Cu Sith, too."

"So, you think whoever was poisoning you killed you in a former life?"

"I don't know for sure. But I do know how to find out. We've got to get to that cave. I remember when my da and I were there, we found strange objects. Machines that didn't belong in this world. My da thought they were used for mining cerecite."

"Mining tools?" I questioned.

"Yes."

Something had happened in that cave. I was one step closer to learning the secrets of Ithical, but there was more I needed to know. "I don't understand. If this person wanted you dead, why waste their time slowly poisoning you?"

The bed sheets rustled as he shrugged. "Maybe they didn't want me dead. Maybe they wanted me to forget about Isaac and how he died."

Moonbeams drifted through the window as I pondered his words. "Do you remember how to get to the cave?"

"Yes. It's a day's ride out to the canyons on the velocipedes."

"When would we go?" I asked.

"We'll have to do it before the coronation." He paused. "Tomorrow."

I lifted my head to stare him in the eyes. "Won't they notice when we leave?"

"Not likely." He smoothed the back of his hand over my cheek. "Aunt Tremayne will be busy setting up for the ceremony. It may be the only time we'll get to sneak away."

A cloud moved across the moon, darkening the room. The window's glass pane shielded us from the rest of the world, from the secrets that lay buried beneath the soil.

19

I collapsed on my bed when I finally made it back to my room. Exhaustion settled in my bones as I stared blankly at the wood-paneled ceiling. My hands tingled with warmth where Morven touched me. Closing my eyes, I couldn't chase away the butterflies flitting through my stomach.

My gaze went to my leather pack sitting by the bed. I'd have to communicate with Fifteen.

Wonderful.

Should I tell him I was falling for the prince of Ithical Island?

I'm sure he'd be thrilled to hear it. Grumbling, I sat up and grabbed my bag. After pulling out the scroll and scanner, I placed them in my lap.

Nervousness twisted inside me, and I gripped the scanner's cold metal, my mind churning with questions.

Vortech owed me answers, but was I prepared for them?

With a reluctant sigh, I pulled the scanner apart, revealing the glass screen. I placed it aside to grab the scroll. The lines and dots created a tapestry, the letters swirled, and the date, and the date now read *seventeenth of May*.

I closed my eyes. This place, this mission, the world, was it all a dream? Would I wake up and find I was back in my bedroom? Would Dad be waiting for me in the kitchen as he sat over a cup of coffee and a newspaper? His eyes were tired, sad and haunted, yet he always managed a smile just for me as he looked up from the headlines.

I opened my eyes, pressing my feet to the floor as I sat on the musty bed cover, the clock ticking on the nightstand.

Mustering my courage, I grabbed the scanner.

After positioning the glass screen over the scroll, I pushed the button. The laser beam streamed from top to bottom. The scroll morphed. In its place sat a pearlescent orb of pure cerecite.

I picked it up. Its smooth, glassy surface warmed my hands, but thoughts of the radiation nagged at me, so I quickly stuffed it inside my bag. I glanced at the leather bracelet on my wrist, took a deep breath, then pressed the metal disc.

"Agent Fifteen, this is Harper. Are you there?"

"I'm here," he answered after a pause. "It's good to hear from you, although it's been a while. Is everything okay?" His voice held an edge of formality.

"I'm okay. I found the next object. It was disguised as a star chart."

"Excellent. I'm glad you're making progress. However, I must warn you that this was only the third object. You still have four more to go."

My shoulders slumped. "I know. Sorry, but I've had some setbacks."

"What sort of setbacks?" he asked.

I glanced at my bag. Anxiety squirmed in my stomach. "I learned some things about this world." I paused. Might as well get this over with. "Were you aware that I'm not on Earth?"

A second ticked past. "Where did you hear that?"

"I found out. I had some help."

"From whom?" he asked.

"I'd rather not say."

"Agent Harper," he said. "Do I need to remind you that it's not your mission to get involved with the people of this world? I've said before that they hold to a superstitious belief system."

"This isn't superstition. It's science."

"That's debatable."

"Actually, it isn't." I sat up tall. "Tell me truthfully, do you know where I am? Am I on Earth?"

"That information is classified. It's on a need-to-know basis."

Was that so? "All right, then. I need to know. If you expect me to find the last four objects, I'll only do it if you're honest with me."

"Agent Harper, think about what you're saying. If you fail to find the objects, you won't return home. Worse, our power grids will be overwhelmed in the next flare. Is that what you want?"

My anger rose. I fisted the bed covers, scratchy fibers abrading my skin. He held the second flare over my head like a noose. "Fifteen, where am I?" I ground out.

The silence grew heavy as I waited for his answer. "We don't know. But we do know that the gateway you entered did more than usher you into an alternate reality. You walked through a wormhole. When you stepped through the gateway, you were transported off our planet and to an unknown plane."

A what? "Unknown plane? What does that mean?"

"The little we could gather from our other agents suggest you are still in our solar system, although we don't know much more than that."

My mind raced. "Could I be on a spaceship?"

"If so, then it's more advanced than any technology we're capable of creating."

I breathed deeply to keep the panic from overwhelming me. "You really don't know where I am, then?"

"No." The severe tone of his voice suggested I not argue, but I had to know the truth.

"Then I'm not in an alternate reality? I never have been."

"That's correct."

"So." I clenched my teeth. "You lied to me."

"Some would call it withholding the truth for your own good. Believe what you will, but there's a reason I asked you not to go down this path. The only agent to have taken my advice was Nordgren, and consequently, he's still alive."

Anger pricked me. "Rosa is dead, then?"

"We never found a body, but most likely, yes."

A wave of dejection overwhelmed me. "Was she murdered?"

"Perhaps. As I said, we don't have a body. There's no way to say for sure."

Rosa's journal sat on my bedside table, and I picked it up. I ran my hand over the leather cover, frustrated that she'd never been found, that she'd been trapped on this world, wondering what her family believed had happened to her. Would the same thing happen to me?

A hard knot tightened in my throat. Tears blurred my vision. What if I never made it home?

My heart hurt for Dad who'd already lost his spouse and his mom. Would he survive losing his only child?

I gripped the journal.

I will go home.

Although I held Rosa's journal, I didn't open it. In my mind, I reviewed the remaining clues.

Matter. Light. World. Poison.

What were the chances not a single object was left inside the castle? I'd combed through each room, marking them off on my grid, until none remained. If Rosa had gone to the cave, she'd likely brought the objects with her. What if some of them remained there?

"Can you confirm you are looking for the next objects?" Fifteen asked.

I paused before answering, imagining my tiny room closing in on me like a trap. One that had only a single exit. "I'm considering it. But I don't like it. You failed to disclose the truth when I stepped through the gateway. When I get out of this, the first thing I'm going to do—after reuniting with my family—is file a lawsuit."

"Don't be so quick tempered, Harper. There were reasons behind our actions, I assure you. Solid reasons that will stand on their own in court. I realize you're most likely emotionally compromised at this point. That's to be expected. Don't be so hasty to throw out terms like lawsuit. You must realize Vortech has the most qualified lawyers in the nation. I should also inform you that Vortech has been supplying your father with the means necessary to afford his mortgage while you're away. If you sever employment, I can no longer guarantee it will continue. And the flare—"

"Stop," I said. "You've done nothing but bring up the flare every time I question your motives. Tell me truthfully, is a second flare really happening? Or is that a lie, too?"

His silence spoke volumes, and a stone dropped to the pit of my stomach. They'd used me. This whole time I'd been nothing but their puppet.

"There's no second flare, is there?" I asked.

"Agent Harper, another flare will occur. We know that with certainty. However, since you want the truth, you might as well know why Vortech has advanced knowledge of why such an occurrence will happen. Have you ever thought it a coincidence that the first flare occurred only a month after Agent Rodriguez crossed through the gateway?"

Realization hit me. "You created the coronal mass wave when you sent Rodriguez through the gateway." Shock punched me like a fist to my stomach. "You caused the first flare."

"Yes."

"And the second flare will happen soon." I remembered to breathe. "Because you caused a second wave when you opened the gateway to send me through."

"Yes," he repeated.

"You used me," I said with heat in my voice. "You're murderers. You killed millions. My mother and grandmother died because of something you did. And now my father will die because of something *I* did."

I should have never walked through that gateway. If only I had known.

"It was never our intention," he argued. "We sent thirteen agents prior to Rodriguez without any problem."

"What changed?" I demanded.

"You tell me," he challenged.

Shattered glass and busted metal surfaced in my memory. "Someone destroyed the gateway on this side, meaning that when we opened the gateway on our side, a negative charge must've been sent into your reality. Someone destroyed the gateway before Rosa came through, and it stayed that way when I came through. But Fifteen... why? Why doom the entire planet again to send me through? It doesn't make any sense."

"Because we don't intend for the second flare to impact us. Once you return with the cerecite, we'll save our world from the second flare."

"That's an awfully big gamble." My thoughts turned dark. "But I must admit, a lucrative one. How much will you get to replace every power grid on the planet to operate on cerecite? Tens of trillions? Hundreds of trillions?"

"I'm not at liberty to reveal the amount."

I shook my head. Betrayal warred inside me.

I remembered what Ivan had called me when I'd first met

him. A lab rat. Yes, he must've known all along. He was in on this, too.

I ground my teeth. A sense of overwhelming hopelessness settled in my chest. If I failed at finding all seven objects, the world died. Vortech had used me, and I would pay the ultimate price for it.

Words escaped me. Panic tried to engulf me, so I closed my eyes. There had to be some silver lining to this situation.

Something Fifteen said surfaced in my memory.

"Fifteen," I asked tentatively. "What happens if I manage to open the gateway on this side? Could it reverse the coronal wave and stop the second flare from happening?"

"There's no way to know for sure, but that's a possibility."

"Then I have no choice, do I?"

He didn't answer. He didn't have to.

Either I found the seven objects and opened the gateway, or the world died. And we all died with it.

20

I dreamed of Dad. He stood across a bridge, calling for me, and when I started to cross, the bridge collapsed. The sense of falling woke me. I couldn't get back to sleep after that. Dark thoughts nagged at me. The queen, Rosa, the poisoned porridge, the missing cerecite... something wasn't adding up, and I planned to find out the truth.

I got up, dressed in my uniform, and grabbed a bowl of porridge from the kitchen. I had an idea in mind, and setting a trap was part of it.

I knocked before entering Morven's room, but I didn't wait for a reply as I opened the door. When I stepped inside, I stopped abruptly. Morven's aunt stood by the open window. Thick clouds obscured the sky, and the sunlight didn't stream inside as it usually did. She clasped her hands in front of her, as if she were a mannequin.

"Miss Harper." She said my name with an icy tone.

"Queen Regent." I held the bowl in front of me. "I'm surprised to see you here."

She bobbed her head. "Indeed. But let's be honest, you shouldn't be too surprised." She fingered the silver key around her neck. "Did you think I wouldn't notice when you stole my key and escaped the palace?"

I narrowed my eyes at her. How had she found out? My annoyance turned to anger as I looked at the prince's empty bed. "Where's Morven?"

"Why do you care to know?" She ambled toward me. "You've not done what I asked. I instructed you to study the scrolls I provided, and you haven't reviewed one."

"That's not true. He already knows those scrolls backward and forward. I don't understand why you think he needs to study them."

"Because he's to be king!" Her voice turned sharp. I hoped she hadn't seen me flinch. "I've no doubt he can recite the information, but does he know it? Understand it? Will he use it when the time comes?"

"I think you're worrying too much. He'll be a better king than you think."

She gave me a condescending glare. "Is that so?"

"Yes. If you'll allow it. Where is he?"

She pinched her lips. "That's none of your concern. Return to your room, Miss Harper. Collect your things. I no longer have any use for you."

"You're firing me?"

"Yes." She spoke in a detached tone.

I balled my hands into fists. I'd only found three objects. What was I supposed to do now? But none of that seemed to matter anymore. I was almost certain the last four weren't in the palace, anyway.

"Have you harmed him?" I demanded.

"Harmed him?" she asked, her eyes wide.

"Yes. Harmed him. The way you've been harming him for half his life. I found out about the poison." As if to prove my point, I lifted the bowl of porridge.

Her gaze narrowed. "Are you accusing me of poisoning him?"

"Yes."

"What a ludicrous thing to say. To think I invited you into my home. You're to leave from this palace now, and I expect you to never return. I never want to see your face again. Is that clear?"

"No, it's not." I ground out, standing tall, anger burning like wildfire through my chest.

"No?" she asked.

"I won't let you hurt him any longer."

"Hurt him? I've done nothing but help him since his parents died. How *dare* you accuse me of doing such—"

"His porridge was poisoned. You're the only person who has motive to hurt him, to make sure you can control him. If you can't do that, what then? What would you do if he weren't forced to sit in a chair all day and do what you demanded?" I took a step forward. "If he got stronger, if he could walk and do what he pleased, then what? You'd have no other choice but to kill him." I stood over her, my hands balled into fists. "What did you do with him?" I demanded.

Fear flashed through her eyes. "Nothing," she hissed.

"Then where is he?"

"He went downstairs to the swimming bath after I told him I was dismissing you." She stuck her nose in the air.

"Truthfully?"

"Yes," she bit out. Her eyes turned icy. "Believe what you want, but I'm telling the truth, Miss Harper."

"But someone was poisoning him. I found yellow cerecite in his porridge. You're the only person in the castle who would benefit if he died."

She shook her head. "I don't know anything about that."

"You must know something. How could you not know he was being poisoned?"

She stiffened as she locked me with her gaze. "How did you know?"

"I tasted his porridge."

"Well, that's something I never did."

Confusion plagued me. Why did I get the impression she was telling the truth? If she wasn't poisoning him, who was?

"Did you really not know he was being poisoned?" I asked.

"No. How could I know? I spend my life toiling over the affairs of this palace and the lives of my subjects. Do you know how hard it is to run a country? No. I suppose you don't. I worry about my nephew. You may not see it, but I love him dearly. He's like a son to me."

I shook my head. "How could I possibly believe you? You've been horrible to him since I arrived here. You've done nothing but bully and belittle him."

"No," she snapped. "That's not true. I'm pushing him to become a better person."

I almost laughed at the absurdity of her comment.

"When Morven's parents died, and they left him to me, I didn't know what to do," she explained. "He was this young, innocent child, and I was certain that whatever I did would never be enough." She turned to stare out the window. Her voice became wistful. "Do you know how hard it was for me when his parents passed?"

"I suppose I don't."

"I was completely unprepared to raise a son," she explained. "Let alone raise a child who would become king. Something broke inside me the day his parents died. I remember standing over their caskets, heartbroken that my sister and brother-in-law had left me so suddenly. I'd never been a mother, never ruled a kingdom, yet it was all thrust on me in that single day. I've never been the same since then." She shook her head. "I know I'm harsh. Some might call me cruel. I know I said things to the prince that I can't take back." She twisted her hands. "But poisoning him? How could you possibly accuse me of such a thing?" Her tone turned sharp.

"How, Miss Harper? When all I've ever done is protect him? How dare you!"

Her words gave me pause. "Then… it really wasn't you who poisoned him?"

"No," she said shrewdly. "I would never do such a thing to harm my sister's child. Gwendolyn meant the world to me."

"Then who would've done it?"

Her eyes shifted. "Any number of people, I'm afraid, including the miners, who have wanted to take the palace for a long time. Although…" She pressed her eyes closed, as if pained, then opened them again. "I do appreciate you bringing this to my attention. Your astute observation may have saved his life."

"You're welcome." I gave a single nod. "Does this mean I'm no longer dismissed?"

"No," she said with a strained smile. "I'm afraid you must go. There's no other option at this point. You're too much of a distraction to my nephew, and that's the last thing he needs right now. However, I will allow you to tell him goodbye. He's down in the swimming bath. By the conservatory."

Hmm. Still the same old queen regent, just perhaps not as evil as I had supposed.

"You should leave now." She straightened once again and threaded her fingers together, then turned away from me to stare out the window at the gathering storm.

I left the bowl on the table by his bed, then I walked out of the room. A mixture of relief and confusion warred within me. The relief came from knowing she was most likely not behind the poisoning—the confusion coming from wondering who was.

Hallways blurred as I passed through them from one level to the next, worries tugging at me like a hook caught in a fish's mouth, pulling me to some unknown place where I would finally discover the truth.

I made my way down the stairs. My footfalls echoed

through the domed chamber as I walked from one passage to the next.

I spotted the bathing pool down the hall from the conservatory. Lightning streaked through the sky, and a gray pallor glowed through the glass domed ceiling as I entered through an open door.

A pool filled with dark blue water took up the center of the room. With the greenery, the trickling waterfall, and the hovering trails of mist, I felt as if I'd wandered into a jungle. Humidity permeated the air.

Scanning the water, I searched for Morven, but only a few ripples broke the surface. Where was he?

A head of dark hair rose from the water near my feet, and Morven looked up at me. Water streamed down his face as I knelt beside the pool's edge. Tiny ripples splashed against the stones surrounding it.

"What are you doing here?" I asked.

"I always come here." He smiled.

"Really?" I questioned. "I didn't know you could swim."

"There's a lot you don't know about me." He wiped the hair from his eyes, water dripping. "I swim all the time—mostly when I'm angry, which happens quite frequently. Sometimes multiple times a day, especially when I've been in the presence of my aunt." His face turned grim. "Did she speak to you?"

I nodded, glancing away. "She was in your room. I thought she'd hurt you—or worse. But it turns out you were taking a relaxing swim."

"It was this or kill my aunt. I thought this was the better option." He sighed, looking past me to stare out the windows. "I asked her not to send you away, but of course, she never listens to me. She only does what's best for her. Since I wasn't becoming more submissive and obedient to her will, she took it out on you. I'm sorry, Sabine. This is my fault."

"You don't have to apologize. I have a feeling she would've

found any reason to let me go. No one will ever be good enough to be your caretaker."

"Caretaker," he said, chuckling. "What a ridiculous title. Makes me feel like I'm a child in need of tending."

I straightened the strap on my bag. "Are we still traveling to the cave?"

"We'll have to be quiet about it, but yes." He rose from the water. Droplets streamed down the exposed skin of his chest. Sinewy muscles flexed in his back as he turned away from me to grab a drying cloth resting on a rock. He wore black shorts that hugged his thighs, exposing his skinny, underdeveloped calf muscles. His body was an odd amalgamation of strength and frailty.

"How were you able to swim when you were paralyzed?" I asked.

"It wasn't hard. I used my upper body. When I swim, I feel free, because I can move wherever I want to go. Even now, although I can walk again, it takes a lot of effort. It's exhausting. If I had my choice, I would swim all day. But I hardly have any choices here." He ran the cloth over his head, and I tried not to notice the way his biceps flexed as he moved, or the beads of water clinging to his chest.

My cheeks burned. I took a step away from him. What was wrong with my head? I wasn't supposed to be attracted to him. Or to anyone. Not while I was on an unfamiliar world, with the possibility of never returning once I found a way to leave this place.

What happened when I found the seven objects and crossed back to Earth? It was what I wanted, wasn't it? I had to see Dad again. That was a given. But what about Morven? Was I supposed to just leave him behind?

"What's the matter?" Morven asked, approaching me, the drying cloth slung over his shoulder.

"Nothing," I said, tempted to tell him the truth—that I came from another world, that I was pretending to be someone else, that this thing we had—whatever it was—could never last. As far as he knew, I was a commoner from a fishing village, and he would have to keep believing it. "I suppose you should get changed."

"Yes." He wiped his face. "It won't take long. I brought extra clothes. Meet me by the velocipedes?"

I stuck my hands in my pockets. "All right. I've got something I need to take care of anyway."

He gave me a second glance, like he was trying to decide if I was okay. I turned away from him, pretending to be interested in the view outside the window. He got the hint and turned toward a doorway which I assumed led to a changing room.

When the door slammed shut, I headed to the exit, past the pool, where the rippling water had grown calm, its surface smooth and glassy.

I treaded on quiet feet through the hallways, passing a few people. When I neared the prince's room, a female's silhouette appeared at the end of the antechamber. She quickly stuffed something into her pocket, then brushed her strands of long blonde hair over her shoulders, as if to act casually.

Justine.

What a coincidence to find her here.

"Miss Sabine." She gave me a surprised smile. "Fancy seeing you here."

I narrowed my eyes. "Same goes to you."

"Me?" she said with mock disbelief.

"Yes." I nodded toward her apron's pocket. "What did you put in your pocket just now?"

"My pocket?" She shook her head. "Nothing."

"You're lying."

"Excuse me?" She placed her hands on her hips.

"You work in the kitchens all the time, don't you?" I asked. "You must've known what was going on in there. What was going into His Majesty's food, and what you must have snuck into his food just now. Were you working alone, or was someone paying you to do it?"

She shook her head. "I had nothing to do with his porridge."

"I didn't say anything about porridge." I ground my teeth. "I only called it his food."

Her eyes widened. "Good day, Miss Sabine," she mumbled as she attempted to march past me, but I grabbed her arm.

She whipped around. "What are you doing?"

"Tell me the truth. Did someone hire you to poison the prince?"

She tightened her lips, not speaking.

"Tell me," I repeated with heat in my voice.

"What do you think?" Her cheeks flared red. "It wasn't my plan to poison him, but I wish it were. He despised everyone. There was a time I had eyes for him, and he wanted nothing to do with me. He ignored me, as he should've done to you. He'll get what's coming to him. He deserves it." She jerked her arm away, then turned and marched down the hall, her skirts swishing.

I caught up to her and blocked her path.

Anger burned in her eyes. "Move," she demanded.

"No. First, you tell me who gave you the poison to put in his food."

She fisted her hands.

"Tell me, Justine."

She pursed her lips and didn't answer.

I balled my fists. "Was it a miner?"

She hesitated. "I don't know."

"You're lying."

"No, I'm not," she snapped. "Leave me alone, Miss Sabine, or you'll be sorry you ever met me. You're worried about the prince being poisoned? You should worry more about yourself. *Don't* follow me." She pushed past me and stomped away.

I watched her go, her words ringing in my head.

I still didn't know the identity of the poisoner, but one thing I knew for sure. Someone in this castle wanted Morven paralyzed or possibly dead. And they most likely wanted the same for me.

21

A fter traveling for hours, Morven and I rode into a canyon. Steep walls hid the sunlight and kept us in shadows. The incessant vibrations of the engine made my legs cramp. Wind gusted with a shrill wail, and strands of hair battered my cheeks.

White patches of crystals grew from crags along the canyon's floor. I got the impression that I was seeing this world as it really was for the first time, not hidden by the contrived plants—the real ecosphere—wherever it was. A planet? A moon? If so, then which one?

The sound of the engine's humming echoed through the chasm—an empty amphitheater carved by nature. We rode up a steep incline and onto a plateau. Craters punctuated the rocky surface, as if we traveled on the moon—or on *a* moon.

What if…?

When we stopped for a brief rest, I sat on a stone and sipped warm water from my canteen.

I wiped the beads of sweat from my forehead, then motioned to the landscape. "This doesn't look anything like the city."

Morven propped against a stone, his eyes roving the land-scape. "No, it doesn't."

"Do you think we could be on a moon?" I asked.

"I doubt it. For us to be on a moon, we'd have to be near a planet, and I've never seen one. If it were one of Jupiter's moons, for example, the planet would be hard to miss. It would take up half the sky."

I glanced up at the purple-tinted dome overshadowing us, mimicking the sky. "What if the dome were hiding the planet?"

"No." He shook his head. "We'd still be able to see something out there."

"Haven't you seen anything that would give us a clue to our location?"

"Maybe." He rubbed his neck. "But I can't be sure yet. We need to get to the cave."

We mounted our bikes. Morven sat nimbly, his black hair whipping in the wind. He focused on the horizon, eyes shining with intelligence, as if he held the clues to Ithical's mysteries.

As the sun reached its zenith, the landscape changed once again, from a desolate waste to the familiar trees and grass. The emerald green hues looked so odd against the purple-tinged sky. It didn't take a wild imagination to realize we were somewhere other than Earth.

Hills became more frequent as we rode. My engine sput-tered, slowing down. I pushed the handlebars forward. The engine clanked, but it didn't speed up.

"Morven," I called, riding next to him. "There's something wrong with my velocipede."

We stopped and dismounted. Morven knelt by the vehicle, removing a side panel to inspect the engine chamber. Inside, glowing tubes swirled around a small yellow crystal encased in a glass box. The light pulsed, dimming, then glowing bright once again.

"It's what I thought." Morven wiggled the box. "We'll

both be having this problem soon. The engines are using up more cerecite than what they're used to. It's the atmosphere out here. We'll have to stop in Edenbrooke for more."

"Do you think we'll make it?"

He replaced the panel. "Yes. It's off our path, but we're not far. Half an hour, maybe."

We climbed on our velocipedes. My engine sputtered as I pushed the handlebars, though managed to crawl forward and eventually speed up.

As the wind whipped past, my mind wandered, conjuring images of Dad working on his tractor in the barn, the smell of grease heavy in the air, working for a life he'd never have. One with Mom in it. I remembered the way she made him laugh— a genuine sound of happiness. I hadn't heard him laugh since her death, as if she'd taken his joy with her when she'd died.

We crested a knoll. Castle-like turrets rose over a village of thatched-roof houses. Grass cushioned our velocipede's tires as we rode down toward the settlement. Windmills fanned the air, creaking as they rotated. Cows grazed in the fields. The barnyard scent brought back memories from my childhood, of following Mima June down the trail to the dairy barn. What would she think of Morven? Did I care what she thought of him? Yes. I supposed I did, and I desperately prayed she'd like him, though I wasn't sure why it mattered so much.

We stopped our velocipedes and walked into the village. A few people passed us, wearing plaids of bright green or red. We drew a few stares. Was it careless for us to be wandering around the village like this? Would any of them recognize the prince? But Prince Morven never got out. Ever.

Church bells rang in the distance. Children laughed and played in a nearby garden. Astonishment struck me at the thought that I wasn't on Earth. Life existed out in the universe, and I'd never known. No one had known.

We parked our velocipedes outside a building made of stones and log planks. A sign swinging on a pole shone with paint in metallic colors of yellow, blue, and green, creating three interlocking circles.

Morven pointed at the sign. "Should be a cerecite resupply post. Stay close." His voice dropped. "Never know what kind of people to expect in here."

I followed him into the building, my eyes slowly adjusting to the dimness. The air held a musky smell. Lanterns glowed blue from the center of round tables where people crowded, casting an eerie light on their grizzled faces. Some talked in quiet voices, others held tankards as they watched us cross through the room.

Rows of glass jars filled with azure and emerald-colored crystals lined a row of shelves. They sat behind a long counter running the length of the back wall. Other jars held an amber-colored liquid, an alcohol of some sort.

A man with a stocky frame and bald head stood on the opposite side of the bar, wiping the wooden top with a discolored rag. Sweat beaded on his head and streaked the white fabric under his arms. He scratched his stubbled chin as he took in our appearances.

"Welcome to Edenbrooke Post." He spoke with a gruff, rasping voice, his Scottish accent thick, as he wiped his hands on his grease-spattered apron. "I don't believe I've ever seen you two before. Are you outsiders?"

"Yes," Morven answered. "From the south."

"I see. Travelers, then." He adjusted his apron over his protruding middle, then started wiping the counter once again. "We don't get many of those. Where'd you say you were from?"

"The south," Morven repeated, an edge of warning in his tone.

"Ahh." The man gave Morven a long glance. "I see. Why've you come all the way to Edenbrooke?"

"We've come to purchase two vials of yellow cerecite."

"Two?" He stopped wiping the counter. "That's a might

lot. We've had shortages of yellow cerecite. You've no doubt heard about the trouble with the mines. It's volatile, too. I'm afraid I don't keep much on my shelves. Not wanting to blow the place up. I can part with one, but that's it. It'll cost you twenty silver."

"But we need two," Morven said. "And I can pay for it." He placed four gold coins on the countertop. The man's eyes widened a fraction.

He rubbed his chin. "Forty gold?"

Morven nodded.

"Let me see what I've got." Coins clinked as he placed them in his apron's pocket, then he turned away and entered a room at the back.

As we stood at the counter, the room grew quiet. Only a few people spoke in hushed whispers. A chill prickled my back as their stares lingered on us. A gleam of silver in a man's belt caught my attention. The turquoise, curving handle of a weapon peeked from a holster.

The shopkeeper ambled back to us. Yellow crystals sparkled from a vial he carefully placed on the counter. "This is all I have."

"That's it?" Morven asked.

"I'm afraid so." He cleared his throat. "As I said, there's a shortage. But the good news is that you can take this, no questions asked, so long as I keep the gold."

"But we paid you forty gold," I said. "You only asked for twenty silver."

His eyes glinted. He focused on me, as if seeing me for the first time. "Yes, but as I said, you can take this one with no questions asked. That might be a useful benefit to travelers such as yourselves."

"We'll take it." Morven snatched the vial off the counter.

"Morven," I hissed. "He's robbing us."

The man crossed his arms over his broad chest, casting me a gloating look.

Morven snatched my arm, and I followed beside him. "Let's go."

"Morven," I whispered. "You can't just let him take your money like that."

"It's fine." He glanced over his shoulder. "It's better if we leave now, anyway."

All the eyes in the room followed us. Some of the men spoke quietly to each other. A man sitting near me clasped his hands atop the table, his fingernails dirty, his hands stained with greenish powder. I catalogued the other men's hands, zeroing in on each pair, all with the same stains.

We exited the building with the glass of yellow cerecite. The sunlight blinded me, and I shielded my eyes against its brightness.

Morven worked quickly to add the yellow cerecite to the engine chambers, only adding a few crystals to each one, and placed the vial back in his pocket when he was done.

He straightened, eyes lingering on the sign creaking in the wind. "We'll have to hurry."

"They're miners, aren't they?" I crossed my arms.

"Yeah, but I don't know why so many are here. Edenbrooke's a dairy town, and the mines are more than fifty kilometers away." He shook his head. "Nowhere close."

I grabbed my velocipede's handles. "Why do you think they're here?"

His eyes darkened. "Most likely because this town is remote, and it's also closer to the capital."

"They're planning to do something, aren't they?"

His calculating gaze locked on me. "It wouldn't surprise me." He sat on his velocipede and started the engine. I did the same, then I pushed the ignition button.

It roared to life, and we rode through empty streets paved in gravel.

I steered close to Morven so he could hear me over the engines. "Can we do anything about the miners?"

"Like what?"

"Go back to the capital?" I answered. "Warn your aunt?"

"It wouldn't do any good," he said.

"Why not?"

"Because she already knows of the threat. The best thing we can do is go to the cave. If we find the origins of the cerecite, then maybe it will benefit the miners. Maybe find alternate ways of obtaining it. Safer ways. Maybe it will keep them from revolting."

Steering our bikes out of the city, we rode over the dirt-packed ground, careful to avoid the larger stones. The sun began its descent toward the horizon, turning the sky to shades of molten copper. Rust-colored crags punctuated the landscape. Massive round spheres lit the world around us in blazing turquoise green.

We rode our velocipedes up a steep path, then into a canyon. A cave's entrance, a dark spot in the rock, split through the canyon's wall. Giant crystals grew from the ground, gleaming with a milky-white light around towering piles of round stones.

We stopped our bikes, my ears buzzing at the sudden silence. A shrill wind howled. My spine tingled as I stared into the cave.

"This is it?" I asked, my voice drowned out by the wind.

"Yes." He pulled a scroll from his bag, clouds of dust spiraling around us. I shielded my eyes as I followed Morven to the mouth of the cave. When we stepped inside, the walls blocked the wind. Except for our echoing footsteps, silence stretched. Stone encased us in a cocoon.

Boulders piled along our trail gave us enough light to see the cavern's ceiling.

"Why are there so many stones here?" I asked. "I've never seen so many in one place."

Morven glanced at the piles towering around us. "I don't know." His voice echoed.

Except for their glow, their size and shape matched the boulders on Champ Island. We followed the trail of rocks, like breadcrumbs leading us to the truth of not only Ithical's origins, but Champ Island's as well.

A trickling stream of water cut a path through the cavern floor. Sand shifted beneath our feet.

"These formations." I pointed to the crystals. "What are they?"

"Salt crystals," he answered. "They're all over this cave."

"Salt?" I asked.

"Yes," he answered with a nod.

"That's odd." Some of the stone-like crystals towered over me. Salt. Was it a clue to our true location? What planets did I know of that contained salt? Shaking my head, I couldn't think of a single astronomy book I'd read mentioning salt.

"This place hasn't changed much." Morven's whispered voice echoed through the immense chamber. "I remember my da and I found the mining tools just ahead, past a ravine and a waterfall."

I shot him a sidelong glance. "A ravine?"

"Yes. Don't worry." He gave a brief smile. "I brought ropes."

His smile caught me off guard, and that fluttering deep in the pit of my stomach returned.

To stay distracted, I adjusted my bag's straps, recalling its contents. I'd put my scanner and Rosa's journal inside. It seemed she and I had taken similar paths, and it wasn't a coincidence that my journey had brought me here. Had Rosa discovered what was inside this cave? If so, what had she found? Were the final objects here? Or had she found something more?

A nagging voice warned me I was getting too involved in mysteries that should've remained unsolved. But Vortech had lied to me about this mission from the start, and I couldn't help but wonder if they might've been part of Rosa's disappearance. Had Ivan had something to do with it? He'd kept things from me. I knew that for certain. And he'd been watching me.

The humidity made my clothes stick to my skin. The roar of a waterfall came from up ahead where water thundered to the bottom of a deep ravine. Mist hung in the air, and cold droplets splashed my skin as we stood looking over the drop.

"We'll have to rappel down," Morven shouted. "Do you know how?"

"Yes," I answered, omitting the part about learning it from Vortech.

"I'll get the ropes."

He opened his bag and pulled out two coils. "Here." He handed one to me. "Tie this off on one of the larger salt crystal growths."

I hefted the rope. "This'll hold our weight?"

He nodded. "They're strong enough. It would take a lot more than us to break them."

"Got it." I walked to one of the taller growths of crystals. Three beryl-shaped stones protruded from the ground. I ran my hand over the surface, cool and smooth to the touch. I was struck with the image of the living crystals, something that must've been native to Ithical and not a man-made cerecite creation.

After securing the rope to the pillars, I tied loops around my thigh, across my body, and over my shoulder. Good thing I'd passed Vortech's rappelling course. I stood beside Morven on the ledge.

"Ready?" he asked, tying his own rope around his waist and legs.

"I guess so." I adjusted the rope around my shoulder. "I've only been rappelling a few times. I wasn't very good at it."

"You don't have to be good at it." He tightened a knot. "You just have to do it—and preferably without dying."

"Good point."

"Besides." He shrugged. "You're talking to the boy who's been mostly paralyzed for the last ten years. I've just started to walk again, and now I'm rock climbing. I'm not sure if I'm brave or stupid."

He paced to the edge and turned to face me. He held to the rope, then took a careful step backward. As he lowered, I stepped to the edge. My head spun as I stared down at the dizzying drop. How many feet was it? Eighty? Ninety? Exhaling, I turned around and took a step down.

I moved slowly with the rope in my hands. Stones crumbled under my feet, and finding footholds took patience. I did my best not to glance down, taking slow and steady breaths to stay focused. I'd never been a fan of heights. Climbing in a remote cave on a foreign world wasn't exactly on my bucket list.

Still, I needed answers, and that thought kept me moving as I descended to the bottom.

I could have kissed the ground when my feet hit bottom. Morven stood beside me as we left our ropes behind and turned to a flowing river.

Mist dampened my clothes. The swift river churned alongside us, its water inky black in the dark cave. Only the occasional salt crystals or glowing turquoise spheres gave any light.

The river's water calmed. The pathway broadened to reveal a domed chamber. Salt crystals grew taller than any I'd seen before. They lit the area in a pale glow.

Grains of white crystals coated the ground. The taste of salt lingered on my tongue. The eerie stillness of the alien world made chills prickle the back of my neck. I tried shrugging the feeling away, but the deeper we traveled into the cave, the stronger the foreboding became.

Did Morven feel the same way? He fixed his eyes straight ahead, trancelike. Neither of us spoke. It seemed if we did, we would break the spell haunting this place.

Ahead, bones protruded from the sand. As we drew closer,

I stopped abruptly, staring in shock at a human skeleton. Its empty eye sockets stared blankly overhead, the jaw unhinged, as if screaming.

I pointed. "Do you see that?"

"Yeah," he answered.

We neared the skeleton. Its teeth remained intact, the bones still fitted together, unmoved by scavenging animals.

"Is it Isaac?" I asked cautiously, my stomach churning with unease.

"Could be." He knitted his brows. "But maybe not. I wouldn't be surprised if someone, maybe a hiker, had fallen into the ravine."

"You think so?" My voice echoed, although I'd barely spoken above a whisper.

He nodded. His eyes remained fixed on the skull. "The ravine is deadly. It would be easy to slip and fall."

I brushed some of the sand away from the skull, revealing the curving lines dividing the cranial plates. "How long do you suppose it's been down here?"

"I don't know. Most bodies would stay fairly preserved because of all the salt. It could be thirty-five or forty years old, but that's just a guess." He sat back. "Which means this most likely isn't Isaac. His remains would be considerably older—if we even find them at all."

I brushed the salt off my hands. "Do you think we'll find him?"

He nodded. "That's why we're here."

I followed him away from the skeleton, around piles of stones that stretched into the darkness above.

"Look." Morven pointed to a reflective, triangular object straight ahead. As we approached, its mirror-like, metal sheets came into focus. Solar panels covered the pyramid, a few inches taller than Morven.

"Solar panels," I said. "Why would anyone need those?"

"What?" He gave me a questioning glance. "Solar panels?" he said the name slowly. "What are those?"

"Well…" I stumbled, realizing my mistake. "I've seen something similar in my village. Some of the townsfolk used them to collect energy from the sun."

"Energy from the sun? Why would they need that?"

"Because… I don't know. I guess they thought yellow cerecite was too volatile. Wanted to find something less dangerous." I hoped he bought the lie.

He frowned, looking at me with a shrewd, calculated glance, then he ran his hands over a panel. "Solar energy," he mumbled to himself. "I've theorized it could be possible." He chuckled to himself. "Perhaps the villagers aren't as backwards as we thought." He scrunched his brow. "But how did something like this get down here?"

"I don't know. It wouldn't have been easy. I can't imagine anyone getting it down the cliff we scaled. It would've had to have been brought down in pieces."

"I agree."

We walked away from the pyramid structure and entered another chamber. I gasped, stopping short.

A corpse lay on the ground.

Black hair fanned out around her decaying face. Her clothing was torn in places, yet her skin was only a little mottled. Around her wrist, she wore a leather bracelet, exactly like mine.

My stomach lurched.

Rosa?

22

I stood over the body.

The bracelet clung to the tendons and fibrous skin of her wrist. A round, silver disc stood out against the leather band. It had to be Rosa. Who else could it be? Hands shaking, I hugged my arms around my chest. I had to know for sure if it were her, but how could I do that with Morven here?

"Well," Morven said. "I'm guessing that's not Isaac."

My nervous laugh filled the cave. "Yeah."

"But who is it?"

"I'm not sure." I hoped I sounded convincing.

He eyed me, but he didn't say anything. We knelt over her. I cataloged everything about the corpse: the smell—stale and sickly sweet, though not overpowering. Her clothes: a dark blue shirt and leather pants, dusted with sand, the fabric gone stiff. Her skin: Brown and leathery, no moisture remaining, as if the salt had mummified her.

Her eyes: Empty sockets, nothing but the smooth ridges of bone remained.

What color had they been? Had they been gray like mine? Had they watched as she'd written in the journal, saw the same round orbs of white cerecite, looked through a scanner, and recognized the same differences in the objects we searched for. Now, the eyes were gone. Eaten by decay, destroyed by time.

Was I looking into a mirror?

Morven touched her wrist. "What's this?" He fingered her bracelet. "It looks like yours."

I scrambled for a response. "Strange. Must've been from the same merchant."

"Very odd." He eyed me shrewdly. He had to be onto me now.

"Yeah, what a coincidence."

He looked at me a second longer than necessary. I shifted uncomfortably under his gaze until he turned back to the corpse.

"Look at this." He pointed to a square of black canvas beneath her. "I think she's wearing a bag."

"A bag?" I spoke with an even tone, though I tensed with anticipation.

"I bet we could learn who she is if we look inside," Morven said. "Will you help me lift her?"

"Lift her?"

"Yes."

"Morven, no." I couldn't let him look in the bag. What if something inside gave away my identity? I'd already cut it too close with the bracelet. I couldn't risk it, at least, not with him around. "We're wasting our time. She's probably just some random hiker who fell off the cliff and her body washed up here. Let's leave her alone."

"Don't you want to know who she is?"

"No. I think we should keep moving."

He gave me a pointed stare. "Sabine, we came here to find out what happened to Isaac, and now we've found a second corpse. What if they were killed by the same person? We need to know more about her." He lifted her shoulder. "I was right. It's a bag. Help me get it off her."

"I can't."

"Why not?"

"I already told you. I think we're wasting our time."

"No, we're not. Here, just grab her shoulder."

"All right," I conceded. Sand particles stuck to my fingers as I helped Morven lift the body. He pulled off her bag as I held her. A strand of her hair tickled my nose.

When Morven pulled the bag's straps off both her shoulders, I lowered the body back to the ground and scooted away.

Morven propped the bag on his lap. He opened it and pulled out a rock.

He shot me a questioning look.

"Maybe she was collecting rocks?" I suggested.

He weighed it in his hand, turning it one way and then the other. "It looks like an ordinary stone. Wonder why she'd want to carry around something like this?"

I had an idea, but I wouldn't tell him. "May I look at it?"

"Sure." He held it out and I took it from him. The rock was a dark gray color, smooth and oval-shaped.

"Strange," I said. "It must've been important to her if she was carrying it around."

"Maybe she'd meant to use it in self-defense?" he suggested.

"Yeah, maybe so. Is there anything else in there?"

He opened the bag and reached inside, then pulled out a metal tube, a replica to my scanner, except the two halves were smashed, and the screen cracked. "What's this?"

I shrugged, though a clammy sweat broke out on my skin. "No idea. It looks broken."

He tapped the screen, but it remained blank.

"Interesting," he said. "I wonder where it came from— what it was used for."

"I wish I knew. It's very odd."

"Let's check the next chamber," he said. "Maybe there's more that will explain all this."

"Good idea. But I want to check here for a moment longer, see if we missed anything."

He gave me a sidelong glance. "First, you didn't want to help me find out about her, and now you want to keep checking? What's going on, Sabine?"

I sat straight, not wanting him to see my fear. He was onto me. It was only a matter of time before he found out, but could I keep him off my trail a little longer? "Fine. You were right. There is something unusual going on, and I think this corpse has something to do with it."

"So, you're admitting I'm right?"

"Yes," I said, sighing. "Happy?"

"I am." He smiled, a teasing expression that made his eyes sparkle. This guy was full of himself.

"Would you like to stay here and help me check it out?" I tried to sound as calm as possible.

"No. I'll go. But I think it's a good idea to check it out more thoroughly. I'm just glad you conceded that I'm right."

"Would you shut up about it already?"

"All right," he said with another smile. "Let me know if you find anything. I'll be in the other chamber."

I nodded, and he stood and walked away, while I stayed with the body. When he disappeared, I grabbed the stone, cataloging every detail: coated in gritty sand, lighter on top, as if it had been sitting in water. The smooth texture. Two small divots carved from dripping water.

My hands warmed the stone. I couldn't help but glance at what remained of Rosa's fingers, gray bones peeking beneath strips of leathery skin. Had they once warmed this same stone?

I turned the rock over another time, but it remained unchanged. Was it an object or not? I could scan it to find out for sure, but I didn't dare use my scanner with Morven lurking.

Holding the rock carefully, I opened my bag and stuck it inside. With any luck, I'd found another object. I ignored the shiver tingling down my spine as I reviewed the last items, those that had been written in her hand, while I sat by what remained of her corpse.

I browsed over the remaining items.

Light.

World.

Poison.

Only three to go. What were the chances they were here in the cave somewhere?

"What are you doing?" Morven asked.

I jumped. My bag slid off my lap, spilling the contents. The rock and my scanner clattered to the cavern floor. The two ends sprang open, revealing the screen. My heart stopped.

Morven crouched beside me. I reached for the scanner. He grabbed my hand. Unspeaking, he stared from the object in my hands to Rosa's matching scanner on the ground.

Understanding lit his eyes.

I froze.

"Who are you?" He attempted a calm tone.

"You already know."

Shrewd calculation darkened his eyes. "Tell me, Sabine. No more lies. Why are you carrying an object that looks like the one in the corpse's bag? Why does your bracelet look like hers? How did you know the name of those panels?"

I swallowed my fear. "I can't tell you."

"Why not?" he asked.

"I just can't."

His grip tightened around my wrist. "Who are you?"

"Morven—"

"Tell me!"

I tried to pull away from him, but he held tight, his eyes

livid. If I told him, then what? Would he hate me and never trust me again? Or would he understand? There was only one way to know.

"Fine," I said, my quiet voice echoing. "You're right. I'm not who you think."

"Are you a space traveler?"

"I-I don't know."

"What do you mean?"

"I'm not from Ithical. I'm from outside the dome."

His eyes widened. "How is that possible?"

"I came through a gateway. I was sent by a corporation called Vortech. They hired me to come here and locate seven objects of white cerecite." The words freed me. I'd hidden behind the lies for too long.

He studied me with narrowed eyes. "You're telling the truth?"

"Yes."

His expression remained passive and unchanged—calmness hiding the storm. "If that's true, then why didn't you tell me sooner?"

"Because I'm supposed to keep my identity a secret. I wasn't the first one to come through." I motioned to Rosa's corpse. "She came here before me, and there were others before her."

"What?"

"It's true. I'm supposed to find seven pieces of white cerecite, and so was she, but she never found the seventh. Then, she died. I think someone killed her."

"Who?"

"I wish I knew."

He kept my wrist clamped.

"Would you release me now?" I asked.

"No." His grip tightened. "I don't know who you are. What's the importance of that rock?"

"I think it's one of the objects I'm searching for."

"So, you're not from Fablemarch. You're not even from this island. Is your name even Sabine?" His voice grew louder, teetering on the edge of anger.

"Yes."

"You've been lying to me."

"Only because I had to. Please believe me. I lied because I had no choice. Someone killed Rosa."

"Rosa?"

I nodded at the girl on the floor. "Her. Agent Rosa Rodriguez. You may've known her as Rose. She was a maid for your mother ten years ago."

His face remained blank, eyes narrowed with suspicion, but I plunged forward anyway.

"There's a good chance they'll be after me once they find out I'm searching for white cerecite. That's why I had to keep my identity a secret. If anyone discovered my true purpose for being here, I'd end up like her."

Finally, he released my wrist. "You really think someone killed her?"

"Yes."

"I see." He worked his jaw back and forth, the way he always did when he was thinking seriously. "Then you'll probably want to see what I found in the next chamber. Just warning you, though. It will be disturbing."

I eyed the corpse. "More disturbing than this?"

"Yes." He didn't look at me when he spoke. "Much more."

I placed the scanner in my bag, praying I hadn't damaged it, and followed Morven to the next chamber. We left Rosa's body behind. I still wasn't sure how she'd died. I was sure Vortech would've told me she'd lost her mind and come to the cave in a compromised state, then slipped and fallen to her death. But I suspected something more sinister had happened. Someone had murdered Rosa Rodriguez, but I still didn't know who had done it. Ivan? He'd been here ten years ago. I wasn't sure what motives he would've had, but maybe something in the cave would give me those answers?

Morven led me through a narrow tunnel to the next chamber, which opened up, domelike, to an expansive space. My gaze trailed up to a towering gateway. Soot blackened the inner edges, the metal blasted open in places. Shattered glass and debris littered the floor. Some of the wreckage lay in huge chunks.

It was destroyed. Just like the first gateway. "The other gateway." I walked toward it.

"You know what it is?"

"Yes. It's like the structure I stepped through to get here. But it's ten times as big."

Seven niches, about the size of mailboxes, lined the gate-way's inner frame. The buttons and lights surrounding them looked the same as the ones on my scanner. I placed my hand inside one of the metal-lined niches, the surface bumpy and covered in tiny circuits.

Interesting.

We walked away from the gateway. I glanced over the debris, the twisted and charred pieces of metal too destroyed to discern their purpose.

A vessel came into view. I stopped, blinking.

A spaceship?

The supple, streamlined craft stretched as long as a bus. From all the documentaries I'd watched, I'd never seen a ship like this. The word *NASA* had been engraved into the metal. The letters connected, unlike the usual logo's style with blocky characters.

"What's NASA?" he asked.

"It's a space exploration program. What is something like this doing here?" I brushed my fingers over it, colder than I expected. The oblong-shaped craft had no rocket boosters or a propulsion system. It could've been an alien vessel. But if that were the case, why was the word NASA printed on it?

I paced to the anterior of the ship where a thick layer of dust clouded a windshield. Brushing the grime away, I peered through the glass.

A corpse sat in the front seat.

I jumped back and grabbed Morven's hand.

"What?" he asked.

"Look inside."

The cavern remained eerily quiet as we stepped to the ship and peered through the dust-smeared glass. The corpse wore a navy-blue jumpsuit with the word NASA stitched to the left breast pocket, a knife's handle protruding from his chest.

"That's Isaac," Morven said, his voice quiet and haunted.

"Are you sure?" I questioned.

"I think so." He brushed the dust away. "It's hard to see through the glass."

"What if we opened the ship?" I offered.

"Do you know how?" he asked.

I eyed the shuttle. "Maybe there's a door somewhere."

We circled the vessel, looking for a way to open it, but the craft had no seams or doorways. We stopped by the glass shield when I noticed a black square pad beside it.

"What's this?"

I pressed my hand to the square, and it flickered with blue light. The glass unsealed, releasing a pressurized hiss, as if everything inside had been in a vacuum. Morven helped me open the shield, which swung on hinges.

Without the glass blocking us, we got a better look at the corpse. It—*he*—rested his hands in his lap. Except for the gray skin, he looked untouched by decay. His dark hair, square jawline, and straight nose resembled Morven.

Dried blood clung to the knife sticking out of his chest.

My stomach churned. "Who did this?"

Morven didn't answer. I turned to him, and he stared at the body with a slack-jawed expression, his skin nearly as pale as the corpse's.

"Morven?"

He shook his head, as if coming out of a trance. "I don't know. The memories… I remember feelings, fleeting images. Fear, pain. Then the grayness. My next memories are from the Mystik wolf, roaming the land, the scents and sights through the wolf's eyes. I don't remember anything else until my own childhood."

"Is there any way for you to remember more?"

He leaned forward, touching the stiff shoulder of the corpse. His fingers ran over the uniform before he jerked his hand away.

"What is it?"

"I thought…" He turned to the panel of switches and buttons in the cockpit. "Maybe." He touched a silver disc.

Static came from speakers. Morven knit his brow as he listened. "…collapsing…too much energy. Going to recalibrate…Can't. It's not working…"

Static whirred, then silenced.

"There was an explosion," Morven said. "Unexpected. We were caught off guard."

"Do you remember anything else?" I asked.

"No." He closed his eyes. "There's nothing after the explosion."

Silence pressed in around us. The blackened gateway loomed, as if challenging us to discover its secrets. Morven stepped away, squaring his shoulders. "But this isn't what I was going to show you. There's more over here."

"More?" I asked.

"More corpses."

Morven led me around the maze of debris. The images of Isaac and Rosa lingered, haunting me. I shook my head, trying to clear my thoughts, instead focusing on every sight, cataloging it as I went. I could always depend on my overactive photographic memory to override emotion.

Fiberoptic wires and wheels looked familiar, but others I had trouble describing. Metal plates, green glass squares, and tool-like objects of various sizes. In the debris, I spotted a small black pyramid with shimmering golden bands—a match to Cade's.

Had Cade's father gotten the pyramid from this cave? Or were there other caves with the same technology lying dormant under the soil?

Morven stopped as we reached the far side of the chamber near the giant gateway. Fear raced down my spine as a pile of corpses came into view. I grabbed Morven's arm to keep steady. Bile rose into my throat. Bits of tattered clothing clung to their decomposing flesh.

"There are twelve bodies here," Morven said. "The skeleton near the water makes thirteen. And the other body we found—Rosa—makes fourteen."

Fourteen. There had been fourteen agents before me. I was fifteen.

Blood drained from my face. My hands grew cold. I couldn't make them stop shaking.

"I don't feel well." My head spun as I sat on the ground.

Morven sat beside me, concern showing in his dark irises.

"What happened here?" I asked, my voice a fearful whisper.

"Someone killed them all. They hid their bodies, hoping no one would find them. It's a good spot, really. No one comes here because of the superstitions."

I glanced at the machinery that lay discarded like the corpses. "What is this place?"

"It was a mine once, I think," Morven said. "There are drill bits back there." He pointed to the far wall. "And some machines with scoops. It looks like they were mining the cerecite."

"Who?" I asked, pleading, fear running cold through my blood.

"I have no idea. But they were here long before us. Some of this stuff could be at least two-hundred years old."

"But... that's not possible. NASA didn't even exist that long ago." My head pounded, and I pressed the palms of my hands to my forehead. "Have we traveled in time or something? Where are we? *When* are we?"

"I think I might know," Morven said quietly. "At least, I think I know *where* we are."

I glanced up at him. "You do?"

He nodded. "I told you I'd discovered the location of Earth, and I've been doing some research since then. I mapped the location of all the planets near us—the closest being Mars and Jupiter. Actually, we're rotating between the two."

"Between them?" I thought back to science class in elementary school. "But there isn't anything between them except the asteroid belt."

Morven nodded, his face solemn.

I gasped. My head spun. "We're in the asteroid belt?"

"I think so. Here, I'll show you." He stood, holding out his hand. I took it, wanting to close my eyes, wake up, and be back in a normal world again.

I gripped Morven's hand, feeling as if he was my lifeline to reality. The smoothness of his palms, and the slightly rough calluses on his fingertips, felt warm against my cold flesh. If not for him, I might've lost it completely. Like Rosa.

"Here," Morven said, crouching over a piece of debris. The bronze plate was the size of a shield, and engraved words scrolled from one edge to the other. *PROJECT CERES.*

"What does it mean?"

"Ceres," Morven said. "Are you familiar with this name?"

"Yes. She's a goddess, right? From mythology."

"Yes. Greek mythology. The goddess of grain. But it's also the name of a dwarf planet in the asteroid belt. It's the only sphere-shaped planet that exists among the asteroids. Some have speculated it contains rare minerals that aren't found anywhere else in the solar system. Minerals like cerecite."

"*What?*"

"Sabine, we're on Ceres."

Ceres. Cerecite. The name had been here all along, in the very objects I searched for. I studied the metal shield, noticing hairline circuits running through its surface. Kneeling beside it, I ran my hand over it, my fingers smearing the dust, feeling the ridges where the wires were. Was this some sort of electronic device? I turned it over, revealing a blank screen.

"Do you think it still works?" I asked

"Yes, if it's powered by cerecite, there's a good chance we can turn it on."

I spotted a button on the bottom right corner. With shaking hands, I pressed it. The screen lit up.

My heart skipped a beat.

A hologram rose up from the screen, the colors faded, yet still discernible. The image resembled the cavern we were in, with the gateway taking up the back of the space, yet machines covered the floor, some crawling on track wheels, carrying loads of colored crystals.

Other machines rose several stories tall. Belts carried rough ore crystals to conveyor belts where they were blasted with high-pressure water jets until they turned to round spheres, then loaded on spaceships.

The turquoise stones ran down belts and were discarded in piles that remained in the cavern.

We watched as one of the ships rose off the ground. It hovered before gliding toward the gateway.

A portal formed and engulfed the craft until it disappeared.

The image froze, and the words: NASA: PROJECT CERES appeared where the image of the portal had been.

"Welcome to Project Ceres," a soft female voice said, her words accented with an Indian inflection. Music played in the background—a peppy, electronic noise that set my teeth on edge, out of place and eerie in the hollowness of the cavern. "You are part of an elite group of astronaut pioneers," the woman continued. "You have been chosen to supply Earth's demands for cerecite, which will benefit generations to come in multiple industries, including healthcare, robotics, agriculture, and the energy market.

"When the first astronauts arrived on Ceres in the year 2447, cerecite was discovered. Its benefits were plentiful, and mines were built shortly thereafter, but problems arose. The costs of shipping and production almost bankrupted operations, but a solution became available with the invention of Dr. Fernoulli's wormhole gateway portal, the first invention of its kind to introduce wormhole technology into the spaceflight industry.

"We are excited to announce the opening of the Ceres Gateway. It is the latest in modern technology and will be an expedited process for shipping cerecite from Ceres to Earth, drastically reducing the costs of shipping, and dropping transit times from seven years to only 3.4 seconds.

"We are proud to introduce you to Project Ceres."

The screen blanked. The music continued, then shut off abruptly.

I remembered to breathe.

2447?

That was four hundred years in the future. My mind raced. A clammy sweat broke out over my skin, and my stomach soured. How would I ever look at anything the same after this?

"It opened a time rift," Morven said, pointing to the gateway.

"Yes," I answered robotically, my mind still reeling.

"The original immigrants were on the ship in the Atlantic when the rift opened. It created a behemoth of a storm. Their ship got sucked into it and transported to the island. Then, they found the wormhole's entrance from the cave on Champ Island to Ceres. They came here and never knew they'd left Earth."

"Incredible," I said quietly, staring up at the wormhole gateway. "It's a manmade wormhole, and with enough energy, it becomes a time portal. Vortech must've built the portal on the island I originally came through, but I can't go back that way because someone destroyed it. Assuming this gateway still works, this is the only way out. Plus, Vortech caused a solar wave when they sent Agent Rodriguez through. Months later, a devastating solar flare hit Earth. It killed millions." I shook my head. Heaviness weighed on me. "Another flare will happen soon."

"Why?"

"Because Vortech caused another wave when they sent me through. But there may be a way to stop the second flare." I glanced up at Morven. "If I open the portal, it may stop the solar wave in time to keep the next flare from hitting Earth."

He stared up at the towering gate. "And if you don't open it?"

"It could take out Earth."

Silence stretched between us.

"Earth is through there," Morven said quietly, almost to himself.

"Yes." I spoke quietly. "My home."

"Your home," he repeated, his eyes wide with wonder. "What's it like?"

"Different," I answered. "We have technology that would amaze you. We've been to the moon, Morven. We've sent robots to Mars."

His eyes widened with fascination, the gears clicking in his head, as he peered up at the gateway. "How do we open the wormhole?"

"I don't know. I'm still working on that one."

The towering structure loomed, taunting me, my only way home.

"Whenever you open it, I'm going with you," he said.

I eyed him. "You are?"

"Yes. No one's left this world. Not since the first explorers came here. We'll be the first."

"But you're about to become king," I reminded him. "Can you really just leave?"

"It's fine." He waved his hand, dismissing my argument. "Aunt Tremayne would love to be the permanent ruler anyway."

I crossed my arms. "I think we're getting ahead of

ourselves. We can't leave unless we find all seven objects. I've only found three—hopefully four—pieces of white cerecite. There are three left. There may be more here in the cave. The objects are disguised. The only way to tell if it's an actual piece of white cerecite is to detect small changes in its appearance, and then I'd have to scan it."

"But how did white cerecite get here in the cave in the first place?"

"Rosa brought some of it. The rock—for one. She must've had the other pieces when she came here. I suspect she may have hidden some it before whoever killed her stole the rest. The remaining pieces ended up back in the palace. Those left have something to do with light, world, or poison."

His gaze roved over the cave, back to the spot where the corpses were piled. "I think I might've spotted something. There was a candlestick back there. It seemed out of place."

"A candlestick?"

He nodded. "Do you want me to show you?"

"All right," I answered, though I had no desire to return to the heap of bodies, imagining my own body stacked on that same pile.

We moved away from the hologram screen to the far side of the cave. Debris littered the ground near the corpses. The teak-colored wood of a candlestick stood out against the rusted gears and wheels. Morven picked it up and showed it to me.

"You're right," I said. "It does look out of place. I don't know why a candlestick would be here when they obviously had more advanced technology than this." I hefted the smooth-grained wood, scanning every detail. Small chisel markings dotted its surface. Seventeen of the divots in total. Melted wax clung to the top where a candle would have been placed.

Soft paraffin had dried around the top, molding to my thumb. Cradling the wooden piece, I scanned every curve and marking, counting the divots, positioning them until I knew the location of every dent—when one disappeared.

I arranged the candlestick on the ground, then took off my bag and placed it on the floor. After opening my bag, I removed the scanner, praying it worked.

"What are you doing?" Morven asked.

"I'm going to scan it."

"You think it's cerecite?"

"Yes, look at this." I held it out for him to inspect. "One of these markings disappeared. It was here a second ago."

"You noticed something like that?"

I nodded.

"That's pretty incredible."

I wouldn't have used those words, but I didn't argue the point as I opened the scanner, the ends separating with a mechanical whisper.

"What's that device?"

"It's a scanner. Vortech made it to detect cerecite. Once it does, it's able to reveal the object's molecular nature and break it down to its original form. The only problem is that I dropped it. I'm not sure if it still works." I clicked the button. The laser skimmed from top to bottom, dimming, then growing bright again. Buzzing came from the machine. That didn't sound good.

Please work.

The light clicked off.

"Was that supposed to happen?" Morven asked.

"Um, no." I pressed the button again, cursing myself for dropping the stupid thing. The light scanned the candlestick once again, glowing from top to bottom. The wood morphed, transforming to a ball of white cerecite. Its shimmering, opal colors reflected off the ground.

I exhaled a sigh of relief.

"Wow," Morven said. "That's really white cerecite?"

I nodded.

"I've only seen it displayed in cases. I've never actually touched it. May I pick it up?"

"Yes, don't keep it for too long, though. It's radioactive. I'll need to put it in my bag soon."

He lifted the glowing sphere. "Amazing," he whispered. "You know this substance is said to contain the properties of all three types of cerecite. I didn't think it was capable of existing."

"Why is that?"

"Because once two types of cerecite are combined—green and blue, for example, their properties are negated. They become like ordinary stones. That's why you see so many turquoise boulders laying around everywhere. But white cerecite contains all the energy of the other colors. Its state is always fluctuating. It has so much power, it has to shift its appearance to release part of its energy."

"Interesting." I glanced around, in awe at the technology scattered around us. "I wish I knew who these people were who built all this."

"What about the company you work for?" he asked. "Vortech. Would they know?"

I sighed. "Possibly. Will they tell me? Most likely not."

His forehead wrinkled. "Then why do you continue to serve them?"

"Good question" I answered. "I have to finish this mission so I can go home." My heart ached at the mention. "But now that I'm here, I have to find the seven stones to get home."

"Then we'll find the last two stones," he said. "And you'll get to go home."

I smiled up at him. "I like that idea."

"Good." He crossed his arms. "And I'll go with you."

I shook my head. "I didn't say that."

"But how will you stop me?" he asked.

I pondered his question. "I guess I can't."

"Then I'm coming," he said firmly. "We'll find the last two

pieces of cerecite, then we'll return here and open the gateway, assuming it's functioning. We'll go to Earth together."

"Fine," I answered, though his plan troubled me. There were so many things that could go wrong. His coronation, for example. Could he just avoid it? Was he okay with leaving Ithical in the hands of his aunt?

Also, there was the business of the murdered agents. The first agent had been killed more than forty years ago, which led me to believe the murderer wasn't a single person working alone, but a group who'd been around for a long time.

Could Vortech be killing their own agents? Is that the reason Ivan is still on Ithical Island? Was he the executioner for agents who discovered the truth? That thought chilled me the most, and I did my best to put it out of my mind. I couldn't go there. Not until I had more proof.

"Let's go," Morven said. "It'll be morning soon."

"Wait, I've got to do one more thing."

I walked back to the gateway. *I wonder…*

I opened my bag and pulled out Rosa's rock. As I examined it, the stone still hadn't changed appearance. With my scanner on the fritz, I may never get the chance to test it. Maybe the gateway was my answer to determining whether it was pure cerecite. I placed the rock inside one of the niches, then pressed the button on the right-hand corner.

A laser skimmed over the rock, the same way my scanner had worked.

Morven stood beside me. "What are you doing?"

"Testing a theory. If this works, I won't have to rely on my scanner."

The stone morphed into a glowing white orb.

"It worked," Morven said.

"Yeah. I got lucky." I removed the orb and placed it in my pack.

"How did you know to do that?"

"Call it desperation."

Morven gave me a questioning look. "One day I'm going to demand you explain how this all works."

"I'm not sure I'm the best one to ask, but sure."

I followed him out of the cave, past the piles of debris and Rosa's corpse. I had the urge to go to her, to bury the body at least, but there wasn't time, and I had no way of digging a grave. I left her behind with nothing but a silent prayer—that her passing wouldn't be in vain. That I would find the last two pieces of cerecite, open the portal, and avenge her death. It was the least I could do.

We arrived at the gorge where our ropes were tied. Climbing up was harder than rappelling down, but we managed to make it without falling. I couldn't shake the image of Rosa's corpse, the gateway we'd found, or the NASA technology.

Mud caked my hands as Morven and I climbed to the top of the ridge, then we stood and coiled the ropes. After Morven replaced them in his bag, we continued to the cave's exit. A dark gray sky greeted us as we walked into the crisp morning air.

We paced away from the cave's entrance, our footfalls echoing through the canyon, a brisk wind cold on our cheeks.

"Where are the velocipedes?" Morven asked. "We left them here, didn't we?"

"Yes."

"Did someone take them?" he asked.

"Who?" I questioned. "This place is deserted."

Pebbles fell, echoing through the gorge. A shadow darted behind a looming boulder at the opposite canyon wall.

"There's someone over there," I whispered.

"Where?"

"There." I pointed to the rock, but the darkness made it hard to see anything. "Who do you think it is?"

"Miners, most likely."

I grabbed the knife from my boot, the hilt warmed by my body heat.

Footsteps came from behind me. I spun around when a flash of silver blurred in my vision. A pistol hit me hard in the face. Pain exploded through my skull. My knife hit the ground with a thud.

The world went black.

I woke with a pounding headache. As the sunlight entered my eyes, the pain grew worse, and I forced them to close. The rumble of an engine vibrated beneath me. Ropes burned my skin where they'd been tied around my wrists and ankles. As I moved, I realized I was laying on the seat of a motorized carriage.

Wind and sand battered my cheeks. We must've been in the desert. Where was my knife? And Morven? Had they killed him?

Surely they hadn't.

Please don't let them kill him.

My skull throbbed, and my consciousness ebbed. The blackness took me again.

"WAKE UP," A GRUFF VOICE BARKED. A SHARP KICK DUG INTO my ribs. I cried out, opening my eyes to a dimly lit room. Rough stones comprised the walls and floor. A man hunched over me. He ran a hand over his slick, bald head. A nauseated stomach and a bitter taste in my mouth added to my pounding headache.

I tried to sit up. Ropes bound my wrists and ankles. I managed to prop my back against a wall behind me. Slime coated the stone, soaking into my shirt. Water dripped in the distance. The dampness burrowed in my bones.

"Where are we?" My dry throat rasped as I spoke.

"Beneath the palace." His rough voice rumbled from a barrel chest. He knelt to be eye-level with me.

"Who are you?"

"My name's MacDowell."

He kept his hands clasped in front of him, his skin covered in green soot, his fingernails caked with the same substance. A miner.

"What do you want with me?" I asked.

"You're collateral."

"What does that mean?"

"You're our guarantee the prince does what we ask. If we've got you, he'll do what we say."

"What do you want him to do?"

"Simple. Kill his aunt. Give us the throne. Stage his own suicide. If he doesn't cooperate, you die."

Fear ran cold through my veins, but I didn't want him to see me afraid, so I sat tall, meeting his gaze. I had to play it cool if I wanted to get out of this. "I think you're underestimating the prince's stubbornness. You'll never get him to do what you want."

He grabbed my neck, jerking me toward him. Rough hands constricted my windpipe. "You will *not* talk to me that way," he seethed. "Do you understand?"

He gripped my neck so tightly, stars spun in my vision. "Do you?"

"I…" Black spots crowded in.

"Answer me!"

I choked. Didn't he know I couldn't breathe? How did he

expect me to talk? Bootsteps thudded as another man approached us. "We're ready."

MacDowell shoved me against the wall, finally releasing me. I gasped as he gave me one last glare, then stood and marched away, talking quietly to the other miner as they left the room.

I rubbed my neck and inhaled deeply, trying my best to remain calm, though I'd seen the look in MacDowell's eyes. He would have no problem killing me.

How long would they keep me down here? I closed my eyes, resting against the wall, trying to think of a way to escape.

Did I have my knife?

I tucked my fingers into the top of my boots but felt only an empty sheath.

A stone dropped to the bottom of my stomach. I'd lost Mima June's knife. A hard knot in my throat made it hard for me to swallow. *I'm sorry, Mima. I didn't mean to fail.*

After a deep, stuttering breath, I sat up and pushed my regret aside. Escape was my only thought as I worked my hands back and forth, the ropes rubbing through my skin. Hot blisters formed, but I moved faster, ignoring the pain. If I didn't get free, I'd have more to worry about than blisters.

Heavy boot steps came from the corridor ahead. MacDowell and several other men ducked into the room, hat brims shading their faces. I froze as they walked into the firelight. Wolfish, hungry gazes locked on me. Dirt-smudged shirts and coveralls formed to their heavy frames.

MacDowell pointed at me. "She'll come with us."

Two men grabbed my arms and hauled me to my feet. They dragged me into the corridor to a metal door at the end. Rusty hinges squealed as they opened it and tugged me into a room where the prince lay in a heap on the floor. Blood covered his forehead and streamed down his cheeks.

My breath hitched. "What did you do to him?"

Without answering, the men shoved me to the ground. I slammed onto my knees. Someone kicked my back, and I pitched forward, smacking my face on the rough paving stones. Stars spun in my vision as I attempted to sit up.

Someone grabbed me under the arm and jerked me upright. The iron taste of blood seeped into my mouth where my teeth had cut inside my cheek.

MacDowell's face loomed in my vision. "Convince him to do what we ask. I'll let you imagine what will happen if you fail."

He stood and exited the room with the others behind him. When the door banged shut behind them, I scooted toward Morven. His eyes fluttered open as I drew nearer.

"Thank goodness you're alive," I whispered.

A hint of a smile ghosted across his face.

"What did they do to you?" I asked. "You look awful."

"I suppose they beat me, but I don't remember most of it."

"They want you to kill your aunt," I said.

He sighed. "Yes. I know."

"I don't get it. Why don't they do it?"

"It wouldn't work in their favor." Wincing, he worked his jaw back and forth. "For them to legally take the throne, the royal family must be deemed unfit to rule. A parliament would then be formed, and the monarchy would be put on trial by the people. If I were to kill my aunt, then they could classify me as a danger to our kingdom. But they wouldn't want me to stand trial or the truth of what they're doing would come out, which is why they want me to stage my own suicide. It's a fairly solid plan, except they're all idiots, so it won't work."

"Why won't it work?"

His eyes darkened. "Because they're dealing with me."

"Still overconfident, I see."

"It's not overconfidence. It's reality. They wanted things to change now. Once I became king, I would've done everything

I could to fix their situation, but they weren't patient enough. They should've waited."

"What do you intend to do?"

"I'll start by escaping this cell."

I eyed him. He laid flat on his stomach, and he hadn't moved anything but his mouth since I'd been thrown in here. "Escape? Can you even sit up?"

He sighed, closing his eyes. "No. To be honest, I can't currently feel my legs."

"O-kay," I drew out the word. "That would be a problem."

"My strength will return. It always does."

I pursed my lips. "How many times have you been beaten by miners?"

"Never, unless you count just now," he answered. "But that's beside the point. Will you help me sit up?"

"I would." I shrugged my shoulders. "Except my hands are tied."

"Good point." He nodded to his legs. "Look in my boot. There's a knife in there."

"A knife?" I glanced at his shoes. "The miners didn't take it?"

"No, they've been in a thoughtless rush this whole time. They're making mistakes because they've never done anything like this before. We'll use that to our advantage."

I scooted toward him. Maneuvering my hands to his boot, I reached inside and fished for the weapon.

My fingers brushed over wood and steel. I grabbed the handle and pulled it out. Holding the knife as best as I could, I worked the blade over the ropes, up and down until one snapped.

My shoulders ached, and wrists burned as I tossed the rope aside, but at least I could move again. I turned to Morven who still hadn't shifted an inch.

Grabbing him under the shoulders, I hauled him upright

and propped him against the wall. I sat facing him for a moment too long, just enough to set my insides on fire the way they always did when he was near. The square line of his jaw and his full lips danced in my vision. If I only leaned a little, I could kiss him.

A mischievous grin lit his face.

"Why are you smiling?" I asked.

He shrugged, upturned lips revealing his amusement. "No reason."

"You're being threatened with your own death yet you're smiling." I shook my head. "I'll never understand you."

I scooted away from him, distracting myself by untying the rope around my ankles.

"What?" he questioned. "You never pictured us growing close to one another while locked in a cell awaiting our death? Some would say this is quite romantic."

"*I* wouldn't say that. This whole situation has gotten out of hand. We've got to escape." I picked up Morven's knife, its blade barely longer than my hand. It didn't compare to Mima June's. Heaviness weighed on me at the loss of my weapon— as if I'd lost my last link to her.

Morven leaned his head against the wall, the color drained from his face, streaks of dried blood standing out against pale skin.

I scooted toward him. "Are you sure you're okay?"

His eyes shone with pain. "I've been better."

I glanced at the low stone ceiling overhead and the rusted metal door barring our path—the only exit from the room. "Where are we, exactly?"

"In the dungeons beneath the palace. They tunneled their way inside. Probably took months. But they are miners, after all. The guards haven't come down here since we sealed off the dungeons decades ago." He sighed, staring at the ceiling. "Last week, they snuck inside my room to capture me when I was asleep, but I wasn't around." He laughed quietly. "They went back to Edenbrooke to come up with a new plan, and I came to them. Fell right in their laps."

"That's convenient," I said with sarcasm.

"Yeah." He barked a cheerless laugh.

I crawled to the door and grabbed the handle, rusty metal flakes sticking to my sweaty palms, then I pushed the lever down, but the door didn't budge.

"What are you doing?" Morven asked.

"I hoped someone left it unlocked."

"They're not that careless." He rubbed his neck. Pain shadowed his eyes.

Yells echoed from the hallway. I backed away from the door as MacDowell burst inside.

Standing, I blocked him, holding Morven's flimsy knife between us. Rage burned in my chest.

"Not another step," I seethed. "Do *not* touch him."

MacDowell laughed. "Or what?"

"Or you'll regret it."

"Is that so?"

My training came back, as if I were in the facility again, as I tightened my grip on the handle. In one swift motion, I lunged for him. He sidestepped, but I spun around, slamming the blade into the flesh of his shoulder.

He howled, rounding on me, madness in his eyes as he grabbed my hair. Pain shot through my scalp as he yanked a clump from its roots. I bit back a scream and thrust my knee into his stomach, hard enough to rupture his kidneys.

MacDowell fell back with another scream. I ran to Morven, tugging his hands to help him stand, when more miners entered the room.

"Get her!" MacDowell yelled.

Three men rushed at me. Two grabbed my arms, squeezing painfully tight, dragging me backward. One of them pressed the cold metal of a steel blade to the back of my neck.

"Don't move," he growled in my ear.

The other man yanked Morven to his feet. When the prince stumbled, the miner socked him in the stomach with a tight fist, the loud *punch* echoing through the small space.

"Don't hurt him," I shouted, rage burning through me.

"Or what? He's killing himself anyway." His laugh grated in my ears. Morven collapsed. Another man came forward, grabbing Morven's other arm. The two men held him between them.

MacDowell got to his feet. He ripped my knife from his shoulder with a ragged scream. Spots of dark blood dripped to the floor from the blade. Menace lit his eyes. "You… will regret that." With the knife, he pointed to the door. "Take them!"

They marched me out of the cell, the men holding Morven following us.

Glimpsing behind me, I saw Morven's eyes focused on the ground, his face paler than it had been in the cell, his feet dragging.

The tunnel's dim light revealed stones slick with slime. Its moldy scent lingered. Sweat clung to my skin, and my hair stuck uncomfortably to my neck.

We made it to a narrow staircase. The men gripping my arms pushed me up. With the knife pressed to my back, I had no choice but to climb. Heavy footfalls followed behind us. The sound of Morven's body being dragged up the steps made my rage burn like wildfire through my chest.

I set my jaw, focusing straight ahead.

Morven was right. They would pay for this.

When we reached the landing, we stepped into a hallway. The men holding my arms shoved me through an open door and into another passage. We climbed more stairs until my legs burned, and my scalp ached where MacDowell had ripped out my hair. Sconces burning with blue cerecite shimmered from the walls. We passed the hallway leading to the kitchens, then approached the stairs leading to the bottom floor.

"Where are you taking us?" I asked.

"Throne room," was his only answer as he marched me down. After making it to the floor, we stepped into a hallway that ended at a wooden door set into an alcove.

A miner opened it, revealing a staging area behind the throne room, a curtain taking up the back wall. Clutter crowded along the walls—tables and chairs alongside buckets, mops, and stacks of folded banners and tablecloths. Muffled voices came through the curtain.

One of the miners shuffled to the curtain and peeked through. When he returned to us, the miners moved us out of the staging area, back into the hallway, shutting the door.

"The queen isn't on the throne yet," the miner said. "Could be a minute or two before she's seated. I counted five guards inside."

MacDowell clenched his jaw. "Fine. Once the queen regent's seated, we'll move the prince behind the curtain. He'll stab her then."

"I won't…" Morven breathed. "I won't kill my aunt."

MacDowell whipped his head around. "Like hell you won't."

"Monster," I spat through clenched teeth.

Cold metal chilled my neck as the man holding me pressed the blade to my throat. "You shut up."

"Kill your aunt or she dies," one of the men holding Morven said. "Your choice."

"Then I choose… neither." Morven shifted on unsteady legs.

"Not an option," MacDowell replied. He pulled out Morven's blade, thrusting it in Morven's hand. "Kill her with this."

"But he can't even walk," I pleaded.

The man holding me slapped my face with the flat of his

blade. My ears buzzed. I blinked to make the room stop spinning.

"Stop," Morven said, his voice a quiet warning. "Don't lay another finger on her or I swear I'll never do what you ask."

"You really want me to stop? Then do what I say," MacDowell barked. "Kill your aunt, or I kill the girl."

"Morven." Panic strained my voice. "You don't have to do this."

"No." He stood straight. "I'll do it. I'll kill her. But you can't lay another finger on Sabine, or I swear you'll regret it."

"Morven, no!" I demanded. "I'm doomed anyway. Don't do this."

"Sabine." He looked at me, his dark eyes glittering with stern acceptance, yet I saw a glint of something else there. "I'll do it."

"Fine," MacDowell ground out. "Get him to the curtain. He can crawl to the queen regent if he must. I don't care how he does it if he gets the job done. I want everyone to see it was him who killed her. And whatever you do, keep her quiet."

Someone shoved a gag in my mouth, tying it so tightly behind my head, my jaw ached. The coarse fabric tasted of sour sweat.

A miner opened the door and two men dragged Morven into the staging area. They kept me close behind. The carpeted floor muffled our footsteps, and the darkness closed in around us as the miners shut the door behind us.

Sticky blood stuck to my neck where the blade had cut me. My heart pounded with each footstep as we crowded inside. Unintelligible voices came from the other side of the curtain.

Morven clenched the knife, his knuckles white.

My hands trembled. He wouldn't seriously go through with this, would he? But how would he ever get out of it?

MacDowell grabbed Morven's arm, dragging him to the curtain. The miners holding me kept me against the far wall, away from Morven.

MacDowell shoved Morven to the ground.

"Do *not* move." The miner holding me pressed the cold blade to my skin. Stinging pain punctured my flesh, making tears spring to my eyes. Warm blood trickled down my neck.

A miner stood at the curtain, parting it to peek through. Morven's aunt's voice carried from the other side. The miner gave MacDowell a single nod.

"Go," MacDowell hissed, shoving Morven forward.

Morven crawled to the part in the curtain.

The light glowing from beneath the door highlighted the fear in Morven's eyes. He separated the curtains and peered through. His chest rose and fell as he knelt. Sweat beaded on his brow. Pale skin contrasted with the dark metal of the blade.

Please Morven. Don't do this.

"Go," MacDowell urged. "I'll give you three seconds before I slit the girl's throat."

Morven clenched the knife. An unspoken warning sparked in his eyes.

He pulled something from his pocket and smashed it in MacDowell's face. Glass shattered, pungent smoke exploding in a yellow cloud. Noxious fumes choked the air. Violent coughing racked MacDowell's body. Tears streamed down his face. He fell to his knees, gagging and sputtering.

Morven sprang to his feet. He grabbed me and tugged me outside, though the miner holding me didn't let go. In the hall, Morven slammed the door shut on MacDowell and two others inside. Only the miner holding me remained, and he tightened his grip on my arm, knife held at my neck.

"Not any closer," he shouted at Morven.

Gargled screams came from inside the antechamber when the door burst open. Miners fell to the ground, choking on fumes that billowed in a yellow cloud.

In the hallway behind us, the queen's guards sprinted to us. "What's going on?"

Morven pointed to MacDowell and the others. "They're trying to take the throne. Take them!"

Yellow smoke thickened, obscuring the hallway. The miner dragged me into the fog of fumes. My eyes watered and my lungs burned, demanding I cough, but I only gagged with the cloth tied in my mouth.

Smoke fogged around the queen's guards crowding in. I lost sight of Morven. Scuffling and shouting came from every direction. The man holding me dragged me down the hallway. Tears blurred my eyes, still stinging from the smoke. Shouting rang in my ears. Bodies pressed in around us from all directions as the palace erupted in chaos.

Guards rushed through the packed bodies. Hallways blurred past.

Where are you taking me? I wanted to scream but couldn't speak through the gag.

Chilly, blustering wind picked up as we stepped outside the palace. Across the lawn, the dome of the greenhouse rose against the backdrop of the gray wall and a looming stormy sky. Thunder rumbled with a drawn-out growl.

Dozens of people poured out of the castle. Some had yellow-tinted eyes and dirt-smudged faces. Metal glinted in their hands as they aimed their weapons for the crowd. Shots exploded. People screamed. A few fell to the ground while others ran frantically back to the castle.

The miner dragged me away from the crowd, holding me against his body. I twisted, using my shoulder to loosen my gag. I wriggled in his grasp, but he grappled me down. I kneed his midsection. Screaming, he fell back, and I tore the gag from my mouth.

The miner cursed as he grabbed for me.

Adrenaline fueling my movements, I stomped the man hard in the groin, then I spun around and sprinted toward the greenhouse.

Bullets whizzed. One hit the greenhouse's glass panels.

Shattering rang in my ears. I burst through the doors and ran inside. Humid air thickened around me, dampening my clothes and skin. Echoing voices came from outside, muffled by the greenery growing on either side of the pathway.

"Sabine," Cade called, his surprised voice coming from the back of the greenhouse. I followed the path to the source of his voice. His white shirt and blond hair stood out against the greenery. "Back here!"

I dodged the rows of plants and tables. Gunshots echoed outside. Screams and shrieks of pain cut through me like a knife. How many people were dying because of this?

"What's going on out there?" he whispered frantically as I crouched beside him.

"The miners," I answered in a rush. "They're taking over the castle."

His blue eyes widened. "*What?*"

"They captured the prince and tried to force him to kill his aunt. It didn't work. We got separated. I have to go back for him. They could've…" I was going to say *killed him*, but I couldn't bring myself to do it. "He could be hurt. I have to save him."

"I'll help you."

I eyed him. "You will? You realize there's a good chance we'll be killed?"

"I think our chances of that are already pretty high."

"Good point," I said.

Cade pulled a pen knife from his pocket.

"Is that the only weapon you've got?" I asked.

"Yeah, sorry. I only use this for whittling." He knitted his brows. "We could arm ourselves with the gardening shears, I suppose."

A shot blasted. Glass shattered, raining shards. I held my hands over my head, sharp particles cutting like razors as we ran to the door. Adrenaline pumped through my blood. We reached the open exit and raced outside.

Flames crackled from the palace windows, and smoke billowed from the open doors. People sprinted, screaming, from the castle.

My breathing labored, with the scent of pungent smoke, I searched the faces for Morven.

A behemoth of a guard blocked me. He held his pike inches from my face, his lips drawn into a tight line beneath a thick mustache. The plaid over his shoulder and his broad frame reminded me of a genuine Scottish highlander.

"Ye're not to enter the castle," he barked with a deep voice, his accent thick.

"She's searching for the prince," Cade said behind me.

His bushy eyebrows knitted together. "The prince?"

"Yes," I said haltingly. "I have to find him."

The guard grunted. "The prince and his aunt have been escorted to an undisclosed location."

Smoke stung my eyes. "They're hiding?"

"Maybe, but ye didn't hear that from me."

"Please," I pleaded over shouted orders from inside the palace. "Can you take me to him?"

The guard shook his head. "Nay. Move along. The castle is being evacuated."

"No! I can't go. I have to find him. Please, take me to him. I'm his caretaker."

"His caretaker?" He scrunched his brow. "Ah, yes. I've seen you around the palace. His Majesty the prince has been in much better spirits since you've arrived. Miss Sabine, is it?"

"Yes!" My hands shook, so I balled them into fists. "If you'll take me to him, I promise I won't cause any trouble. I'll leave."

The guard sighed. "Very well, lassie." He leaned closer, motioning me to him. "But only because you're his caretaker. I wouldn't do this for anyone else. You're not to repeat this. Understood?"

I nodded, my pulse thrumming lightning fast.

"They've been taken to a safehouse in the southern district," he whispered. "I don't know where it is exactly. But ye can ask around. I'm sure some of the locals will know more."

"Thank you," I said, stumbling away from him. "Thank you so much. I won't forget this."

He gave me a solemn nod.

A combination of happiness, relief, and anxiety flooded me, my head spinning.

Cade and I raced away from the palace, dodging the crowds until we reached the main gate. I glanced back as we crossed under the cold shadow of the portcullis. Black smoke billowed into clouds, and the charred scent of death carried on the wind.

25

Cade kept a brisk pace alongside me. Velocipede engines rumbled through narrow lanes. Stone and brick buildings towered over us, their windows tinted orange in the waning sunlight.

"The southern district," I said. "Do you know the fastest way there?"

"Yeah, I can get us there. Just stay close." He cast a nervous glance over his shoulder. "Miners could be anywhere."

My breathing came in labored gasps as we made it to a bridge. Water gushed beneath the arching structure. Our footsteps echoed over stone.

"Sabine," Cade said as we crossed. "How did they capture you and the prince in the first place?"

"Morven and I were out in the desert near a cave when they found us. We'd stopped in Edenbrooke. They were organizing, which we thought seemed strange. Then they must've followed us, because they caught us and brought us back to the city."

We dodged a passing velocipede.

"What were you doing in the desert?" Cade asked.

"Checking on some information people in this world will want to know. I shouldn't say more than that."

He only nodded and didn't press the issue as we crossed the bridge. The water running beneath us made it seem as if I were putting a chasm between me and my brief life in the palace. Would I find Morven again?

Yes. I had to find him.

Cade led me down the busy streets until we took a narrow lane. We strode to a quiet district where two story, thatched-roof homes stood along cobbled lanes. I couldn't stop looking behind me, thinking the miners would be following, but only an empty street stretched into the distance.

Our footsteps echoed the blood pounding in my ears. As my adrenaline drained, exhaustion caught up to me.

Cade ran his hand through his tousled blond hair, his expression pinched with anxiousness, which didn't suit him. I much preferred carefree Cade.

"My mother lives in the southern district," he said. "We can stop by her house and see if she knows where the royal safehouse is."

"Do you think she'll know?"

"No idea. But she usually keeps up with the other locals. If anyone will know, it'll be her."

"Then we're lucky she lives there."

"That's one way to look at it." His eyes met mine, bright mesmerizing blue, but his handsome face only served as a reminder of the man I'd lost.

I glanced back, wondering if I'd be better off searching for Morven and his aunt on my own, but it would take too long, and I didn't know where to start searching in the first place.

"It's this way." Cade led me down another lane, this one narrower than the others. Buildings rose on either side, the sunlight only hitting the upper stories, casting the ground in shadow. Bits of ash floated around us. Charred gray bits, feather-light, gathered on the benches and lamp posts.

Yells echoed. Behind us, firelight flickered from a mob of men carrying torches.

Cade's face fell. "I think the miners are torching the city."

"Why would they do that?"

"I don't know. I suspect they've been angry for so long that they're doing anything to take out their rage. Hurry." He ran ahead, and I followed. The maze of buildings spun in my vision. Muscles cramping, energy drained, I ran because I had no choice.

"Up there," Cade said breathlessly. We stopped at a building made of red bricks. Cade led me inside, through the front room, and into a kitchen.

Stillness settled in the small space, as if we'd entered a refuge from the world. It reminded me of my own home. A wooden butcher block took up the center of the area. Garlands of garlic and pearl onions hung from the open cabinets, scenting the room with their spicy aroma. Earthenware bowls and mugs crowded the shelves. We sidestepped casks of dried beans and oats as we paced through the kitchen.

"Mam," he called, searching the house. I walked with him through the silent rooms. All empty.

"Where is she?" I asked.

"I don't know." He shrugged, attempting to act casually, though his worried gaze revealed his emotion. "It's possible she's hiding at her sister's house in the market district." He shook his head. "I hope she's okay."

"Cade," I said, daring to rest my fingers on his. I wasn't sure how he'd react, but it seemed like he needed it. "I'm sure she's okay."

He gave me a single nod, eyes softening a bit at my touch.

Outside, enraged voices echoed. Cade clasped my hand and we crouched behind the butcher block. Through the window overlooking the sink, the crowd of miners marched past. Flames crackled from their torches. I prayed they didn't set fire to the house.

Cade held tightly to my hand. I wanted to tell him to let go, but I couldn't move. Fear paralyzed me as I watched the mob trample past.

The miners disappeared from view, their shouts echoing behind them. Seconds ticked past. Silence replaced the yells. I let out my pent-up breath, finally pulling my hand free of Cade's, my fingers stiff and cramping.

He made no argument as he continued to stare out the window, as if he weren't sure if they were really gone.

"What do we do now?" I whispered.

He paused before speaking, his eyes wide, haunted. "I've got to find Mam. She could be in danger. I'll go down to the market district and look for her. You'll have to hide here until I come back."

"Are you sure?" I questioned. "What if the miners catch you?"

"I know the back passages. I'll be safe enough." His glance darted. "I hope."

"Shouldn't I come with you?"

"No." He shook his head. "Stay here until I return."

I gave him a concerned glance. "You're sure?"

"Positive."

The idea of hiding while he went to the streets on his own unsettled me. He could be killed. But common sense told me that this was the safest place for me, and if I went with him, I could be killed, too.

He stood, grabbing a knife from a kitchen drawer before he crossed to the door. "Stay here," he said firmly. "Don't leave. I'll be back soon." He turned to go, then stopped. "Sabine, I…"

"Yes?"

He glanced down at his crumpled white shirt, then brushed at the dirt smudges.

"Cade, what is it?"

He shook his head. "I know we never had time…"

I eyed him. "Time for what?"

"I just…" He shook his head, as if reconsidering what to say.

I cast him a sidelong glance, and he pursed his lips, then crossed the distance between us and took my hands. Warm fingers brushed a strand of hair behind my ear, his fingers trailing down my cheek. "Take care, all right?"

Confused, I nodded. As I looked up into his bright turquoise eyes, anxiety squirmed through me, the touch of his skin too overwhelming. All I could do was wish I were looking into Morven's eyes, and feeling his hands instead of Cade's.

As if sensing my unease, Cade released my hands. Without another word, he stepped away from me and crossed the room. As he swung the door open, a smoke-filled sky came into view, then he left, closing me off from the world outside.

A leather chair sat in the parlor, and I collapsed on the seat. After pulling an all-nighter, being beaten, and fleeing from crazed miners, weariness seeped into my bones, compelling me to close my eyes. But how could I possibly rest?

Glancing at the door, I had the urge to run outside and try to find the queen and Morven on my own. I could knock on every door in the district until I found them. But rationality overrode my emotions. The miners had almost killed me once. What would happen if they caught me again?

Lightning flashed, an electric burst that glowed through the window, giving a purplish luminosity to the room. Thunder rumbled in the distance. An uncontrolled chill shook my body. My head still ached, and the gouges on my neck stung. I gingerly touched the cuts, blood sticky beneath my fingertips. Was there anything in the house I could use to clean the cuts? Better yet, maybe I could find some green cerecite.

Shelves lined the wall across from me. I crossed to the books and knickknacks arranged along the rows. Labeled jars rested in a neatly arranged row, labels facing out. *Oil of prim-rose. Seeds of lavender. Herschpringer's potion.*

A painted skull at the end of the ledge caught my eye. A depiction of Ithical Island decorated its cranium. Golden lines connected around the capital to form the major rail routes. More lines spread across the curve of the skull, out to the other cities. Each landmark and township were painted in golden calligraphy. Bright blues, greens, and yellows glowed in pearlescent colors to form fields and mountains, all in such vivid detail, I had to run my fingers over the bumpiness of the paint.

I cradled it between my hands and lifted it off the shelf. The chill of the smooth bones unsettled me.

I replaced the skull on the shelf, glad to have it out of my hands. Why would someone paint something like that on a skull? Then again, this was a foreign land. Perhaps decorations like that were commonplace.

Taking a step away from the shelf, I searched the rest of the house, looking for healing ointments of any kind. In the water closet, I found a washbasin with a lump of soap placed atop the wooden bowl, and I cleaned my wounds as best as I could.

Anxiety squirmed through my stomach as I paced back to the front room. *Cade and his mother will be here any minute now,* I told myself. And if they weren't, I had no choice but to go back and search for them.

I reflexively reached for my bag, only to remember I'd lost it, most likely taken by the miners. I had no choice but to get it back, but how?

Another flash of lightning lit the room in a bright glow, followed by a booming crash of thunder, rattling the skull on the shelf. A chill crept down my spine at the sight of the object —and of the white dot just above its left temple.

When I neared the shelf, I reached for the skull, but hesitated. The dot had been there a moment ago, hadn't it?

I blinked in disbelief. Hesitantly, I lifted it up. A white circle stood out against the greens and blues. Beneath the marking, the words *Project Ceres*.

What?

I studied the location of the white dot on the map. West of the capital. Just north of Edenbrooke.

Cradling the skull, I collapsed on the chair.

My breaths came in shallow gasps. This was wrong. Everything was wrong. This skull must've been the sixth piece of cerecite. What had the last clues been?

It came back to me in complete clarity, as if Rosa's journal were sitting on my lap.

Mundo. World.

I didn't like where my thoughts were taking me. I needed to get out of this house.

Tucking the skull under my arm, I raced for the door when it boomed open. Cade's silhouette stood out against the dark sky behind him. His eyes sparkled blue, the strange color I'd noticed when I'd first met him.

"What are you doing with that?" He stepped inside, his gaze fixed on the skull I carried.

"I…" My mouth grew dry.

"What are you doing with it?" he repeated.

"I'm…" Behind him, wind gusted from the open door. My escape. Could I make it past him?

He stepped toward me. "I'll ask you one last time, what are you doing with that skull?"

"Cade, please," I begged. "I need to leave."

"Leave?"

I rushed past him when he caught my arm. He pushed up my sleeve to reveal my bracelet, then he gripped the metal disc and pried it up until it revealed the *V* logo etched on the back.

"Vortech," he hissed, eyes narrowing. "I should've known."

He squeezed my arm.

"You're hurting me," I gasped.

"I'll do more than that," he growled.

My eyes widened. "What?"

"You're Vortech." His cheeks burned red. "*Vortech*! Sabine, how could you? Don't you know who they are?"

"Cade, no…"

"Listen to me, Sabine. They're the enemy. *You're* the enemy." He looked to the ceiling. "How did I not see it?"

"Cade, let me go."

"No!" Rage burned in his eyes. "I can't do that. I don't care who you are. I'm so sorry, Sabine. I have to kill you."

"What?"

"I have to kill anyone from Vortech who comes here. I have no choice but to kill you, too."

He slammed the door and dragged me into the parlor, then shoved me on the ground. I fell, landing hard on my back. He kicked the skull away from me, knocking it out of my reach, then he knelt over me, pinning my arms above my head, pressing my fists into the ground.

"Cade, stop!"

"No! You brought this on yourself. You've been lying to me this whole time. I knew something was off when you said you'd gone to a cave with the prince. I thought surely it couldn't be the wormhole cave. Vortech hasn't sent anyone for ten years. They'd lost all their past agents. They wouldn't dare send another one. But I knew if you were Vortech, you'd take the white cerecite. So, I tested you. Look what I found. You. With the white cerecite, attempting to steal it from me."

"Cade, no," I pleaded. "It's not like that."

He struck me across the face so hard I felt my teeth reopening the cut in my lip. Warm blood swirled in my mouth. "I should've killed you when you first arrived here. I'd grown lax."

"Why did you kill them?" I asked, gasping through the

pain. If I kept him talking, it would buy me some time. At least, that was my hope.

"I had no choice. I couldn't allow them to open the wormhole."

"Who are you?" I asked.

"I was a miner." He nodded to the skull. "So was Isaac."

"You know of Isaac?" Panic squeezed my lungs. How had this spun out of control so quickly? "How?" I demanded. "Who are you?"

"Why should I tell you?" he barked. "You're with Vortech. Do you have any idea what your people want to do to this world? How they want to exploit it? They'll take all our cerecite and leave us to die." Tears brimmed in his eyes. He choked on his words. "Do you think they care about us? Our lives? The families here? They don't. They want power—the kind cerecite can give them."

I shook my head. "I didn't know. I promise I had no idea."

He laughed, a mirthless sound, devoid of humor. "You expect me to believe that?"

"It's true. They sent me here. They said they wanted the cerecite as a power source." I spoke quickly, my words tumbling out all at once. "That's all I knew. I promise. Cade, who are you?"

His eyes narrowed, as if he were trying to decide if I told the truth. A knot I couldn't swallow formed in my throat. If I died, what happened to Dad?

"Tell me," I whispered. "I want to know the truth."

Not speaking, he studied me, then he released my hands and sat back. He wiped the tears from his face with his shirttail.

I sat up and scooted back.

"Stop," he seethed. "Don't move another muscle." With a flick of his wrist, he pulled a knife with a crystal yellow blade from his pocket. He grabbed my wrist and slid the blade under my leather bracelet. The band severed with a snap.

Tossing it aside, he stood, stomping on the metal disc. Crunching came from beneath the sole of his boot as he crushed it to pieces. My heart fell. He'd taken away my communications.

"Do *not* try to escape." He held the knife for me to see.

I only nodded, sitting up and scooting away from him until my back hit the bookshelf. Without my bracelet, emptiness settled inside me.

He knelt over me, the knife in my face. I reached out and placed my hand over his.

"Cade, please," I said softly. "Tell me what's going on. Tell me who you are."

His gaze lingered on my hand covering his, as if that one gesture had reminded him of our friendship.

"Okay," he breathed. "I'll tell you what I know. I was born in the future…"

26

"I was born in the future," Cade repeated, his voice hollow as we sat in his home, eerily silent compared to the destruction raging outside. He hesitated, as if unsure he wanted to say more.

"When?" I asked, keeping my hand on his, managing to keep from shaking.

His gaze wandered. "Four hundred years. The year 2437."

His words forced me to take a deep breath. "Four hundred years? How is that possible?"

He shrugged. "It's not so complicated. We opened a time rift. It sent us back in time to the year 1887."

"Where are you from?"

"Earth. Montana, actually."

Montana. The word sounded so familiar.

"Growing up, all I ever wanted to do was to leave," he said, gaze distant. He shook his head. "I've never told this to anyone."

"But you can tell me," I encouraged him.

He bit his lip, then continued. "I never got along with my parents, so I signed up for NASA's Cerecite Project to become a miner. It sounded adventurous. Maybe I just wanted to explore. When I got here, it wasn't what I expected. The place was a nightmare. It didn't look like the world it is now. It was a barren rock. The living conditions were miserable. We ate freeze dried food, never anything fresh. We never saw sunlight except to adjust the pyramid panels—spent all our time underground. Our only task was mining cerecite, day in and day out."

His gaze wandered, his tone wistful, as if he were there again. "But once we started learning more about the mineral, we got better at using it. We created plants and food. Water. Before long, we made the dome, and recreated a world like Earth. Sun and clouds. Thunderstorms. All the things you think you'll never miss but you do."

He shook his head. "Things changed, though. We weren't getting the shipments of cerecite back to Earth fast enough. People were hungry for money. They demanded we speed up the process or they would only pay half price." His words turned sharp. "That's when the scientists created the wormhole. What had taken years and millions of dollars to ship cerecite back to Earth would now only take seconds. But they'd rushed the building of the wormhole, cut corners, never properly tested things.

"When they opened it, the wormhole worked fine for a time. But not for long. One day we tried to open it. Something went wrong. The explosion killed everyone except two of us. It was so powerful it ripped a hole in the fabric of time, from here to an island north of Russia. It blasted stones from our project through the gateway, covering Champ Island.

"That's where the stones came from?" I asked. "The wormhole?"

He nodded.

"Yes, the explosion was so massive, it sent me and the other miners back in time. That's how it seems we arrived in the past. When really, we come from the future." He pulled the pyramid pendant from under his shirt. The bands of gold sparkled against the black, mesmerizing, and now I knew why. It was made in another time completely. In the future. To me, it might as well have been magic.

"Wow." I rested my head against the shelves, my world turned upside down.

"After the settlers arrived, they wanted to find a way back home. But the portal was damaged. Only seven pieces of cerecite could make it function again. By then, the pieces had been lost. They forgot trying to get home when they started helping us clear out the rubble from the explosion. We helped them create a new home, one patterned after Scotland, down to the stars in the dome. We used cerecite to create everything. It was perfect. A paradise.

"Nearly two centuries later, a traveler arrived. He said he was an explorer. He'd built a cavern that brought him through a wormhole portal to here—the same cave you must've entered to get here.

"The explorer was welcomed for a time, until he started stealing white cerecite. When he brought the objects to the larger cavern, I knew his true purpose. He was attempting to open the main gateway. I found out he was an agent for a corporation called Vortech. Just like you. After I killed him, more came. I didn't want to kill them all. I destroyed the machine in the smaller cavern, trying to stop them from coming through, but they still managed to enter our world because I couldn't destroy the machine on their side.

"I knew what they wanted, and I couldn't allow them to have it. Everything we'd worked for would be destroyed. They'd mine our cerecite, take every last bit of it for themselves. We'd have nothing left. Cerecite isn't a renewable material. It works fine here, sure. But for an entire planet the size of Earth? No. You know what the people on Earth are like. They use every resource until nothing is left. They'd do the same here. Take everything and leave nothing for us. So, my only choice was to kill them. Every single one who came through."

"And now their bodies are discarded in a cave," I said. "Their families never knew. Rosa's family never knew."

"Rose, yes. She came before you. I tracked her into the cavern. She never found the seventh piece of cerecite, but she was desperate to go home. She tried opening the gateway with only six pieces. It didn't work. I slit her throat with this." He glanced at the knife.

My fear turned to revulsion. "You're a murderer."

He clenched his jaw. "No," he snapped. "I'm a soldier. I protect our world. If there was any other way, I would've taken it. I tried to stop them. But protecting Ithical and the tens of thousands of lives here is more important than one single person."

The room wouldn't stop spinning. "Where's your mother?"

He heaved a deep sigh. "She's not real. I lied about her. This is my home. Has been for more than a hundred years."

Of course, it was. That's how things worked in this place.

"Where's Morven?" I asked with heat in my voice. "Did you kill him?"

"No." He locked his jaw. "Unfortunately, I can't kill him."

I cocked my head. "What do you mean?"

"I stabbed him when he was in his first body. Isaac. But the cerecite reprocessed his DNA. He became the wolf, then the prince. If I killed him, he would be recycled again. My only choice was to erase the memories of his last life by giving him yellow cerecite."

His words brought me back to the first day I'd entered the palace. "You led me to the kitchens the first day I was at the palace. You told me you were on your way there, but what business did you have there?" I laughed at my own stupidity. Why hadn't I seen it sooner? "You were there to slip the poison into his food. You must've been handing it off to Justine and making her do your dirty work for you."

"It was the only way to make him forget."

"Forget what?" I demanded. "Why are you doing this?"

"Because…" His eyes darkened. "He was the other miner who survived. He wanted to repair the wormhole, so we could travel between our worlds, but I knew what would happen if it was opened. They would take everything and leave this world a wasteland. Don't you understand, Sabine?" he pleaded. "My only choice was to mask his mind from his former life. I didn't *want* to kill him. I never did."

I rubbed my temples, his words overwhelming me. "How are *you* still alive?"

"The cerecite, of course. When I survived the explosion, it changed me. The cerecite became part of me. Something similar happened to Morven, but instead of never aging, like me, he was changed to a spirit wolf, and then he was reborn with all his former knowledge." His eyes darkened. "But it seems he started to remember his past if he traveled to the cave with you. What did you do there?"

"Nothing," I answered.

"Nothing, really?" he asked skeptically.

"We were exploring," I explained. "Trying to find out the nature of this world. We didn't know what was going on."

Suspicion riddled his face. "You didn't try to open the gateway?"

"No," I said firmly. "I couldn't have anyway."

He nodded. "Because you don't have the seventh piece of cerecite. And you never will. No one has found it. Not any of the other agents. Not you. And it will stay that way." His eyes shifted to his knife. Yellow cerecite glittered in the reflection of his pupils. "Still," he continued. "If I were smart, I would kill you myself, but…" He hesitated, his chest heaving as he took a looked from me to the knife. "Of all the people, why you, Sabine? We were friends!"

"Then don't kill me," I spoke with slow, measured words, fearing anything I said would provoke him. "Please. There's been enough bloodshed. We can find another solution."

"There is no other solution." He glanced away. "Except…"

"Except what?"

"No." He hung his head. "There's no other way. You've left me with no other choice. I don't deserve your forgiveness for this. I'm so sorry, Sabine."

He took a step toward me, the knife glinting.

"Stop!" Adrenaline flooding my blood, I bounded to my feet and drove my knee into his groin.

He cursed, falling back, and I sprinted for the door. I grabbed the handle when he tackled me from behind. I pitched forward, Cade on top of me, the wind knocked from my lungs as I hit the floor.

He rolled me over. I grabbed for the knife when the blade sliced down my palm. Sharp pain stabbed through my flesh. Screaming, I pushed away from him, shocked at how much blood pooled in my hand and ran down my arm, staining the floor.

The pain fueled my adrenaline. Vortech's training hit me with sharp clarity.

I was there again.

Fighting for survival.

Rising to my feet, I faced Cade.

"Sabine, please," he pleaded. "Stop fighting me. You're making this harder than it has to be."

His words meant nothing to me. I thrust a sharp kick at his hand. My boot connected with his fingers. Bones snapped. He screamed, the knife flying from his grasp.

His weapon landed with a clatter at my feet. The yellow blade spun on the tiles, creating a shimmering pattern, like a kaleidoscope.

Yellow cerecite. Poison. The clue to the seventh lie.

Warm blood seeped from my cut palm. I didn't feel the pain. I grabbed the knife as he staggered toward me. He cradled his broken hand to his chest.

"Give me the knife," he demanded.

"Why?" I answered with equal sharpness. "Because it's the seventh lie?"

"Give it to me now!" He rushed at me.

Fist clenched around the knife's hilt, I let him come. I side-stepped his attack, spun around, and drove the blade into his stomach.

Screaming, Cade fell, his knees hitting the ground. He clamped his hands around the hilt, dark blood seeping from the wound.

A moment of panicked desperation hit me, as if time had slowed, and my actions replayed in vivid clarity.

Had I killed him? Swallowing the fear rising in my chest, I knelt by him.

He gasped shallow ragged breaths. His face drained of color. "Sabine... I..." He ground his teeth, then grasped the blade in his abdomen. With a muffled scream, he yanked on the handle, pulling it out with a sickening, sucking sound.

The knife fell, hitting the floor with a ringing echo. Bloody fingers fell limply beside the weapon. Cade's breathing turned to quiet gasps.

I reached for him. "Cade...?"

"Sabine," he pleaded, grasping my hand. "Please. I'm so sorry."

"Sorry?" I almost laughed. "You tried to kill me. If you had another chance, you'd try to do it again."

"No," he groaned. "No, you're right. There's another way. I should have told you. But... please. Don't let me die..."

"I thought you couldn't die."

His eyes flicked to the weapon. "The knife. Cerecite... it's the only thing that can kill me." Sweat created a clammy sheen on his overheated skin. Pain etched his face. He grabbed my hands in a death grip, his fingers cold. Icy blue eyes set with firmness locked on me. "If you swear to protect… my world, I can help you… but…"

"But, what?" Desperation bled through my words.

"I broke your bracelet." His voice turned to a whisper. "He'll be here soon."

"What do you mean? Who will be here soon?"

His eyes closed, and he shook his head.

"Cade," I repeated. "Who will be here soon?"

"I—I'm sorry…"

I shook his shoulder. "Cade."

"Sorry…" his voice faded.

"Cade." I shook him again, then cupped his cheek, his skin shockingly cold. "Can you hear me?"

He didn't respond.

"Cade!"

He remained motionless, eyes closed. I sat back on my heels, my mind reeling, the cut on my hand throbbing, Cade's last words replaying. *He'll be here soon.*

I picked up the knife. Yellow facets refracted around the room. Cade's blood dripped from the blade to the floor.

Behind me, the door boomed open.

Ivan stood inside the entry, his bulky frame blocking most of the doorway.

He glanced past me where Cade had fallen.

"Ivan?" I asked, shocked. "What are you doing here?"

"I saw your communications get cut off." He held up his bracelet. "I thought you must be in trouble, so I followed you to the bracelet's last known signal." He cleared his throat as his gaze snagged on the gardener. "Got him, did you?"

"Yes," I answered, casting him a sidelong glance, suspicion clawing at me. Fear trickled down my spine as Cade's revelation made sense.

Ivan would be here soon. That's who he meant.

But what did Ivan have to do to with Cade? How had Cade known he would come?

I clutched my bloody hand to my chest.

Bushy eyebrows narrowed over his eyes. "You're hurt?"

"Just a scratch."

He pulled a length of rope from his belt and entered the room.

"What're you doing?" I asked.

He nodded at Cade. "He's coming with us. We're going to the wormhole. Going home. Assuming you've found the seventh object?"

I nodded. "I found it, at least..." I glanced at the knife. "I'm pretty sure."

"Good." Ivan nodded, then stalked to Cade, his furs billowing in the wind gusting from the open doorway, his bootsteps heavy on the wooden planks.

"Ivan, wait," I said. "He's dying. He needs green cerecite."

"Dying?" He chuckled. "Good job, Harper."

He slammed his boot into the side of Cade's face. Bone crunched.

My stomach sickened, and I had to look away.

He reached into his furs and pulled out his canteen, took a drink, then knelt by the gardener and grabbed his face between his hands.

Cade's cheek was swollen and misshapen where Ivan had crushed him. I forced myself to calm down, think rationally, and try to control this situation as best as I could.

"Ivan, tell me again how you knew I'd be here?"

"Eh?" He glanced up for a brief second. "Your bracelet. I've been monitoring your communications with your AI unit. Saw you'd broken it. Knew you must be in trouble so I came as soon as I could."

I knelt to be eye-level with the big man. "You were monitoring my communications? Why didn't you tell me?"

"Didn't think you'd mind. It's my job to make sure you

stay alive." Ivan lifted the gardener's head and pressed the canteen's opening to the man's lips. "Help me here, will you?"

Anger and betrayal warred, making my chest feel impossibly tight. Ivan had been monitoring my communications? He had a history with Cade? What else had he thought wasn't important enough to tell me?

But I had to make sure Cade survived, so I knelt to help Ivan as green liquid pooled in Cade's mouth.

I knelt, resting my hand on his shoulder. "Cade, swallow it," I nudged.

He remained still, with only the rise and fall of his chest to tell me he was alive.

"Cade. It's green cerecite."

"Sa—Sabine…" he whispered.

"I'm here. Drink the cerecite."

He gave a slight nod. His Adam's apple bobbed once, then twice. Ivan placed Cade's head down and hid the canteen in his furs.

"I bloody well hope this wears off soon." Ivan chuckled, though the sound didn't hold any humor. "Probably should've warned you, but the gardener can't be trusted. He hasn't aged a day in the thirty years I've been here."

"Why didn't you tell me sooner?" I asked, my tone sharp. "How much do you know, Ivan? How is it you stayed alive when all the other agents disappeared?"

"Do you really want to ask so many questions when I'm here to rescue you? Maybe you're not as brilliant as I thought." He hefted a rope, then tied it around Cade, and fastened a gag in his mouth.

"Why are you doing that?"

"Can't trust him not to run."

Really? Or was it that he didn't want Cade talking?

"Now." He grunted as he hefted Cade on his shoulders. "Are we going to stand here and play twenty questions, or will you let me do my job and help you?"

I stood to face the man. Indecision clouded my judgment. Cade had tried to kill me. He killed the past agents, so why was Ivan's sudden arrival bothering me almost as much?

"Look." Ivan sighed. "You're right to question me. If you've found all the objects, you must've gone out to the spirit caves, maybe figured I knew Rosa and the others were buried there. But I'll have you know I had my reasons for not telling Vortech what happened." He shook his head. "Vortech isn't who you think."

"What do you mean?" The cut on my hand throbbed, and I kept it close to my chest. Thinking through the pain sent knives needling through my skull.

"I'll explain it all when we get to the gateway."

"But we can't go yet. I've got to find my backpack. It's got all the other pieces inside. Also, the prince and his aunt... I have to find them. They're missing. I have to know they're safe."

"Don't worry so much. I've got this figured out. I've done all the grunt work for you." He chuckled softly. "Follow me and you'll be fine."

His words grated on me as he spun on his heel and walked away. Seeing Ivan in this new light made my skin crawl, and I wouldn't allow him to dominate me.

I stood tall. "No," I spoke firmly.

He spun around. "No?"

"I won't go with you," I said. "Leave Cade with me. I'll find my own way to the caves."

His blue eyes narrowed to icy slits. "You're making the wrong decision. It so happens my house was designated as the royal's safe house in the event anything went awry at the capital. Can you believe who came to me less than an hour ago? And guess what they brought with them? Your bag. I've got the first five objects, and the prince and his aunt are with me as well."

"What?" I questioned. "Where?"

"In my rover." He nodded to the door. "Just outside."

"You're telling the truth?"

He let out a deep-bellied laugh. "Why would I lie to you? I want to get off this damn rock just as much as you. You want to go home, don't you?"

Home. It's what I wanted, didn't I? To see Dad again. To complete my mission. To stop the flare.

I held Cade's knife in my injured hand, yellow blade warmed by my pulsing blood. A second passed, and the jewel facets changed shape. A tiny glimmer so subtle, no one else would've noticed it.

My hands trembled. I held the seventh lie.

I had everything I needed within my grasp. All I had to do was follow Ivan, and I would go home.

"Follow me." Ivan called as he turned. "We've got to get that wound tended."

I stood unmoving. Choices raged a wicked battle in my head. But what choice did I really have? Stay here and bleed?

I placed the knife in my boot's sheath and cradled my bloody hand. With my good hand, I grabbed the skull and rushed to keep up with Ivan, following the trail of Cade's blood into the street.

Outside, clouds hid the stars. Rain pelted me in a steady drizzle. Pools of hazy light lit my way. Ivan stood with Cade thrown over his shoulder beside a tank-like vehicle, its engine rumbling quietly on the street. Its rugged, metal dome and track wheels seemed suited for an alien terrain.

A muffled groan came from the gardener as Ivan opened the door and tossed Cade inside. Ivan reached inside the carriage and pulled out my leather pack, then shoved it in my face.

"What did I tell you?" he said. "I've done everything for you. Follow me and you'll be fine."

Biting back my retort, I took my pack from him.

"Where did you find this?" I demanded, holding up my bag.

"I didn't. They did." He nodded inside the carriage. "Now get inside. We don't have time to lose."

At the thought of seeing Morven, I hurried to the carriage. Inside, Cade lay on the floor. Morven and his aunt sat on the back row of seats. The queen regent didn't look at me, keeping her gaze focused forward.

Morven's eyes widened as he saw me. "Sabine?" He sat forward.

I climbed over Cade and made it to the seat beside Morven, hugging him tightly. His warmth surrounded me. I inhaled the woodsy scent of his clothing. Was this really him? I could hardly believe it. When we'd been separated, I knew something bad was bound to happen, but here he was—whole and uninjured.

"Your hand," he said as he pulled away.

"He cut it." I nodded at Cade. "But I stabbed him. I think we're even."

"Not even close," Ivan said, climbing inside to the bench across from us. He pressed a button on a panel to the right of the door, and it slid closed. "Take us to the caves," he said. Lights blinked from the ceiling, as the carriage rolled forward with a gentle lurch.

"You'll have to tend to that hand," Ivan said. "It's been poisoned with yellow cerecite." He pulled a roll of gauze and a bottle of green liquid from his bag, then leaned forward.

I pulled away from him.

"I can do it myself."

Bushy eyebrows rose. "Touchy one, aren't you? Let me see it."

"No."

Morven leaned forward and grabbed the supplies from Ivan. "Here," he said gently. "Let me."

With a nod, I held out my hand, and he set to work,

cleaning it, rubbing the ointment in my palm, then wrapping it with the gauze. When he finished, I sat back, the pain and exhaustion starting to catch up to me once again.

Morven took my good hand, threading his fingers through mine. Our eyes met, and his unspoken gaze said everything. We were together again, and we were alive.

The carriage rolled through the lanes, the rhythmic clicking of the track wheels lulling me. Outside, the shapes of the buildings came into view, illuminated only by the infrequent streetlamps. I spotted the palace's single spire rising above the rest.

"Did they take over the castle?" I asked Morven quietly.

"Only in name. They have no real power. We'll get it back."

Morven's aunt sat straight, and her face turned resolute. "We will," she echoed him.

The sun rose as we approached the canyon. I'd managed to catch a quick nap, and we'd shared a meal of some breaded potato cakes and a few sips of water. The carriage halted. Outside our window, the shadow of the cavern's entrance loomed.

Cade lay motionless on the carriage floor. He hadn't moved since we started. Already his face had healed, and the stab wound to his stomach was knitting back together, leaving only a raised purple scar.

Despite a few hours to process everything, I still had trouble understanding what Cade had told me about this world. About him being from the future. About the wormhole and time rift it had opened.

My stomach churned with queasiness.

Ivan's threat to kill Cade bothered me. And although Cade had tried to kill me, I knew his reasons. Would I have done the same in his situation? Maybe.

Ivan opened the doors. The early morning sun shone down on us as we exited the carriage. Ivan hoisted Cade over his shoulder. Morven and his aunt followed us. Sand shifted beneath my feet as we trekked into the desert toward the cave.

I searched for my knife in the swells of sand but saw nothing. Mima June's heirloom was lost to me—but that didn't mean she was gone. Her memory would live forever with me, at least, that's what I told myself, hoping one day, it would feel like the truth.

The skull and the yellow cerecite knife sat in my pack along with the other five pieces of white cerecite. My scanner had stopped functioning, but at the gateway, I wouldn't need it.

We entered the cave, our footsteps echoing. Salt crystals lit our path. Morven walked beside me, though he didn't speak. He kept his eyes on Cade. Was he starting to recollect their time together in a different life?

The floor rumbled.

"What was that?" the queen regent asked, stopping beside me.

The cave shook again. Small pebbles dislodged from the ceiling, sailing to the floor, and smashing to pieces.

"Keep moving," Ivan said.

We continued walking, though the tremors increased until we made it to the drop-off. Ivan removed a collapsible, metal-pieced ladder from his bag, attached it to the lip of the gorge, and allowed it to unroll until it reached the bottom of the drop-off.

After making sure the ladder was secure, Ivan untied Cade and removed the gag, though kept a knife at his back.

"Try to run or do anything stupid, and I push this blade through your heart." His furs rustled as he gripped the blade's handle. "Understand?"

Cade only nodded. I half expected the gardener to fight Ivan. But he only stood stoically, blue eyes focused straight ahead.

We took turns climbing down the ladder, the cavernous room trembling around us. Morven and Ivan helped the queen regent, who made it down more spryly than I thought possible while wearing her black dress and heeled slippers. Several times I lost my grip on the damp metal, but I managed to regain it. I breathed a sigh of relief as my feet connected with the ground.

We reached the underground river, following the same path Morven and I had taken. The cave shook more violently. Larger stones crashed from the ceiling, landing with loud splashes in the water. Cold droplets sprayed my exposed arms and face.

"Why is the cave shaking?" I asked.

"The white cerecite," Cade answered, his voice barely audible over the rumbling. "There are seven pieces together. It's too much energy. It'll tear the cave apart. It'll do the same to our world."

I adjusted my bag's straps on my shoulders. The quiet clanking of the cerecite made me too aware of what I carried inside.

We passed through the room with Rosa's body. The queen regent gasped, though the rest of us continued to the final chamber as she trailed behind. I heard Morven speaking quietly to her, perhaps explaining this strange underground world we'd come to.

Cade only briefly glanced at the body, then focused straight ahead, his face unresponsive, a guise of composure.

As we entered the largest chamber, the gateway loomed over us. Ivan stopped when we reached the bottom of one of the giant pillars comprising the looming rectangular structure. The mirror-like panels, the rectangular slots, and the wall of blackened rock behind it, brought back memories of the first time I'd crossed. My stomach knotted with apprehension.

"Tell her how it works," Ivan demanded, his knife at Cade's back.

"It's operational?" I asked.

"Yes," Ivan answered.

"How do you know?" I asked.

Ivan straightened his furs. "Because I fixed it."

"Fixed it? I thought you said you didn't meddle with any of this. That's how you stayed alive."

"No. The way I stayed alive was by telling no one what I was up to. Including you."

Cade shifted in Ivan's grasp. "Let me go and I'll help her open it."

"Not a chance," Ivan barked. "You'll stay right here with my blade at your neck."

"Tell me how it works," I asked Cade, my voice calm. "Please."

His chest rose as he inhaled. His eyes roved the gateway. "The seven spaces in the pillar here." He pointed. "That's where you'll put the pieces. Once you do, you'll have to punch the code into the screen. Two-four-three-seven-Alpha-Lima-Juliet. When it switches to the next screen, scroll to INITI-ATE. Make sure to transform all the objects into their original forms, and they'll open the gateway. Do you understand? It's important each object is in its original form," he spoke slowly, enunciating each word.

I studied his face. An unspoken communication lingered in his eyes. Blue eyes that seemed lit from within—strange and beautiful—the color of cerecite.

I nodded to him—a single gesture to let him know I understood. "I'll make sure," I said. "*All* seven will be in their original form."

"What are you waiting for, Harper?" Ivan demanded. "Do it now!"

I opened the bag. White light shone, enveloping my hands and face. I pulled out the first orb, then cradled it in my hands. Tremors rumbled while I placed it inside the slot. With a mechanical click, it slid inside the niche. A beam of white light lit the two side pillars and top of the gateway. A low hum resonated.

I repeated the same process with the next four orbs, the

mechanical whirring growing louder. When I got to the skull, I transformed it the same way I'd done with Rosa's rock, until six beams glowed from the structure.

As I lifted out the knife, the ground shook violently. A thunderous clatter filled the air. Everyone fell to the floor. The queen's screaming overpowered the smashing rocks. I landed on my back, dropping the knife. It slid away from me.

Ivan crawled for it and picked it up, but Cade loomed over him.

"Give it to me," Cade demanded.

"Are you crazy? I'll kill you first!" Ivan lunged. Cade side-stepped, and the big man rounded, his furs flying, pure hatred and anger lighting his eyes.

Rocks fell from the ceiling with deafening thuds.

He attacked again, slashing with a wide glancing blow that nicked Cade's arm.

"Stop," Cade seethed. "I told Sabine I would open the gateway for her. But I won't do it for you. You helped me kill Rosa, but then you broke our bargain. You said you would protect the gateway so no one else would come through. You were supposed to protect Ithical, Ivan!"

"I had a change of heart," he yelled. "Thirty years is a long time to be here. It's time for me to go back, to start what should've started a long time ago. I'll bring Vortech back here and mine this stuff. Do you know how much money is in this industry? Billions. Trillions!" He laughed. "And I'll own it all."

He took a step backward, then another, until he reached the gate.

Anger at Ivan's betrayal seethed in my blood. I couldn't let him take another step. "Is that true?" I called to Ivan. "You helped him kill Agent Rodriguez?"

"It doesn't matter anymore," Ivan goaded. "We're about to open the gateway, Harper. Don't you want to go home?"

I stood facing Ivan, the glittering knife held between us.

Home was all I could think about for the past six months. Without it, my life was meaningless.

My nails cut my palms as I clenched my good fist. I'd sworn I would do anything, *anything* to go home. But Dad's words rang in my ears.

Harpers finish with honor.

Maybe I couldn't go home, but I could finish this, and do it with a little honor in the process.

When Ivan turned around, I rushed at him. I threw my body into his back so forcefully, he toppled sideways. The knife flew out of his hand and hit the floor with an echoing clatter.

Cade rushed in and caught it as it spun over the ground.

The world quaked. Boulders fell from the ceiling, smashing what remained of the mining equipment and spaceships.

Morven approached the three of us. "This place is getting torn apart," he called. "We've got to get out of here!"

"We're opening the gateway first!" Ivan yelled back. A chasm split the floor, a seam breaking through the rock that cracked and bent living stone. He held out his hands to keep his balance.

"No," Cade yelled back, the chasm between them. "I won't let you harm this world. Ithical will stay protected. Forever." He tossed the knife into the open chasm. It sailed with a whoosh until it clattered to the bottom dozens of feet below.

"What?" Ivan bellowed. "You bastard! What did you do?" He edged his bulky frame to the lip of the chasm when another quake hit, this one stronger than any of the last. Chalky clouds blinded me.

"Help!" Ivan screamed. "Help me. Please." His voice faded. "Please…"

I laid on the ground with my hands over my head, blinded by the dust, my pulse thrummed so loud, it overpowered the quaking stones. Rocks jabbed my back. Dust choked my lungs.

When the tremors stopped, I sat up. Gasping for air, I climbed to my feet. A hand found mine, and I recognized the warm skin, the callused fingertips.

"Morven?" I asked.

"I'm here," he answered.

An aftershock made me lose my balance. Morven caught me as I fell, his hands cradling me.

"You ready to go?" he asked.

My heart felt like the floor opening with millions of fissures. I couldn't leave Dad alone, but I couldn't doom Ithical either. "Yes. I'm ready."

The dust settled, and I found the shapes of giant glowing rocks in the debris. Cade limped toward us, holding the queen regent as she staggered beside him.

I searched for Ivan, but I didn't see him in the debris.

"Ivan's unconscious," Cade called.

When he reached us, I was shocked at the red blood streaming down his face from a cut near his hairline. He handed the queen regent to Morven.

"Take care of her," he said. "She protects our world better than you think. You'll need her when you take the throne back from the miners."

Morven nodded, releasing my hand as he wrapped his arm around his aunt.

I took a step forward. With Ivan gone, maybe I could go home—the way I should've all along, with the aid of the actual seventh lie.

"Cade, will you help me get home?" I asked.

His chest rose and fell. He smeared the blood on his face as he attempted to wipe it out of his eyes. "Are you sure you still want to go?"

"Yes. My promise stands. I won't allow this world to be stripped of its resources."

The cut seeped with bright blood. His eyes burned with

intensity, the bright blue of cerecite. On his forehead, the gash shifted a millimeter to the right.

Excitement raced through my blood. My suspicions were confirmed. "It wasn't the knife, was it?"

He shook his head. "No. I created the knife to be a decoy."

"You're the seventh lie," I said. "Aren't you?"

He gave a single nod.

I scrutinized him. "How is it possible?"

"It happened during the explosion. The first one," he said. "Some of the cerecite became part of Isaac, and it became part of me, too. That's how I'm able to live so long."

"But… if it's you, this isn't good. We'll never be able to remove the cerecite from you."

"No. There's a way," he said solemnly.

"How?" I asked.

"It's him," Morven whispered beside me.

"What?" I asked, focusing on him for the first time.

"He can change his form. Just like me. A wolf." He nodded at Cade, and a look of understanding passed between them.

Cade's eyes flicked to the gateway. Its six rows of lights shone through the dust clouding the room. With a deep exhale, he turned back to us.

Tears brightened his cobalt eyes. "You'll remember me?"

"You won't be forgotten," Morven said earnestly. "You never have been."

"Thank you," Cade answered. Light glowed from his skin, igniting as if he were on fire. A greenish glow surrounded him as cerecite attached to DNA. I shielded my eyes as he transformed. Shimmering bands that reminded me of braided DNA formed translucent wings. His body morphed, his head and neck elongating, a tail growing from the lean, reptilian frame, all connected by the glowing ladder-like cords, the building blocks, the bridge between living and non-living.

"The green dragon," I said, my voice subdued by awe.

We stood and followed the dragon to the gateway. When he reached it, he pumped his wings, leaping into the air, flying in a low circle.

"He's opening the gateway," I said. "Just like he promised."

Warm wind brushed my cheeks as the dragon sailed overhead. Seams ripped through the floor, throwing me off balance, though Morven caught my hand, helping me stand straight.

Together, we stood and faced the gateway. The dragon screamed a primal sound of power as he sailed for the gateway's opening, toward the wall of stone. As he approached, the light glowed brighter. I shielded my eyes against the onslaught of heat radiating from the doorway.

The seventh light ignited around the archway as the dragon flew through it. Digital lights with the code appeared on a screen by the seven objects. The wall of stone disappeared, revealing a snowy landscape punctuated with smooth, spherical boulders, remnants of an explosion that had happened centuries ago, evidence of the bridge between two worlds. The blue sky spanned above, so brilliant it stole my breath.

Morven squeezed my hand.

The queen regent stood beside us. "He did it," she said, her eyes following the dot in the sky. "He saved us. The green dragon saved us again."

I woke before dawn in my bedroom. The warm blankets piled on me kept the chill away, making me never want to move from the bed. I could hardly believe I was here again.

Home.

But I had to get up. I had something important to do today.

I walked out of the room, dressed in only jeans and a faded flannel shirt, my bare feet slapping the wood of the cold floor.

When I entered the dining room, the table caught my attention. Free of the clutter of bills and torn envelopes, the wood grain gleamed in the overhead pendant light. I ran my hand over the tabletop, the surface smooth and polished.

A slim package wrapped in brown paper sat at the table's center, a yellow post-it note attached to it, with the name *Sabine* written in Dad's handwriting in magic marker.

Lifting an eyebrow, I picked up the bundle and unwrapped it, pulling out a *Star Trek* DVD collection.

On the back I found another post-it.

Sabine,

Let's start with season one.

-Dad

I positioned the box on the table's center, aligning its circumference to the grain of the wood, as if it were meant to fit perfectly. When I took a step back, I shook my head. Dad had a funny way of welcoming me home.

A figure stood on the front porch. I slipped on my sandals, grabbed the door handle, and pushed open the screen.

The springs slammed shut with a metal clank behind me, where I found Dad waiting for me. His eyes met mine as I walked to him.

"You're up early," Dad said. "I thought you'd want to sleep in."

I rubbed my eyes, nightmares of collapsing cavern walls still lingering. "Couldn't sleep."

He nodded. The pool of porch light revealed the edge of the rows of green wheat sprouting from the soil. "I gotta get an early start today. Planting a new crop of soybeans in the west field."

I stuck my hands in my pockets. "That's good."

"Yeah." He sat on the swing and patted the slats beside him, so I sat. The rhythmic creaking of the swing was a familiar sound—one that made me feel I'd never left. The smell of old paint came from the worn wood, and the crisp taste of spring lingered in the air.

Dad patted my knee. "I'm glad you're back."

"Me too."

"Mima would've been proud of you."

"I hope so." I threaded my fingers together. "I miss her."

"I do too." He wrapped his arm around me. "What I would give just to have one more conversation with her. To hear her voice as she told her stories. But..." he patted my back. "I'm glad you're back, Beanie Girl." He left unspoken the feelings tugging at my heart, the ones I feared would never heal.

"We'll get through this," Dad said.

"Yes," I answered. "We will."

"What will you do now?" he asked.

I picked at the peeling paint. "I don't know. I'm meeting someone from Vortech today. They're offering me another job."

"Will you take it?" he asked.

"Not sure. Vortech was never honest with me. They still haven't told me what they're using the cerecite for."

"But you're still meeting with them?"

I nodded.

He scratched his chin. "Why?"

I shrugged. "I suppose because I'm hoping for a fresh start."

Glancing at the dark field, I couldn't fight the emptiness tugging at me.

"Is something bothering you?" Dad asked.

I crossed my arms. "There was someone I met. I haven't seen him since I left the airport in DC. It's been a week. I thought... Well, never mind, that's not even worth mentioning, I guess." I crossed my arms as a chilly breeze rushed past. "I've got bigger problems. I don't trust Vortech, yet it's hard for me to leave Ceres behind. I think I fell in love with the place. It became part of me. It's hard to let it go."

The rumble of a vehicle's engine came from the driveway. I stood to get a better look. In the light of the porch, a sleek black sedan drove slowly into view.

"That would be them," I said. When the car stopped, I gave Dad a nervous smile and crossed to the steps.

Dad stood and placed his hand on my shoulder, stopping me.

"You got my gift?"

"I did. Thank you."

"We can watch a couple episodes this evening if you'd like."

"I'd like that."

He smiled, wrinkles crinkling around eyes full of joy and sorrow. "Thank you for coming home."

I only nodded, a hard knot forming in my throat as I hugged him. "I'm glad I could."

He patted my back, then stepped away. "Now, go let loose on Vortech. It's time to give them you're best what-for. Then see what they're offering." He winked.

I squared my shoulders. "I will."

When he stepped away, I faced the car, expecting someone to get out and greet me, but it idled in the dark driveway, silent except for the purring of its engine.

What were they waiting for?

After pacing down the porch steps, I marched to the Jaguar.

The back door opened. A middle-aged woman sat inside. Her knee-length black dress fit snugly on her Hollywood-thin frame, and she wore three-inch pumps to match. Red lipstick stood out against her pale skin. Black-rimmed glasses framed her shrewd, dark eyes. She wasn't holding a weapon. At least there was that.

"Get inside, Miss Harper." She spoke with a velvet-smooth voice, as if she weren't accustomed to emotion.

"Inside? Why can't we speak out here?"

"This will only take a minute. You're perfectly safe."

I took a step back. "What if I refuse?"

"Then I'll leave. But I'd rather not have to do that."

"I don't see why we can't speak in the house."

"Because." She pressed her lips into a tight line. "I'm sharing top secret information with you. I'd like to make sure it stays that way. It's either this or we meet in Los Angeles."

"I'm sick of traveling."

"Then perhaps you ought to get in."

I hated arguing, so I climbed inside and shut the door. The air smelled of clean leather and money.

"My name is Anna Johnson. You can call me Anna. I'm

one of the partners in Vortech. You might know me by another name. We spent quite a bit of time together on Ceres, though only through communications."

I cocked my head. "Fifteen?"

"Yes. Partially." She smiled. "Agent Fifteen is a computer program engineered with the knowledge of the three founders of Vortech. Me, Vincent Fernoulli, and Yusuf Barnak. We created it to have all the knowledge it would need to assist you. I hope he was somewhat helpful."

"Somewhat."

She gave me a tight-lipped smile. "You're a special person, Miss Harper," Anna said. "We had faith in you, of course. You had potential, but I have to admit, I wasn't sure you would make it home."

"I wasn't sure I would either. I was almost killed."

"Yes. *Almost.*" She cleared her throat. "Let me get to why I've come here. I need your help. You should know that I haven't come here on behalf of Vortech. I ask this as myself. Our corporation is being corrupted from the inside. Vortech has already begun the initial mining phase on Ceres."

"What?" My anger flared. "That's seriously the *one* thing I asked you not to do."

She held up a hand. "It's not what you think. We're extremely sensitive to the local population. We're building our facilities underground to keep a minimal profile. Only a few on Ceres even know we exist."

"They don't know you're stealing from them, you mean?"

"It's not stealing if you pay for it, and we are. Half of our production is going back to the miners. They've been equipped with new technology to eradicate their exposure to cerecite poisoning."

I pursed my lips. What did she want me to say?

"But that's not why I've come. I need your help in hunting down a criminal. Someone has stolen a portion of the cerecite. I fear the worst. If they're using it for weapons, I need to know. Your unique gift is unequalled. I want you to return to Ceres with me and another agent."

"Another agent? Who?"

She threaded her fingers together. "Cade MacDougal."

"Cade?" I nearly choked on the word. "A Vortech agent? Are you kidding me?"

"No," she said with seriousness.

I couldn't help but laugh. "I can't believe he's working for you."

"He's doing it to protect his world. He feels it's his last chance to do so." She leaned forward. "He came straight to us once he left the gateway. It was him who negotiated the Ceres mining details, begging us to keep a low profile, making sure we stayed away from populated areas. We agreed if he consented to help us find a criminal. Like him, you will be rewarded. Vortech has paid you for your work, but that amount can't last forever. If you choose to work with me, I will guarantee a steady paycheck, one that won't run dry once you're done."

Could I work for Vortech again? Go back to Ceres? See Morven? He'd come with me to Earth, but he'd wanted to explore; I'd wanted to come home. We were supposed to meet this morning, but I didn't know where we were. Were we in a relationship? I had no clue. But I did know he couldn't stay here forever. He had a monarchy to repair and a city to rule.

She handed me a business card. "Contact me anytime. I wish you all the best, Agent Harper."

Nodding, I clutched the cardstock as I climbed out. The door clicked shut behind me, and the Jaguar disappeared down the road behind the tree line. I slid the card into my pocket.

"That was weird," a familiar voice said behind me. Startled, I spun around to face Morven. His dark eyes glinted with mischief, and the paleness of his chiseled face contrasted the locks of hair falling across his forehead. Someone so dangerously attractive shouldn't have been left to his own devices alone on Earth.

"You scared me!" I said.

"Did I? It was a complete accident, I swear." His teasing grin told me it wasn't.

"You're early."

"Yeah, I couldn't stay away from you." His grin turned to a lopsided smile, showing off his white, perfectly-spaced teeth. "I drove up while you were in the car." He pointed at a classic model Harley Davidson motorcycle propped in the drive behind him.

"Where'd you get that?" I asked

"Rented it," he answered. "I won't be here long, so I figured I'd have fun while I could."

I eyed him. "You're going back to Ceres?"

"Yes, sometime."

I glanced at the empty porch. Had Morven talked to Dad? The idea of Morven chit-chatting with my father mortified me, but it filled me with hope, too.

Would Dad like him? Did I care if he liked him?

Morven walked with me to the whitewashed fence. We stood looking out over the field. The sun rose with streaks of pink against the gray. Dew clung to the green shoots of wheat.

It seemed almost poetic that Ceres should be named after the goddess of grain, when the plant had played such a role in my life—the source of life in the home I'd saved.

Birds chirped in the distance, and I took a moment to savor the fresh air. It tasted of spring—of new leaves, honey-suckle flowers, and a hint of lingering frost.

An ant crawled over the fence post. Morven's curious gaze followed its movements. What would it be like to see an insect for the first time? The ant moved away, down the post and out of sight.

"I wondered where you went." I propped my elbows on

the wooden fence railing. "I came home, and you disappeared."

His genuine, charming grin sent my insides fluttering. He rested his elbows beside mine. "You missed me, didn't you?"

"I didn't say that."

"I think you did."

I playfully jabbed his ribs. "You didn't tell me where you went."

"Well, since it was my first time here, I figured I should catch up with as much as I could. I made a stop in Houston and visited NASA, then to Florida to Cape Canaveral. Did you know your astronomers have discovered more than seven-thousand exoplanets? Incredible."

"So, you've been doing nerdy sciency stuff this whole time?"

"For the most part." A twinkle lit his eye. "But I couldn't stay away from you for long. I couldn't stop thinking about you, to be honest." He brushed a strand of hair from my face, the pads of his thumbs moving slowly over my skin, making me flush with heat. "What do you want, Sabine?"

I eyed him. "Why are you asking me that?"

"Because I need to know. What do you want from your future? Where do you want to go? And... is there any possibility that I might be a part of it?"

"I guess that depends. You're the prince. You've got a lot of work to do restoring your home after what the miners did. Do you *want* me to be a part of it?"

"Yes, I very much do."

I nodded, my stomach aflutter and in every knot conceivable. I reached into my pocket, the card bending under my grasp, and ran my fingers over the embossed Vortech logo.

"I guess I'm going back to Ceres with you."

He squeezed my free hand. "You mean that?"

"Yes. Vortech might be involved."

His eyes widened. "You're serious? I thought you found all the white cerecite."

"Yes, I did." I sighed, picking at the paint on the fence. "But they suspect someone's stealing cerecite and possibly using it for weapons. I don't think I can ignore something like that."

"Then I'll help you find them. We'll do it together."

I nodded. The sun crested the horizon. Its warmth melted my chills.

"I'll never get tired of that," Morven said softly.

"The sunrise?"

"Yes. It's remarkable. I never knew what I was missing until I saw that. This is an incredible world."

"I guess it's not so bad."

"Not so bad?" he asked. "I think you must've lived here too long."

"Maybe I haven't lived here long enough."

He smiled, and I couldn't help but smile back. "You asked me what I wanted," I said. "I want to go back to Ceres. It was me who opened the gateway. I've got to make sure nothing bad happens because of it. I guess there's more out there than just me and my family, isn't there?"

"There's a lot more out there." His voice turned wistful as he studied the sky, then his gaze went back to me. "And I imagine there's a lot more in store for you—and for us."

I rested my cheek on his shoulder, and he wrapped his arm around me. His warmth enveloped me, and I couldn't think of a time I'd ever felt happier.

"I hope so."

He held me close against him. "You were on the news. Well, not you, exactly, but I knew who they were referring to when they mentioned a Vortech agent saved the world."

"I didn't save the world."

"But you made it possible for cerecite to power your grids

for the next several centuries, even through another flare. That's pretty impressive."

I almost laughed at the absurdity of the situation. "Vortech caused the flare to begin with. The whole planet could have died because of it. Did they mention that?"

"Oddly enough, they omitted that part."

"Big surprise, huh?"

I was sick of thinking of Vortech, so I turned my attention elsewhere. The sunrise transformed the sky, tinting the puffy jet trails that tracked across the horizon, a foreign sight to someone who'd spent their life on Ceres. Unhindered by the dome, Morven's gaze fixated overhead, on the freedom he'd never known he was missing.

"Amazing, huh?" I asked.

He turned to me. "More than amazing."

His eyes met mine. My heart raced with anticipation. He stirred my soul so powerfully, I could never let him go.

He leaned in and brushed a kiss over my lips. My senses heightened, the feel of his lips, warm and soft. His hands moved to encircle my back, the palms of his hands drawing me nearer.

Instinctively, I clammed up, dulling my awareness, closing me off before I became overwhelmed.

But with a deep breath, I let go.

When I did, everything in the outside world faded—the sounds of the birds, the scent of green wheat shoots—until nothing remained but freedom.

AUTHOR'S NOTE

Warning: only read this if you're into nerdy sciency stuff.

Kidding. But really, I wanted to share a few details that make this book more interesting—the science behind *The 7th Lie*.

First, Champ Island. Yes, it's a real place. It is indeed located in the Bering Sea north of Russia. It's covered with perfectly-sphere shaped stones ranging from the size of marbles to boulders. As was stated in the book, scientists don't know what causes them to be shaped as perfect spheres. They shouldn't exist in nature. However, scientists were able to discover that the stones were created by water. Everything else is supposition. The shipwreck is fiction, although explorers did find an old wooden ski on the island. Its origins are unknown.

Next, Ceres. It's the only planet-shaped body in the asteroid belt. It's also the closest dwarf planet to Earth. Although not well-known, it was discovered in 1801 and is a fascinating world. Several NASA missions led to the discovery of bright spots on the planet, which were discovered to be made of a salt mixture. It's a geologically active world, with geysers and volcanoes. Scientists have also revealed that Ceres contains ice and could contain liquid water beneath its surface.

If mining in the universe were to ever become a reality, Ceres would be a prime candidate because of its proximity to Earth and abundance of minerals.

I've always been fascinated with the prospect of "what's out there." Are there elements combined in different ways we haven't discovered in the universe? If so, what sort of properties would they have? Would they be something alien and distinct from anything we're familiar with? Thus, the idea of cerecite began, and the birth of *The 7ᵗʰ Lie,* began.

ABOUT THE AUTHOR

Tamara Grantham is the award-winning author of more than a dozen books and novellas, including the Olive Kennedy: Fairy World MD series, the Shine novellas, and the Twisted Ever After trilogy. *Dreamthief*, the first book of her Fairy World MD series, won first place for fantasy in INDIEFAB'S Book of the Year Awards, a RONE award for best New Adult Romance of 2016, and is a #1 bestseller on Amazon with over 200 five-star reviews.

Tamara has been a featured speaker at numerous writing conferences and has been a panelist at Comic Con Wizard World. Born and raised in Texas, Tamara now lives with her husband and five children in Wichita, Kansas.

ABOUT THE PUBLISHER

Babylon Books is a division of Bernhardt Books, a family-owned publishing house founded in 1999 that showcases emerging authors and compelling fiction.

Editor-in-Chief: Alice Bernhardt
    Chief Financial Officer: W. Harrison Bernhardt
    Marketing Director: Ralph Bernhardt

Learn more at: www.babylonbooks.net

Made in the USA
Columbia, SC
20 August 2024

40795746R00190